Praise for Leslie O'Kane
and her Molly Masters mysteries

"Endearing characters, touching family and friend relationships, and a feisty heroine."
—DIANE MOTT DAVIDSON

"O'Kane delivers a satisfying whodunit."
—*San Francisco Chronicle*

"O'Kane is certainly on her way to making her Molly Masters series the *I Love Lucy* of amateur sleuths."
—*Ft. Lauderdale Sun-Sentinel*

By Leslie O'Kane
Published by Fawcett Books

THE COLD HARD FAX
THE FAX OF LIFE
PLAY DEAD
RUFF WAY TO GO
THE SCHOOL BOARD MURDERS

THE SCHOOL BOARD MURDERS

A Molly Masters Mystery

Leslie O'Kane

Leslie O'Kane

FAWCETT • NEW YORK

A Fawcett Book
Published by The Ballantine Publishing Group
Copyright © 2000 by Leslie O'Kane

www.randomhouse.com/BB/

Library of Congress Card Number: 00-190163

ISBN 0-449-00567-4

Manufactured in the United States of America

First Edition: June 2000

10 9 8 7 6 5 4 3 2 1

To my mother, Suzanne Mitoff,
who opened that first library door for me
and started me on this path.
Thanks, Mom!

Chapter 1

Send in the Clones

This silence meant trouble. My usual loquaciousness came from a proud heritage, handed down from both sides of the family. Yet the three of us—my parents and I—had nothing to say to one another as we drove to the school board meeting.

What we now shared—in addition to this heavy silence— was a fear of the unknown. Plus the realization that my father's fate was no longer in his own hands, but rested on the red-painted lips of decidedly unbalanced Sylvia Greene, president of the Carlton school board.

Outside my car window, the leaves of the trees and shrubs were resplendent in their full array of autumnal colors, only partially cloaked by the darkness of evening. Normally, my parents would be leaving their home here in upstate New York to spend the winter in Florida. All that had changed last year when my father became so fed up with the sniping among school board members that he ran for a seat himself— and won.

I shifted my vision to the back of my father's head and smiled at a memory, now many years old, of when my children had drawn a happy face on his bald spot while he napped. Their peals of laughter had awakened him and alerted me to drop everything and run into the room, where I gasped at what Nathan and Karen had done. . . .

My reverie switched to a fantasy, with me marching up to the front of the mini-auditorium that, even now, we were fast approaching. I would grab that fetid prune, Sylvia Greene, by the collar and shout, "You can't do this to Charlie Peterson, because he's my father! Because when my children drew a

1

face on his scalp with Magic Marker, he just laughed and helped them add a mustache and a goatee. And because he's three times the human being you could ever hope to be!"

"Do you think she's bluffing?" my mother asked as we pulled into the parking lot of the Education Center.

"No, but all I can say is she's wrong about me," Dad answered. Mom had asked this question many times since Sylvia had threatened him at last month's meeting. "The most despicable thing I've done was to register as a Republican."

"Why did you do that, anyway, Dad?" Some of my best friends were Republicans, including my husband, but Dad had always been a staunch Democrat.

He glanced at me through the rearview mirror. The lines around his eyes and beneath his white eyebrows were deeply drawn. Even in the small view afforded by the mirror, it was clear what a toll this battle had taken on him. "I wanted to vote in their primaries. The courts must use their registration lists, though, because now I keep getting called to jury duty." He shut off the engine, then sat still, staring at the monolithic Ed Center, soon to become a lion's den. "Serves me right."

"Well, Dad," I said, "I guess if Sylvia does divulge that you registered as a Republican, we'll just have to relocate overseas. That is, if we can find a country that would accept us, despite your checkered past."

Dad sighed and patted my mother's shoulder. She was also in no hurry to leave the car. "Really, Linda, there are no illegitimate children or mistresses in my past. I've given her no cause to kick me off the board."

Mom ran her hand through her salt-and-pepper hair. "I believe you, Charlie. It's just that I'm afraid she'll make something up."

"Whatever happens, we'll deal with it. Together. Just like always." Resolved, the three of us got out of the car, but Dad immediately became distracted by the sight of the left front tire. "Linda? Why didn't you tell me the pressure in your tires was low? We could have taken my car instead."

I glanced at the tire in question and saw only that it appeared to be reasonably round.

Mom straightened and fired one of her patented icy stares in my father's direction. At nearly five-eleven, she could be intimidating and was slightly taller than my dad. He ignored her and, ever the mathematician, went on to say, "Under-inflated tires can cut down on your gas mileage by as much as one-and-a-half percent. All you had to do was—"

"I'll skip a couple of meals and make up for my wanton gasoline usage." She took Dad's arm. Heads held high, the two of them entered the lobby, while I deliberately lagged a step or two behind.

The hum of conversation from the crowd milling in the lobby came to an abrupt halt. They turned their faces away from my father, but not so far as to prevent furtive, sidelong glances. A middle-aged man, notepad in hand, rushed up. "Mr. Peterson, have you decided to resign, or are you going to battle it out?"

"Hey," I interrupted, rushing over to step between him and my dad, "you're the reporter who eavesdropped on my private conversation at the grocery store the other day!"

"My quotes were accurate, Ms. Peterson," he said, his features tensing.

"The name is Masters. Molly Masters. I repeat, that was a private conversation. How was I supposed to know that the"—I resisted the urge to describe him as "silly looking," though with his concave chest and pot belly, that's what came to mind—"guy standing behind me in line was a newspaper reporter? My comments were never intended to be spread across the front page." In the meantime, as I'd hoped, my parents had continued into the auditorium and were safely beyond this muckraker's reach. "Besides which, my saying 'Sylvia Greene should be shot' did not necessarily mean 'to death.' For all you knew, I could have meant a booster shot or a shotput. Nor did you include the 'Amen to that,' which the grocery clerk said at least as loudly as my original statement."

His vision wandered partway through my tirade. "'Scuse me," he muttered and rushed off to join the crowd that had formed as Her Highness Herself entered the building. Incredibly, she was wearing a bright green dress that, with her cotton-candy-processed hairdo, made her look like an overgrown munchkin from Emerald City. Not that one could normally describe her as "overgrown" at five-one or so, not counting her spike-heel shoes. She'd insisted that her chair be raised several inches above all others on the semicircular dais for the school board. Ostensibly, this was merely so "the TV cameras can find me" (board meetings are televised on a local cable network), but I think it had more to do with her insatiable need for attention and power.

From amid the throng of reporters, Sylvia held her hands up dramatically. "Gentlemen, ladies. As the saying goes, *'Nam et ipsa scientia potestas est,'* or for the pedestrians among us, 'Knowledge is power.' "

She had once taught Latin and made a practice of working it into daily conversation. I now regretted never having learned the language myself. I would have loved to march over to her and say, *"Ipso stuffio ein gymsockna entra et,"* but I doubted that my translation was 100 percent accurate.

The small auditorium was packed. Lauren Wilkins, my closest friend, had saved Mom and me seats in the front row. Lauren worked as secretary in the high school and, having predicted how well attended this meeting would be, had come here directly after work. Her daughter, in turn, had gone over to our house after school, where my husband was currently staying home to watch the three children. Or, more likely, was currently watching TV with the three children present.

My father was chatting with another board member in front of the dais. They rounded the string of tables just as I approached. I experienced an unpleasant moment of clarity and pictured my father as others might see him, a nondescript elderly man, his shoulders slumped. He had a hitch in his step as if his hip was bothering him. When had he gotten so old?

I nodded in greeting to Lauren and took my seat between her and Mom. Meanwhile, Dad hung his jacket on the back of his chair in the front of the room, caught our eye, and gave us a thumbs-up. As the newest board member, he'd been assigned the seat at the very end of the string of tables, on our side of the room. He pleasantly greeted the woman beside him, Carol Barr. She was a former electrical engineer with grown children. Her views sometimes annoyed me and sometimes struck me as right on. In this latest battle that had so polarized the board—Sylvia's boneheaded desire to stop funding the music and art departments—Carol was on the correct side. Along with my father.

More to myself than to Lauren, I said, "My dad will brook crap from no man. Or no maniacal woman, for that matter. Then again, maybe I shouldn't have said 'brook crap,' but rather . . ." I was rambling out of nervousness, and Lauren was listening to me patiently, but her eyes had glazed over. "Never mind."

"Tommy's working tonight, or he'd be here, too," she said.

"Too bad," I replied in a half whisper. "I have this strange feeling that Tommy in his police uniform might be just the thing to keep the potential for violence under wraps."

"What's that?" Mom asked.

"I was saying that, last time I was here was for a chamber orchestra, featuring violins doing rap." Well, that made no sense, but Mom wasn't paying attention to my answer anyway.

"Here she comes, the witch," Mom muttered under her breath. The black coat, which Sylvia hadn't been wearing earlier in the lobby, was now carefully draped across her shoulders as if it were her royal cape. She marched down the center aisle and, I couldn't help but notice, avoided proximity to my father by rounding the tables on the opposite side. She then handed her coat to an elderly woman who'd brought two pitchers of ice water to their tables. The woman must have been one of Sylvia's appointed minions, who carried The Royal Coat into a room behind them. The woman returned a moment later and took a seat at a built-in desk next to the board's dais, just below where my father was seated.

Before taking her elevated perch behind the center microphone, Sylvia Greene scanned the crowd. Her vision rested on me and then on my mom for what felt like a full, miserable minute. Her shoulders moved with the weight of her sigh, then she pursed her signature bloodred lips and began to chat with the woman beside her, Gillian Sweet, a member of the pro-Sylvia faction of the board.

"Bet they're planning their sacrifice even now," Mom grumbled.

Before my father had been elected to replace a Sylvia disciple, the seven-person school board voted four against three on every single issue, with Her Highness in the majority. Dad, however, was now the swing vote. He had tried to be impartial and not vote in a block. His evenhandedness was probably why he'd become Sylvia's target. He sometimes voted with her, and therefore her reasons for initiating a smear campaign weren't as obvious to the community as if she'd singled out one of her diehard opponents.

Kent Graham entered the room, muttering "Excuse me" as he rushed down the aisle, narrowed by the standing-room-only conditions. Drat. Sylvia had her quorum.

Kent took his seat, and the other man on the board, Stuart Ackleman, followed suit. Being seated last was some sort of a power trip for Stuart, for I'd noticed he always managed to do so, even when he was first to arrive. In fact, Stuart cast a long, disheartened look at the school superintendent, who was talking with Sylvia's Coat Carrier and had not yet taken his seat beside the dais.

I scanned the faces of the seven board members. Sylvia's dearest disciple, Gillian Sweet, was my age—I had recently turned thirty-nine and would celebrate becoming twenty again next year—and was by far the youngest member of the board. My "by far" would probably have rankled the attractive and elegant Michelle Lacy, but nowadays when I can't easily estimate a woman's age, I assume she's about fifty.

A racket arose from the back, and I glanced behind me just in time to see someone, head covered in a sheet, release a pot-bellied pig down the aisle. The pig came trotting through the middle of the room, wearing a sign around its neck that read, simply, "Sylvia."

The human Sylvia watched the pig with amusement, until she saw the sign. She banged with her gavel and yelled, "Somebody, get that pig out of here! I will not allow an *ad personem* attack here! Nor will someone's juvenile sense of humor make a mockery of my leadership on this board!"

As if anyone needed a pig to do that.

A couple of men in the aisle seats of the audience took it upon themselves to capture the pig, which put up a considerable fight. The superintendent, I noticed, walked right past the fracas toward his seat without lending a hand. Meanwhile Sylvia kept pounding the desk with her gavel. Finally, she laid down the gavel and hissed something in Gillian's ear, causing her to blush.

With the room still abuzz, Sylvia cleared her throat and said, "We need a few moments *ex post facto* to collect ourselves and begin again with *tabula rasa*. In any case, I need to speak to my fellow board members in private."

The audience groaned. I grumbled into Lauren's ear, "Or, as Caesar might have said, were he here tonight, *'Veni, vidi, vomiti.'*"

Sylvia rose, then gestured at the other board members. "Ladies, gentlemen, after you. Let me remind you how poor the ventilation is in that room. It's always a little warm, so we'd best bring our water glasses."

They all topped off their glasses from the pitcher of water and filed toward the door. Sylvia suddenly leaned out and motioned to the bookish young man standing by the wall nearest me. "Sam. I need you to come, as well."

He seemed surprised at the request, but then followed her into the room.

"What do you think she's doing?" Mom asked me. "Why did she bring that man back there with them?"

"I have no idea. Maybe he's her lawyer, who's come with a notice for Dad to sign saying he's resigning of his own free will."

"He's not going to resign of his free will or anyone else's. How can she possibly think that he would?"

"I think Sylvia is counting on the notion that everybody has done something at some point or another that they're ashamed of and wouldn't want the world to know about."

"Not your father. He's the most scrupulously honest human being since . . . forever. Your father is one of a kind."

"He sure is. Sylvia Greene picked the wrong person to mess with." I said those words and meant them, and yet there it was again—that horrid uneasiness that insidiously crept into my consciousness at times—the realization that everybody *did* have something in their past that they'd prefer to keep to themselves. I'd engaged in a few such activities as a college student in Boulder, Colorado. I would be mortified if I had to own up to such things publicly and in front of my children.

Surely Dad, as a college professor, had known more about temptation than most. He'd told us how it infuriated him when college girls would flirt in shameless attempts to shore up their grades. All Sylvia needed was one mild transgression on his part and one blabber, and Dad's life would be made miserable.

At that thought, I found myself grumbling out loud, "I don't really know why anyone bothered to elect Gillian Sweet and Kent Graham. They're nothing but Sylvia's puppets, anyway. She should just have had herself cloned. Then, at the start of every board meeting, we in the audience could start by singing 'Send in the Clones.' "

Lauren chuckled, but Mom clicked her tongue. I found myself trying to picture how I could use that idea in one of my faxable greeting cards.

I changed positions in my seat but found myself growing crankier and less patient by the moment. "None of this would be happening if people just had the good sense to fund education. This makes me nuts! Their school taxes are deductible from their federal taxes anyway. Don't they prefer having their money go to their own children rather than to two-thousand-dollar Pentagon toilet seats?"

"Keep your voice down, Molly," Mom whispered.

The woman in the seat next to Lauren leaned past her to shake a finger at me. "None of this would be happening if Charlie Peterson and the other idiotic half of the board hadn't tried to prevent my sons from being able to participate in football!"

"He doesn't *want* to cut athletics, but he realizes that art and music need our support more. If we don't reverse trends, this country will turn into a cultural wasteland."

"Cutting sports programs will hurt our boys' futures. Do you have any idea how much money a football player makes?" the woman asked me scornfully.

"Yes, I do, and you've just made my point. Do you realize how rare it is for any athlete to actually wind up playing pro sports? But people can play and enjoy music all their lives."

She stood up abruptly, her nose in the air. "Come on, Bob, let's move where the air is a little fresher."

Though I could feel my mother's disapproving eyes on me, I somehow couldn't stop myself from turning to see her reaction. Predictably, she sighed, shook her head, and said, "Oh, Molly."

"Sorry, Mom." She was right; I was only making things worse.

Another couple sat down in the seats the first couple had vacated. The woman leaned around Lauren and said to me, "Good for you. We hate football."

I gave them a wan smile and nodded. Actually, I love football, and my beloved Denver Broncos finally winning those Super Bowls were personal triumphs permanently etched in my memory. I had lived in Colorado for seventeen years, prior to returning to Carlton, New York, five years ago.

The minutes ticked by. The "audience," currently witness to nothing but a closed door and an empty row of tables, grew ever noisier. I noticed the sweaty upper lip of the cameraman, who was supposed to be broadcasting this live for the local cable network. Sylvia had insisted that no commentators be allowed to speak and that every minute of the board meeting be shown without interruption. I smiled at the thought of channel surfers catching sight of the crescent-shaped table and its seven empty seats. This could prove to be their highest-rated broadcast to date.

Some fifteen minutes past the scheduled start time, the door opened. All seven members emerged, followed by the strange young man, who was now staring at the floor. Everyone seemed tight-lipped and red-faced. This time, at least, Sylvia was carrying her own water glass.

"It's pretty obvious they were having quite the fight in there," Lauren whispered to me. "I'd have liked to have been a fly on the wall for that conversation."

"No, you wouldn't have. You'd've spent the entire time frantically trying to escape Sylvia's web." I gave Sylvia a smile as she glared down at Mom and me.

"The meeting will now come to order," Sylvia said, rapping her gavel on the desk with so much venom that several members of the standing-room-only crowd that flanked us flinched.

"Does anyone . . ." Sylvia's face looked flushed and her voice sounded strained. She patted her chest and cleared her throat. "Excuse me." She took another drink of water. "Does anyone on the board have an announcement they'd like to make?"

She looked at the faces of the board members to both sides of her, letting her eyes linger on my father.

Nobody spoke, and my father grimly shook his head.

"Well, then . . . I guess . . . I guess I have no choice . . ." Sylvia's voice faded with each word, and her face was damp with perspiration. She stopped and clutched her throat. "Can't . . . breathe."

My heart started to pound. I felt Lauren and my mother stiffen, and the audience in the room was absolutely silent, attention riveted to the strange scene playing out before us. Could this be yet another one of the Latin-loving drama queen's acts?

"Sylvia, are you all right?" my father asked, rushing to her side.

She struggled to her feet, as if intending to leave the room once again. She scanned the faces of her fellow board members and murmured, *"Et tu, Brute?"*

My father caught her as she collapsed.

Chapter 2

Is There a Mathematician in the House?

Dad, still supporting Sylvia Greene, eased her to the floor behind the table and chairs. He checked for signs of breathing, then began mouth-to-mouth resuscitation.

The stunned silence was broken as Carol Barr leapt to her feet. "Somebody, help!" She scanned the audience. "Is anyone here a doctor?" When nobody spoke up or rushed to the front, she cried in a shrill voice, "There has got to be someone here more qualified than Charlie Peterson. He's just a mathematics professor, for crying out loud!"

My dad gave her a look, but kept working on Sylvia. The elderly attendant who'd carried Sylvia's coat rushed to the fallen board president and instantly started sobbing and wailing so loudly that the school superintendent took it upon himself to practically carry her down the hall.

The various murmurings of the audience—most in agreement that somebody needed to do something—were soon deafening. Mom had gone completely pale. Beside me Lauren cried, "Who's got a cell phone?"

At least sixty people in the room cried simultaneously, "I do." They were all dialing 911 at once. It felt as though we were trapped in some sort of surreal wireless-phone commercial.

"Busy signal," someone shouted from behind me.

"Just one of you call!" Lauren stomped her foot in frustration, then pointed at the nearest person, a fortyish man in an ill-fitting suit. For just an instant a proud smile flashed across his features, until he realized the solemn task he'd been appointed; then he furrowed his brow and dialed.

"Where's security?" someone directly behind me said. "There's got to be *someone* here who's certified to do what that mathematician is doing to her up there."

Kent Graham suddenly turned his attention to the camera that was still focused directly on the dais and all of the flustered school board members. "Cut the cameras! There could be children watching!"

At the sight of the muscular Kent Graham charging at him, the cameraman gasped and flipped a switch. "I was just trying to do my job," he said, flinching as if he expected Kent to tackle him.

Kent soon had his hands full as a couple of reporters and photographers rushed to the podium. A flash went off every couple of seconds. Stuart darted upstage to help Kent, trying to get between the cameras and Sylvia, all the while urging the photographers to "show some common decency."

Meanwhile, Michelle Lacy had knelt beside Sylvia and kept patting the fallen woman's hand. My father said something to her that I couldn't catch, and Michelle nodded and began CPR compressions on Sylvia's chest. Watching her, I felt a pang of guilt at my long-held assumption that, because she was such an elegant-looking woman, she would be the last one to roll up her sleeves and do physical work.

Beside her, the comparatively dumpy-looking Carol Barr had given up on finding a doctor in the room. She now was simply looking down at Sylvia's face and saying, "Ohmigod, ohmigod, ohmigod . . ."

Meanwhile, Stuart Ackleman deserted his attempts to waylay the newsmen and grabbed the microphone. He began urging everyone to "remain calm," which seemed to incite the crowd even further. He pointed at the doors in the back of the room. "Tonight's board meeting is hereby adjourned. Everyone needs to leave the room in an orderly fashion."

Stuart cleared his phlegmy voice and waited. Nobody moved. The problem was that, of all the board members, Stuart was the least able to command authority. He was short, elderly, slightly pudgy, and bald with a bad comb-over. The color in his cheeks was rising, and he gestured with both hands. "You! In the back row. Go. Everybody out. Give the woman some privacy. Clear the way for the paramedics."

For our part, I knew Mom would never leave with Dad in the process of administering CPR. Nor would I leave without the two of them. Lauren, in turn, was no doubt going to wait here until her husband—Police Sergeant Tommy Newton—arrived.

Though many people did leave, more stayed, taking a sideways stance to the stage, as if this were less egregious than to flat out stare at her.

A man with a scarecrow build in a security guard's uniform finally bolted through the side door nearest the dais. "The paramedics will be here any minute," he said, and promptly took over for my father at the artificial respiration. My father reluctantly got up, his face flushed.

As the security man had promised, sirens could already be heard in the distance by the time I followed my mom onto the dais, where she gave my father a hug. My mind was in a daze. Sylvia's last words, *"Et tu, Brute?"* troubled me. I wondered if her words meant that she believed she'd been poisoned. If so, wouldn't my father have ingested some poison himself when he'd put his mouth over hers to try to restore her breathing?

"I don't know if she's going to make it," my father whispered to my mom. "Good Lord. This is just . . ." He let his voice fade away, his face ashen and damp with perspiration.

Two medics rushed into the room with a gurney and took over the CPR. Their presence made the severity of the situation all the more obvious.

The bookish young man who'd been in the private meeting with Dad and the other board members had slowly made his way to the back of the auditorium. Keeping his head down, he pushed his way out the door and left without a second glance. I had a strong urge to rush after him, not only because I was so curious about his role in Sylvia's ad hoc meeting, but also because of his skulking exit.

The large audience soon dwindled to just a few lookie-loos, plus the reporters. I felt like an albatross, or a vulture, even, waiting around and doing nothing during the paramedics' fight to save Sylvia's life. I kept expecting her to bolt upright and slap one of them, but she wasn't moving a muscle. We watched in silence as, finally, the paramedics put Sylvia onto the gurney and wheeled her out of the room.

"Charlie," Stuart Ackleman said quietly, trying to square his rounded shoulders while he looked up into my father's eyes. "Things look bad. Carol, Michelle, and I are going to go on ahead to the emergency room. We'll keep you posted as to the latest news on Sylvia's condition."

"We're heading there, too," Kent said, indicating he meant himself and Gillian. Kent was Stuart's prototypical opposite— a broad-shouldered, agile, middle-aged man, and football coach of the Carlton High School team.

"We don't *all* need to go," Stuart objected.

"Fine," Kent said, running a hand over his thick, wavy, graying brown hair. "Then Gillian and I will go and you can set up a phone tree."

"I thought up the idea of going to the hospital first," Stuart protested under his breath so that the nearby reporters couldn't overhear. He reminded us of their presence with a jerk of his head. "It's going to look real bad if some go and some don't. We either all go, or we all stay away."

"Then it's settled." Kent used a teasing tone of voice that set my teeth on edge. "We'll all go."

With my father still immobilized by his shock, the five other board members started to collect their things.

"Hold it right there," the security officer called gruffly. Until that moment, he'd been occupied at keeping the host of reporters away from the dais. The board members stopped and looked at him. For my part, his words had made me want to raise my hands, as if he were the sheriff in an old western and had me in his sights. "The 911 dispatcher told me she had to send the police, just in case anything looked suspicious. All you folks had better stay put."

"You're just a security guard," Kent scoffed, "one step up

from a janitor. You've got no authority over us." He started toward the door and said to Gillian, "Let's go."

I winced, half expecting the guard to pull out his gun and show Kent that he *did* have the authority, but he merely glared and made no move to stop Kent.

"Let me just get my things," Gillian answered, averting her eyes as if embarrassed by Kent's classless retort.

"Leave your possessions exactly where they are till the police get here," the guard said, stepping toward her.

"But my purse is here," Gillian objected. "I have to take that with me."

He hitched up his belt on his nonexistent hips. "I'll keep an eye on everything, lady. That's my job." He shot another glare in Kent's direction. "I'll have the police bring your things if they decide to interview you at the hospital."

"Us? Be interviewed by the police? Don't be silly," Gillian immediately replied, looking at Kent, her lone political ally now that Sylvia was down and out. "Sylvia just . . . fainted. Mark my words. She's going to outlive all of us."

Which would make it difficult to "mark" her words, since we'd all be dead, but there was no sense quibbling. She started to reach for her purse, but the security man said firmly, "Leave it!"

Gillian narrowed her eyes at him, whirled on her heel, and called, "Let's go, Kent," over her shoulder. She turned back and said, "Charlie? You don't want to be the only board member not going to the hospital. Wouldn't be wise, politically. Whose car do you want to ride in?"

I realized then that the cars—as with all other matters—had been divided into the typical two factions: Carol, Michelle, and Stuart in one car, Kent and Gillian in the other. I couldn't help but grit my teeth at the audacity of turning such a tragic event into yet more political posturing. I honestly didn't understand how Gillian and I could have so much in common and yet hold such diametrically opposed opinions. We lived at far ends of the same subdivision of Sherwood Forest and were not only roughly the same age, but our sons were in the same class in school. The boys didn't like each other either, so apparently this would prove to be generational. The muscles in Dad's jaw were working and I knew he was moments away from exploding.

"Ride with me, Dad. We'll drop Mom off on the way."

"Fine," Dad answered testily. "So much for people bonding in the face of adversity." We followed the others out without another word.

Actually, knowing Sergeant Newton's mind-set so well, I suspected that the security man had been correct. We should stay here, in case Sylvia's collapse struck the police as being "suspicious," which it certainly seemed to be to me. And yet, I was too anxious to get out of the building to voice my concerns.

The night air was now chilly. Dad was shaking, and I didn't want him to drive in this state. We hesitated outside my father's car, my father patting his pockets. "My keys are in my jacket, which is still on the the back of my chair."

"I've got mine," Mom said, reaching into her purse.

I held out my hand. "I'll drive, Mom."

"Your father will drive," she said firmly, as if I were too young to drive at night.

"But I think—"

"Your father will drive," she repeated in her do-as-I-say-or-I-unleash-the-hounds voice. Grudgingly, I got into the backseat. Ironic that, after having experienced motherhood myself for a dozen years now, I still was expected to fill the role of dutiful daughter during such an intense situation.

"I have a bad feeling about this," Mom said the moment we got into our car, nervously running her hands through her short hair.

"Linda, I'm dropping you off at the house on the way home," Dad said as we pulled out of the parking lot. "You too, Molly."

"No, I'm going with you." Remembering who currently wielded the hammer of power within our trio, I added, "Mom wants me to be with you, don't you, Mom?"

"That's right, Charlie. Considering everything that happened tonight, you're not being left alone with those people. Not without a reliable witness."

"Thanks, Mom." At least she trusted me as a witness, if not a driver. Meanwhile, Dad's driving was fine, though a tad overcautious.

After dropping Mom off, we were the last ones to arrive in the waiting area of the emergency room. The five other board members were sitting on the brown, Naugahyde furniture, their relative positions once again determined by political factions: Gillian and Kent on one side of the small room, Michelle, Carol, and Stuart on the other. Appropriately, the only two remaining seats were along a third wall of the room. Dad and I could remain neutral.

Gillian rose and gave my father a smile. "I've already taken coffee orders from everyone. What would you like, Charlie?"

He shook his head. "Nothing, thanks."

She reclaimed her seat, somewhat dejectedly. Everyone except Gillian, and now Dad and me, was sipping steaming liquid from small Styrofoam cups.

"Sylvia's with the doctors by now, I assume," Dad asked.

Kent nodded. "No word yet."

Michelle stretched her long legs. "This waiting room could use some work."

"Work?" I repeated, not catching her drift.

"Redecorating. That's what I do for a living."

"You design waiting rooms?"

"No, I'm an interior decorator. In my real life, when I'm not working on the school board, that is."

"Ah." I nodded. I might have guessed. I had another acquaintance who reminded me of Michelle—attractive and always impeccably dressed—who was also an interior designer. Come to think of it, I had yet to meet a shabby-looking interior designer. If I ever did, I'd make it a point to hire her. She would probably understand and appreciate my lifestyle.

Gillian started pacing and eventually stood beside Dad and me. In a hushed voice, she said, "Why do you suppose

Sylvia's last words were, *'Et tu, Brute?'* You . . . don't think it's possible that she was poisoned, do you?"

So it wasn't just me who suspected poison, I immediately thought, feeling a small measure of vindication.

"No," Carol answered firmly on our behalf from across the room. "She wasn't drinking anything except the water, which we were all drinking. No," Carol repeated, and shook her head in emphasis. "She had to have had a heart attack, is all."

"Is it common for heart attack victims to clutch their throats and say that they can't breathe?" I asked quietly.

"Yes," my father answered.

"Molly," Carol said, "please keep your questions to yourself. You're not helping."

I looked at her, a little surprised that she even knew my name. Perhaps the fact that she was clearly the oldest woman in the room had caused her to act so patronizing toward me— or rather "matronizing"—but I bristled anyway. "I know I'm not helping. None of us are. That's why this is called a waiting room as opposed to a helping room. I'm just trying to figure out what happened."

"Carol told you," Stuart answered pointedly. "She had a heart attack."

Gillian leveled her gaze at Stuart. "Weren't you a doctor once? Why didn't you try to help her?"

"No, I'm not a medical doctor. I'm a Ph.D.—a doctor of philosophy. Did you expect me to administer emergency Descartes discourses till she revived?"

"Sorry," Gillian said, holding my gaze for some reason. "My mistake." I had seen her do that to another parent in a back-to-school meeting recently in our sons' fifth-grade class when she'd disagreed with something the teacher had said. That seemed to be her method for trying to indicate that you were her secret ally. If so, one of us was reading signals incorrectly, for I felt no camaraderie with the woman, whereas Stuart Ackleman had always struck me as upstanding and honest.

We shared several minutes of tense silence. At one point, a

woman in the typical dull green shade of scrubs came in and shut the inner door, explaining, "A police officer called. He said no one from the press is allowed to talk to you before he gets here. We're closing off this room to anyone but you, to be on the safe side."

Kent thanked her, then watched her leave, shaking his head. "The reporters are going to have a field day with this." Kent stuffed his hands into the pockets of his khakis. Despite the cold climate outside, he was wearing a yellow Izod shirt that showed off his muscular build. At length he turned to Gillian, seated beside him. "What did she say to you?"

"Nothing," Gillian said nervously. "Who do you mean? The nurse?"

"No, Sylvia. I saw her whisper something in your ear, just before we went to the private meeting."

"Oh." Gillian chuckled, as if relieved. "That was nothing. She just said . . ." She widened her eyes, then let her voice trail away. "It wasn't important."

"That is so like you, Gillian," Carol said from across the room. "By not telling everyone what she said, you make it seem all the more important."

"Fine, Carol." Gillian's brow was so knotted now that she looked shrewlike. "I'll tell you. She said that it was probably Charlie's henchman who released the pig. And that it bore a striking resemblance to you."

Carol clicked her tongue, but straightened and sucked in her stomach a little. "She did *not* say that. Not that last part, anyway. You made that up to pay me back for my remark about you just now."

Michelle, who seemed all the prettier when seated beside the plainer and older Carol, rolled her eyes and shook her head. "I can certainly see why you two are on the school board. Never did quite resolve the issue of who gets to go down the playground slide first or be the teacher's pet, did you?"

"I won't dignify that remark with a response," Gillian said through clenched teeth.

Carol, too, objected, "Really, Michelle, you have—"

Kent leapt to his feet and pounded a fist into his palm as if we were slackers on his football team that he was trying to energize at halftime. "Stop this bickering! That woman is in there fighting for her life. And all you people can do is argue with one another."

"Congratulations," Stuart said. "You get to be the one to take the moral high road."

"I meant every word I just said!"

"Of course you did," Stuart said in a monotone. "We all feel that way. None of us wants to see Sylvia die. But let's be honest, here. Haven't each of us thought how nice it would be if this meant that she were on an extended leave of absence? She's a difficult woman who's never said a sincere, kind word to anyone in her entire life."

"Speak for yourself, Stuart," Kent retorted, reclaiming his seat, but spreading out in his chair to take even more space. "You obviously don't know the woman the way I do. Yes, she's got a gruff exterior, and yes, she is determined and ruthless. But she gets things done, however much you might not happen to care for her methods. And underneath it all lies a heart of gold."

"Who do you think you're kidding?" Stuart said. The calm monotone was gone. In fact, he was seething. The color in his face had risen so dramatically that even his scalp was beet red and glowed from beneath the long strands of hair he'd combed over the top and plastered into place. "Underneath that gruff exterior lies a gruff interior, and we all know it. Every *one* of us has experienced the Wrath of Sylvia. If the names for hurricanes ever get as high as the letter *S* and there's a Hurricane Sylvia someday, I, for one, am moving into the nearest bomb shelter."

"You just disliked her because you two never agreed on anything."

Stuart pointed a finger in Kent's face. "You're speaking about her in the past tense, Kent. Is there something you know that the rest of us don't?"

Much as I disliked Kent's political views, I respected the

fact that even though he was so much Stuart's physical superior, he stayed seated and didn't shove Stuart's hand away. Or bite his finger, as I think I'd have done were our roles reversed.

"I intended no such thing," Kent said evenly. "I merely meant that in all of your past dealings with Sylvia, you have never understood her position. Perhaps you could profit by taking one of my exercise classes. I teach one for regaining flexibility."

"You steroidal bastard! What makes you—"

"Gentlemen, that's enough," my father interrupted. "Choose a better time and a more private location for your argument."

Kent snorted, and Stuart said, "Well, Charlie, *you're* hardly . . ." His gaze shifted to me, then he averted his eyes and his voice faded into a feigned—I was certain—coughing attack.

Hardly *what*? I asked myself silently. The only sentence ending that was compatible with Stuart's demeanor was: ". . . in any position to tell *us* what to do." Now I regretted the fact that, while we were en route to the hospital, I hadn't asked my father what had happened in the private meeting of board members. Perhaps Sylvia had come up with some truly scandalous charge that Stuart, at least, believed.

Wanting to divert attention from my father, who was looking utterly embarrassed, I blurted out, "Who was that man who came into your private meeting?"

"Sam Dunlap. He was a private investigator Sylvia had hired," Dad said solemnly.

Everyone else found something to look at. There was a sudden flurry of rummaging for magazines.

I should have given more thought as to the precise subject matter for my interruption; the mention of the private investigator had not diverted attention from my father at all. Quite the contrary. But it was too late now. "What was he there for?"

"According to Sylvia, he'd uncovered the dark secret from someone's past, which she was going to have to reveal publicly, unless that person resigned from the board," Dad answered quietly.

Now all eyes were on us. I was not about to ask my father in front of his peers if Sylvia had said what this secret was. Instead, I said, "Maybe one of us should ask the nurse in admissions for Sylvia's status."

My feeble attempt at diversion not working, Gillian let out a haughty laugh reminiscent of someone her child's age. "She meant you, of course, Charlie."

Dad shook his head. "Just as we were leaving the back room, Sylvia pulled me aside and whispered that she had changed her mind. That, actually, the private investigator had recently learned something so much worse about one of you that she'd decided not to act against me."

"Ha!" Gillian cried. "That's a convenient story."

I instantly felt like socking the woman, but Dad said calmly, "It's the truth."

"Whom was this supposedly concerning?" Carol asked Dad.

"She didn't say."

Unable to contain my curiosity any longer, I asked, "But, Dad, you were all in the meeting room for a good fifteen minutes or more. What *did* she say?"

Dad rolled his eyes. "Most of the time was taken by an argument regarding the various ramifications of allowing Mr. Dunlap into a private meeting."

Kent scoffed. "The whole thing was probably another one of Sylvia's political maneuvers. Sam Dunlap probably isn't even really an investigator." Kent scanned the faces of the board members seated along the opposite wall. "He's probably some actor she hired to play dress-up and try to scare one of you into voting to continue financing sports rather than arts."

"Come off it, Kent," Michelle said. "You know full well if this so-called secret had anything to do with one of us in the arts contingent, she'd have revealed it to the entire world. Instead, she sat on the information, probably because it would undermine her support otherwise."

"What do you mean?" Kent asked.

"That this secret had to do with you. Or Gillian."

"That's nonsense," Kent shot back, with Gillian protesting as well. "If it were one of us, she'd have kept it to herself without making any insinuations whatsoever until after the vote."

"Oh, she wasn't as ruthless as all that," Carol said.

Stuart laughed and shook his head as he peered at Carol over his glasses. "So. Already writing her memorial service, are we?"

Just then, all eyes turned to the door as Sergeant Tommy Newton stormed into the waiting room. He was probably upset that we "witnesses" had had the chance to compare stories for quite some time now.

Tommy scanned the faces and took his cap off, his thick red hair suffering from a case of hat-head. "Gentlemen. Ladies." He stared at me for a moment, then added, "Molly."

I couldn't help giving him a glare for acting as though I fit in neither of the other categories.

"I'm going to have to ask you all to . . ." He stopped as someone entered the room.

The doctor, a bespectacled man with blond hair, glanced around. We all sat in silence, staring as he asked quietly, "Is one of you Ms. Greene's next of kin?"

We all turned to look at Gillian, Sylvia's best friend on the board, who rose. "She's been divorced for years, and her teenager died in a car accident five years ago."

The doctor fixed his gaze on Gillian. "We need to contact siblings, parents. Someone."

"Oh my God. She didn't make it, did she?" Gillian asked, with a little too much dramatic flair to be sincere.

The doctor shook his head. "We did everything we could, but it was too late. She never regained consciousness."

I scanned the room. All five of the remaining seven board members—not counting my father—appeared to sigh in relief.

Chapter 3

What's My Secret?

My father sank his face into his hands. He was visibly more upset than were Gillian or Kent, though they were Sylvia's advocates and supposed friends on the board. Meanwhile, her adversaries—Stuart, Michelle, and Carol—seemed to have to work at changing their facial expressions of relief to more appropriate looks of solemnity.

"Are you okay, Dad?" I asked him quietly.

He let his hands drop to his lap but kept his face down-turned. His lips were almost white. He shook his head. "This is . . ." His voice trailed away. He stayed staring at his knees.

Sylvia's doctor muttered some general condolences, then left the room. It was inconceivable to me that all of this was really happening, that Sylvia Greene had died, essentially right in front of me. She'd become such a galvanizing force over the last couple of years—someone who always made reading the newspaper worthwhile, in an effort to see what infuriating, lamebrained scheme she'd cooked up. Now she was dead.

"I'm gonna need to get everybody's names and addresses," Tommy said seriously. He looked more tense than I could recall in the many years we'd known each other. The muscles in his jaw were working. His skin, pale beneath the light dusting of red freckles, was damp with perspiration.

"Why?" Michelle asked gently. "I want to cooperate, of course, but . . . people collapse and die all the time. Surely by now the doctors know the—"

"What's the problem, officer?" Kent interrupted.

Tommy didn't answer, but I began to suspect that he'd

25

already received some damning piece of evidence that we weren't privy to. If that was the case, perhaps his uneasiness was due to the lack of control he'd had over the investigation to this point. The "murder scene" hadn't been sealed; the witnesses had talked among themselves at length.

Though Tommy kept his face inscrutable as always, he glanced at my father, and a second possibility occurred to me that made me all but quake in my shoes. Could Tommy suspect my father? Was that why Tommy seemed so shaken by Sylvia's death?

Just then, a second officer emerged from the hallway. This one, a young, baby-faced man I'd met before but whose name had since deserted me, gestured to Tommy that he needed to speak with him privately.

I craned my neck to watch as they left the waiting room and spoke with a doctor. The doctor who'd given us the news about Sylvia soon joined the three of them. The expressions on all four men's faces were somber, their demeanors understated. After the doctors headed off together down a corridor, Tommy spoke quietly for a moment to the second officer, who nodded as if Tommy had given him instructions.

While watching this scene play out even with no audio, my instincts concurred with my fear: Something indicated possible foul play in Sylvia's death. I was certain of it.

My heart pounding, I looked again at my father. He had barely moved, his eyes still averted.

"Dad? Don't you think you should—"

I stopped when my father shook his head, still not looking up. I'd meant to ask him if he should take charge, as was his natural way when faced with a group of people lacking direction.

My father's inertia was scaring me. All of my life, he'd been so capable and decisive, so ready to quickly choose some course of action and charge forth. Now with his bald head glistening with sweat and his downturned features pale and drawn, he had the bearing of a broken and defeated man. It was so painful to see him like this that my insides ached.

Tommy and his colleague returned and scanned the room.

The moment they crossed the threshold, my father straightened and watched them. Tommy rocked on his heels. Beside him, the young officer watched us warily as Tommy said, "We've got to interview each of you. 'Fraid I got to ask you all to stop talkin' to one another in the meantime."

"Officer," Kent said gruffly, "that's simply unacceptable. We're all very tired, and clearly Sylvia had a heart attack. There's no point in treating this as if it were some kind of a criminal investigation."

"Tell you what, Mr. Graham," Tommy fired back. "I won't tell you how to run the school board, and you don't tell me how to investigate suspicious deaths."

That was more confrontational than Tommy's normal demeanor. So much so, in fact, that I deliberately averted my eyes when he glanced over in my direction. "Mr. Ackleman, could you come with me, please?"

Stuart cleared his throat and meekly shuffled off after Tommy. Kent watched them leave, then muttered, "Bet that officious son-of-a-gun is now going to make me wait and go last."

"Sergeant Newton is just doing his job," the young officer said, sounding as though he'd forced his voice to be a halftone deeper than natural.

"That's all I was trying to do when all of this happened. And *I'm* not even getting paid for doing *my* job."

Feeling trapped, I headed to the pay phone in the corner, anxious to talk to my husband.

"Molly?" the young officer asked. "Who are you calling?"

I was a little startled that the officer knew my name, but reminded myself that we had met before. He probably just had a better memory for names than I did. "My husband. I need to check in with my children and let them know where I am."

"Me too," Gillian said, rising. This set off a minor clamor as the other board members leaped to their feet to get a place in line to call their people, as well.

"Whoa." The officer held up his palms and shook his head at us as if we were misbehaving children, which was difficult to take from someone so much my junior. "I'm going to have to ask you all to wait until Officer Newton dismisses you."

"Dismisses us? Who died and made him school principal?" Kent grumbled, but he sat down nonetheless.

Dad patted my shoulder. "Grandma will have called Jim and the kids."

I nodded and considered how very unimpressed Mom would have been had she overheard her husband referring to her as "Grandma." At least Dad had recovered enough of his composure to speak to me. He still wouldn't meet my eyes, however.

Tommy proceeded to interview each school board member one by one, leaving the young officer in the waiting room with us to make sure we didn't "compare stories." Tommy had spoken with each of the "pro-arts" contingent first: Stuart, Carol, and Michelle.

Despite Kent Graham's pessimism, my dad was the last person to be interviewed. In fact, the others had taken off in their carpools long before he finished. Save for me and the young officer, the waiting room was once again filled with sick patients and their families. I tried hard not to pace, not to stare at the people and play guess-their-medical-emergency games.

Dad was taking forever, more than three times as long as anyone else. He knew Tommy personally. They lived next door to each other.

"This sure is taking a while," I said to my young watchman.

"Yeah."

"Are you sure you're still supposed to wait here? Everyone else has already gone, you know. I was merely in the audience at the board meeting. I didn't see anything important. And even if I had, there's nobody left on the board for me to talk to."

"I'm under orders to stay with you."

"Do you mean that you're under specific orders to stay with me, or just with the last person here?"

"Sergeant Newton said I should keep a close eye on you."

"Why?"

He shrugged and returned his attention to *Sports Illustrated*.

"Is it because he suspects my dad?"

He shrugged a second time and flipped the page.

Taking this as a "yes," I was now thoroughly ticked off at Tommy. He knew full well that I'd had nothing to do with the murder, but was assuming that I'd interfere with his investigation.

Because Tommy wasn't here, I decided to vent my frustration on the next best thing. "Is this what you call keeping a close eye on somebody? Reading a sports magazine? If Tommy wants me to be in the company of a man reading sports articles, I can just go home to my husband and save the taxpayers some money."

The officer tossed the magazine on the table and turned his attention to the small television set suspended near the ceiling in one corner.

"That makes me feel much better," I grumbled.

I picked up the magazine myself, but did a double take as a local television news announcer came on the screen to say, "We interrupt our regular programming to bring you a breaking story. The president of the Carlton school board, Sylvia Greene, collapsed in the auditorium at the Ed Center tonight in front of a packed house, as well as thousands of viewers watching the cable broadcast. Ms. Greene died after attempts to revive her at Ellis Hospital failed. Our latest reports are unable to confirm or deny rumors that poisoning is suspected, and that one of the fellow board members could have been involved in Ms. Greene's death."

My stomach fell. The three couples sharing the waiting room had focused their attention on the TV, as well. The broadcast changed to show footage from the meeting. The first shot was just as the board left together for their private meeting in the back room, with Sylvia filling her water glass. The officer turned off the set.

If the poison was in her water, the pitcher itself had to be uncontaminated. Maybe Sylvia had been poisoned at dinner.

There was no direct indication that she had been poisoned at the board meeting itself.

Just then, another officer entered the hospital carrying what looked exactly like my father's jacket over his arm. I had a feeling that they weren't bringing this out of concern.

"Oh no. Please don't let there be something in the pocket," I muttered to myself.

" 'Scuse me?" the officer beside me said.

As a diversion, I showed him the article my magazine happened to be open to. "How 'bout them Broncos, hey? I used to live in Boulder, Colorado, you know. They're my team."

"I'm a Packers fan myself."

"That's not very risky. How about rooting for the Saints? There's a team that could use loyal fans."

He forced a smile, and I forced myself to stay seated and quiet, all the while with my thoughts in hyper-drive.

A few minutes later, my father looked positively stricken as he emerged from his interview. Tommy lagged a step behind him as they entered the waiting room, and he looked none too happy himself. It was all I could do not to tear into him. I so wanted someone to blame for my father's obvious downheartedness, as well as for my miserable night.

Tommy's and my eyes met, and in a radical departure from his usual eagerness to joust with me verbally, he said, " 'Night, Molly. Try to get some sleep."

"You're being nice to me." My pulse started racing. All was not right with the world. "Things are that bad? You're feeling sorry for me?"

"Huh?"

"It was the coat, wasn't it. My father's jacket that the other officer brought in. He's being framed."

Tommy crossed his arms on his chest and growled, "For Chrissake, Molly! Don't be so quick to read doom 'n' gloom into every little nuance."

"You're angry with me because I'm right."

"No, I'm angry because you're annoying." He pointed with his chin. "Your dad is waiting for you."

I whirled on my heel and left without a word. I could feel

Tommy's eyes on me. I had just verified what it was that had thrown me off balance and made Tommy seem so tense: We were adversaries now. He suspected my father of this crime. And he felt sorry for me and my family.

Dad said nothing when I got into the passenger seat. I asked, "What went on in there? What were you talking to Tommy about?"

Dad didn't answer for the longest time. He kept his eyes riveted to the road as he drove. "You're familiar with the Serenity prayer, Molly," he answered quietly. "This is one of those times when you've got to accept the things you cannot change."

"What do you mean, Dad? You're scaring me."

He didn't say another word, just pulled up in front of my driveway. I got out and he drove away without another word.

I went upstairs to check on the kids and kiss them good night, even though it was too late for them to hear me. Karen was asleep on her back, her forehead slightly damp, her light brown hair framing her pretty face. Nathan had flopped around on his bed, all long limbs at angles, his curly brown hair every which way.

Jim was already in bed. I put on my T-shirt that doubled as a nightgown and got under the covers beside him. Jim stirred a little—when I intentionally jostled the bed, that is. By my book, that was a sign that he was awake enough for me to justify talking to him. "Did you hear what happened at the board meeting?"

He grunted, and I repeated the question. Finally, he woke to answer, "Yeah. Uh. Your mom called. Are you all right?"

"I'm fine. Just tired and discouraged." Not to mention scared half to death by my father's sudden fatalistic approach to this.

"Tried to wait up for you." He yawned. "I've got a breakfast meeting in Albany. First thing in the morning. Seven A.M. How's your dad?"

"I guess he's all right. My gut instincts are telling me that this is going to be a major problem. One of Sylvia's last acts was to ask my father to carry her glass into the back room with him. When we were driving home from the hospital, I asked him what went on in his interview with Tommy. He said that I had to accept the things I couldn't change. I hate to say this, but as much as he keeps denying that he has a deep, dark secret that Sylvia was set to divulge, I'm not convinced. He's acting so ... closed. Secretive, even. What do you think? Has my dad seemed different to you when you've been with him?"

Jim's light snores clued me in that I was talking to myself. I accidentally kicked him with my heel as I pulled the covers up.

In the morning, with Jim long gone for his breakfast meeting, the children were in a whirl getting ready for school. Our cocker spaniel, too, was always full of energy in the morning. Betty Cocker—BC for short—is a beautiful color, all reddish brown fur except for a white blaze on her chest. I dragged myself around the kitchen and made the children's lunches, but couldn't get in sync. Finally, I explained, "Karen, Nathan, I have to tell you some really awful news. Last night one of the women on the school board with your Grampa died, and it's really upset Grampa and me. This is a hard time for both of us right now. I feel so bad having to watch my father go through it."

Karen nodded solemnly. Nathan said nothing for a moment, then asked, "Mom?"

"Yes?"

"Did you and Dad get a chance to discuss my allowance yet?"

I gritted my teeth, counted to five, knowing full well I couldn't make it to ten, then said, "Let's review, shall we? Just now, while words were coming out of my mouth, were you listening to any of them?"

"Yeah, Mom. You were talking about that lady, Sylvia Greene. We already saw her die on TV last night."

"But, Nathan, that was real. It wasn't just a TV show with

actors and actresses playing parts, pretending to die. Sylvia Greene really did die."

His lightly freckled face was guileless as his dark brown eyes stared straight into mine. "So could you just give me my allowance yourself? Dad doesn't need to know, right?"

I winced, tempted to bang my head against the nearest wall, but refrained because the only thing that would accomplish would be to give myself a headache.

"Grampa is still going to be on the school board, right, Mom?" Karen asked.

"Yes, he is. Why do you ask?"

"I think it's cool that he's kind of famous. His picture is on the front page of the paper." She showed me the newspaper, which she'd folded on top of her binder. "Can I bring in the article for my current affairs homework?"

"Not till I get the chance to read it myself," I muttered, scanning the page. The picture showed my father kneeling on the dais, but had been cropped so as not to show Sylvia Greene's body. At least some editor had a measure of restraint. My vision immediately locked on the phrase, *"about to reveal a secret from Peterson's past. . . ."*

"Time for your school buses."

Nathan glanced at the clock on the microwave. "Mine won't come for another ten minutes."

Now that Karen was in junior high, her school day was thirty minutes longer than Nathan's. "Go early," I growled, then realized with a start how much the voice coming from my lips resembled my mother's.

To my surprise, they grabbed their backpacks without complaint and headed out, cheerfully saying goodbye. I was going to have to try to channel Mom more often.

As it seemed I was doing more and more frequently, I sent up a prayer that my current traumas would leave my children unscathed. Karen's bus came right away, and I kept an eye out the front window until the yellow splotches visible between the budding branches of maple trees lining the street let me know that Nathan's bus was at the stop. Then I called my parents, but got no answer.

They might well have gotten so many calls throughout the night and early this morning that they'd turned the ringer off. My parents lived on the next cul-de-sac down from me, and it would be better if I just walked over there and spoke with them anyway.

Ignoring BC's forlorn, take-me-with-you brown eyes, I locked up and headed out, the air brisk on my face. The first fallen leaves were beginning to collect against the various windbreaks. The sky was that shade of gray that doubled as blue for those who'd never had the great fortune of seeing a Colorado sky.

Tommy's cruiser was still in the driveway next door. He must have come home at some point and was now catching up on his lost sleep.

I caught sight of Lauren in her kitchen window. She held up both palms with spread fingers, then pointed at her floor to indicate I should come over in ten minutes. Tommy must have been awake, but leaving for work soon. I gave her the okay sign, then continued to my parents' doorstep and rang the doorbell.

Mom answered. She looked as though she hadn't slept all night. In any case, I decided to attribute her puffy, bloodshot eyes to lack of sleep, rather than to the much more unsettling thought that she'd been crying.

She greeted me with a sigh rather than a smile and stepped out onto the front porch, closing the door behind her. "Molly, I'm sorry, but your father only just now fell asleep, on the living room couch. We've had a rough night. We even had to turn off the phone, because of all the calls we've been getting."

"Curious friends?"

"And nosy reporters." She clicked her tongue. "Speaking of which . . ." She gestured with her chin at the car pulling up behind me into the cul-de-sac. "Bet this turns out to be another one."

Unfortunately, moments later, Mom's pessimism proved accurate. My least favorite newsman—the short, out-of-shape man I'd chewed out last night for quoting my remarks at a grocery store—emerged from his car. He strode toward us purposefully, then hesitated when he spotted me, and forced a smile. "Morning, Ms. Masters. Mrs. Peterson."

"No comment," my mother called to him, then reentered the house.

Watching my mother essentially being chased from her own front porch, I felt a surge of anger and protectiveness toward her that was something of a role reversal. I fisted my hands and glared at the man.

The reporter rolled his eyes and shook his head in frustration. "I'm only trying to do my job here. I'd rather get direct quotes from your parents before I have to resort to using 'sources.' "

"Maybe you need to work on your presentation skills. Besides, my parents and I are close. They know full well how you quoted me out of context the other day, and aren't about to talk to you now. And feel free to quote me when I say that."

He crossed his arms and rocked on his heels; then his lips set in a smirk. "This must be very upsetting for you, Ms. Masters. I'm sure you've heard the rumors that your father is the chief suspect in Sylvia Greene's untimely death."

"No comment," I snarled at him through gritted teeth. "Please leave. And tell your coworkers to stay away from my parents' home, as well."

He spread his pudgy hands, his expression one of wide-eyed innocence. "Hey, lady, let's get something straight here. I'm doing you and your dad a favor. I'm trying to give him a chance to respond to a piece we're set to run in tomorrow's paper."

"What does it say?" Though I tried hard to make the question sound casual, the thought of a possible front-page article accusing my father had shaken me.

"Our sources have already informed us exactly what your father's secret was that the late school board president was about to divulge to the world. But, hey, we'll run it with or without your father's response."

My face felt blazing hot. He grinned at my distress. He

reached into a pocket, then held out his business card and
sneered at me. "Tell your father that if he wants a chance to
be heard, call me before midnight. Otherwise, our article
runs as is."

Chapter 4

My Toilet Runneth Over

I snatched the card from him, barely able to control my rage at his accusations. "You're bluffing, Mister . . . ," I glanced at the business card, "Johnson, and I'm not going to fall for it."

"Am I?" He gave me a know-it-all look and shook his head. "All I can say to that, *Ms.* Masters, is apparently your family isn't as 'close' as you seem to think it is. Have a nice day."

"Thank you. And may you get exactly what you deserve from yours."

He strutted back to his car, probably not realizing that he resembled a sack of mashed potatoes with legs. Watching him, I pictured myself ripping the bumper off his car and beating him over the head with it. Despite the overwhelming temptation to, at the very least, launch into a venomous verbal attack, I knew I had to hold my tongue or risk having a slew of ugly words quoted in tomorrow's paper. For all I knew, he could have a camera at the ready in his car. Inwardly seething, I merely watched him drive away.

Once his car was out of sight, I did my best to calm myself, then knocked softly on my parents' door. Dad would be sleeping right near the sounding device for the doorbell, and I didn't want to wake him. My mother opened the door and stepped out beside me, once again taking care to close the door behind her.

"Did you overhear any of that?" I asked.

"No, you know what a nut your father's always been about

weatherproofing the house. It keeps the place fairly sound-proof as well." Suddenly, her eyes widened. She seemed to somehow rise up an inch or two, despite her already ramrod-straight posture. "Oh, Molly! You didn't get into an argument with the reporter, did you?"

"I . . . didn't say anything that will show up in the papers, if that's what you mean. But he told me some pretty alarming things."

" 'Alarming things'?" she repeated, then asked in a half-whisper, "What did he tell you?"

"That he needed Dad's reaction to the story he was going to run in the morning, which is going to reveal Dad's big secret."

Mom's features clouded with anger. "He's made it clear that he doesn't *have* a secret. You heard him say so yourself last night."

"Yeah, I know. The reporter's probably bluffing. But he gave me his business card and told me to have Dad call him by midnight if he wants his denial to accompany the story."

Mom took the card from me. "Okay. I doubt it'll do much good, but I'll give this to your father when he wakes up. I'd better try to get some rest myself. I'll see you later."

There was something in her facial expression that scared the living daylights out of me. Perhaps it was her reluctance to meet my eyes, as if the truth might be written in hers. Her earlier wording now struck me as a demurral. She hadn't said that Dad didn't have a secret, but rather that *he'd* made it clear that he didn't.

She started to open the door, but froze when I asked, "Mom, did Dad tell you what Sylvia was planning to reveal about him?"

"Why do you ask?" She didn't turn around to face me. "You doubt your own father?"

When you come straight down to it, yes. But I didn't want to say so. I muttered noncommittally, "I'm just trying to help."

She went inside and only then turned to face me. The tears she was trying so hard to keep inside were now welling in her eyes. The sight made my insides knot. "Then go home, Molly."

She shut the door on me.

On the verge of tears myself, I went next door to Lauren and Tommy's, even though Tommy's cruiser was still parked in the driveway, which meant that Lauren and I wouldn't be able to speak freely just yet. I wondered if he'd witnessed any of my confrontation with the reporter, though I would have liked to believe that, if so, Tommy would have come out and helped me encourage him to leave.

Tommy, dressed in his uniform, opened the door just as I reached for the doorbell and seemed a bit surprised to see me.

"Molly. Mornin'. How's your dad?"

I couldn't help but notice that he looked past my shoulder in the direction of my parents' house as he spoke.

"I don't know. He's sleeping late. I haven't gotten the chance to speak to him this morning."

"Uh-huh," he said, a speech affectation of his that only annoys me whenever we happen to be at odds. Though he'd done nothing—yet—to earn my wrath, his response had set my teeth on edge. He stepped aside to allow me to come inside his house.

Lauren must have heard my voice, for she rushed into the hallway, not even noticing that a couple of drops of coffee from her cup had sloshed onto the carpet in the process. "Molly, hi. Tommy was just about to leave for work. Would you like—"

"Tommy, you know my father didn't do this," I interrupted. Though I knew it was rude of me to ignore Lauren, there was a strange vibration that I was picking up, one which refused to let me simply allow Tommy to leave. I was getting the feeling that the two of them had already discussed my father's troubles and that Lauren was trying to run interference for me. "He would never commit a crime of any sort, and certainly not one of violence. You do realize that, don't you?"

He raised his palms in a placating gesture that had the opposite effect on me. "Molly, I can't discuss your father's role in what happened last night. You know how it goes. Nobody ever wants to accept the possibility that someone in one's own family could—"

"Tommy, I don't believe it! You live next door to the man!" I was instantly so furious that I was literally hopping as I yelled at him. "You can't honestly think for one minute that he would do something like this! Obviously, someone is framing him!"

"Didn't I just get through sayin' I couldn't talk to you? That is, not unless you have some pertinent information 'n' you want to come down to the station house with me."

"Molly, Tommy, let's just—"

Once again I ignored Lauren. "That's just great, Tommy. My own father is being set up to take the rap on a murder charge, and I'm just supposed to do nothing."

"Molly, if he's innocent, you got nothing to worry about. You worry more than anyone I've ever met in my life."

I glanced at Lauren. She looked horridly uncomfortable at seeing the two of us go at it like this. I managed to take a deep breath and calm myself down a notch. "Maybe so, but if you'd had the run of luck that I've had—so bad that your neighbors were calling *you* Typhoid Molly—you'd leap to pessimistic conclusions, too."

"Uh-huh. You got a point, there, Moll. If folks started callin' me Typhoid Molly, I'd be downright ornery, too. Not to mention, seriously concerned about my testosterone level."

"Yes, well, if . . ." I had launched into an immediate retort, but I had no comeback. My cheeks grew warm. I could not believe that Tommy had fed me a straight line just screaming for a witticism, and I had none to offer. "He's innocent, Tommy. You've got to help us prove that."

"See, that's the thing, Molly. My job is not to help you or your father prove anything. It's to find Sylvia Greene's killer. I've got to keep impartial. And that's exactly what I intend to do. In fact, if I knew your father any better than just to say hello to him when we happen to bump into each other, I'd've withdrawn from this investigation—"

"Tommy . . ." Lauren started to interrupt, but then she pursed her lips and averted her eyes.

Your testosterone level's already so high it's short-circuiting your brain, I thought, too late to voice the line. That was one of the advantages of composing greeting cards. There, unlike live conversation, you get however much time is needed to come up with a snappy punch line.

Again, he held up his palms. "Sorry. That's the way things have to be." He gave each of us a long look. "If you all want to keep peace, you better not ask me any special favors."

My cheeks were blazing, and I wasn't about to acknowledge that I realized Tommy was right.

Lauren murmured goodbye, and Tommy gave her a peck on the cheek, then brushed past me, got into his cruiser, and drove off.

I turned back toward Lauren, who was watching me with a sad expression on her face. "I'm sorry," I said. "I'm making a horse's ass out of myself this morning. Everything that comes out of my mouth seems to add to the problem." Which was not a metaphor I wished to explore further.

"You're under a lot of stress right now. Anybody in your situation would be struggling. Have you already had breakfast? I made some muffins."

"Great. Thanks." As Lauren realized, I rarely ate breakfast but was always a willing consumer of her homemade muffins. She baked whenever she was upset. Fortunately, I found her baking wonderful comfort food, and our moods often corresponded.

I followed her into the kitchen, and she poured a cup of tea for me while I took a seat at her faux wood linoleum counter. "Lauren, don't you have to go into work this morning?"

"It's Tuesday. Remember?"

"Oh, right." She was only working Mondays, Wednesdays, and Fridays now. Her job as secretary at the high school paid little but allowed her to be home by the time her daughter Rachel was getting out from school. Rachel and my daughter were the best of friends and were in seventh grade together.

"This is a real mess. Not just because of Tommy. My own parents are stonewalling me. As much as I hate to say this, they're acting guilty. And how are we going to prove he's innocent, when even Tommy, who knows my father personally, is acting as though he believes my father killed Sylvia?"

"It's a mess, all right."

She kept her attention focused on the teabag she was steeping for an inordinate amount of time, and I knew she was working out her phrasing for some bombshell of a statement. A minute later she dropped it, after she finally stopped fidgeting with the cup and slid it and some sort of red-berried muffin toward me.

"Molly, I know that there's no way you're going to want to hear this right now, but maybe you should steer clear of the whole thing."

"You're right. I can't hear that, let alone do it."

She tilted her head, in her personalized gesture of a slight shrug. Her round cheeks had reddened slightly. "The thing is, though, Molly, if your father does have something in his past that Sylvia uncovered, he obviously doesn't want you or anyone else to know about it. Maybe you should just respect that and . . . back off. Know what I mean?"

"Sure, but I think that—" I broke off. What if Dad was covering up for some torrid affair that could destroy both my mother and, to a lesser extent, me? "But I just had an encounter with a reporter who claims he's going to run an article about the content of Sylvia's news in the morning. So, if it's going to come out anyway, I'd certainly rather hear it from my father than read about it on the front page."

"Anyone in your shoes would," Lauren murmured.

Anyone in my shoes? Did she know more than she was letting on? "Tell me something. You've known my parents almost as long as I have. Do you have any idea what this secret could be?"

To my relief, she shook her head. "No, but you sound pretty convinced that he really is hiding something. That's different from how you felt last night."

"Not really. I still think it's more than likely that this is all one big smoke screen that Sylvia put up to try to intimidate my father into changing his vote." I blew on the surface of the tea and took a sip, capped off by a bite of muffin, which was delicious—sweet, but with a nice tangy flavor from the berries—then asked, "What's the scoop with the investigation?"

"Tommy wouldn't tell me much of anything. He says he knows I'll go straight to you."

"Well, duh. So what did you find out?"

Lauren searched my eyes, then said quietly, "There was a vial in your dad's jacket that contained some sort of really powerful, fast-acting poison. I can't remember the name of it. Anyway, they did a blood test on Sylvia Greene at the hospital. It came back positive."

"Meaning she was poisoned by the same substance they found in the vial?"

"Yes."

Because this was precisely what I was expecting, I wasn't surprised, but it was still horribly unnerving to have my worst suspicions confirmed. "Were there fingerprints on the vial?"

She shook her head.

Her news left me feeling exhausted and defeated. "I knew it. This is a living nightmare. And Tommy accuses me of being pessimistic."

"He's right. You are."

"Just because you're pessimistic doesn't mean your life is not in the toilet."

Lauren gave me a sad smile and crossed her arms. "Now *there's* a catchy slogan. Used that on any greeting cards lately?"

"You know I always leave the sappy, sentimental cards for someone else to write. Anyway, the thing is, no one was wearing gloves during the meeting, my father included. Someone had to have wiped the fingerprints off and slipped the vial into my father's jacket."

Lauren grimaced and tucked an errant lock of her brown hair behind an ear, her pretty, round face still looking deeply worried. "That's the worst part. I overheard Tommy's phone conversation with another officer late last night. The police examined the videotape of the proceedings last night. Nobody went near your father's jacket the entire time the cameras were on."

"That *is* hard to explain," I murmured, taking another sip of tea and bite of muffin. "But then, the cameras weren't on the whole time the paramedics were there trying to revive her. The killer could have slipped something into Dad's pocket during all the confusion."

"Have you found out who that man was who went back into the room with them?"

"Some private investigator Sylvia had hired to do a background check on Dad. Apparently the investigator didn't say anything during the private meeting, but Dad said that Sylvia had told him this investigator had uncovered something incriminating about another board member."

"So, then, it must have been somebody else on the board who Sylvia was intending to strong-arm during the private meeting."

"Right. But, supposedly, nobody knew who, except Sylvia herself. And, most likely, the person with the terrible secret." And the private investigator! I took a couple more sips of tea, then rose, muffin in hand. "Listen, thanks for the tea and sympathy. Plus the muffin. But I'd better get home."

She walked me to the door. "What are you going to do next?"

"Probably talk to Sylvia's private investigator."

She nodded and said simply, "Be careful."

"Lauren, I do realize that, as the investigating officer, Tommy can't play favorites."

She pursed her lips. "Everything's going to work itself out. Tommy will find the real killer, and if there is something haunting your dad, you'll cope with it."

"I hope so," I said, trying to wage war against my much-deserved and readily apparent pessimism.

She gave me a reassuring hug.

I headed down her walkway, then stopped and stared at my parents' place for a moment, hoping that one of my parents would sense my presence and invite me inside. When they didn't, I slowly walked home, finishing my muffin and stuffing its paper wrapping in my jacket pocket for want of a trash can.

The phone was ringing as I unlocked my front door. As was typical, my little dog was pressed sideways against the door in anticipation of my arrival. I had to ignore her, which was difficult because I had to literally step over her in order to run to the phone. She followed at my heels, no doubt alarmed at my breach of etiquette at not pausing to pet her first.

"Hello?" I panted into the phone.

"Molly," said the inordinately sad female voice over the line. "I saw the papers this morning. I am just so very, very sorry."

I gritted my teeth and yanked my arms out of my jacket sleeves with a vengeance, flinging the coat onto the kitchen chair. There was only one person I knew who could be this syrupy and think that anyone would believe her to be sincere. "Hello, Stephanie."

"Oh, Molly. I can't help but feel responsible, in a small way, at least. You undoubtedly realize that, as Carlton's PTA president, I never miss a board meeting, but Mikey has a bad cold, or at least he did last night. He's much better this morning. And as wonderful as Tiffany is with children, she's not so great with grouchy four-year-old brothers."

"I can imagine," I said. Stephanie's teenage daughter, Tiffany, was our baby-sitter and did an adequate-enough job watching the kids. I wouldn't call her "wonderful," though, and was glad that my children had reached the age where I felt it was safe to leave them unsupervised for reasonable periods of time.

"So, of course, that meant that I had to stay home with my little one. I couldn't very well bring a fussy toddler and, well," she sighed, "this is a difficult time for me. Tiffany is going through something of a difficult phase right now."

As was typical of Stephanie, she had immediately moved the conversation around to herself and her own problems. While speaking, I knelt to rub my cocker spaniel's tummy.

She was so spoiled it was embarrassing—true of my dog, as well as of Stephanie and her daughter.

Taking an educated guess as to what Tiffany's current "phase" might be, I asked, "She's dyed her hair again?"

"Lime green. She looks like the Jolly Green Giant's niece. It just breaks my heart. Honestly, Molly. I am going to sue the company that produces these colors. If they didn't sell them, the kids wouldn't be able to buy them and destroy their appearances."

And if the kids didn't buy them, the company wouldn't produce them. "It was nice of you to call, Stephanie, but I really have to be—"

"Rumor has it that the police think your father is the prime suspect. That must be so devastating for you and your family."

That got my full attention. I rose from my knees and barely contained my temper enough to say, "What makes you say that? Actually, we are enjoying all of this attention immensely."

There was a pause. "Really?"

"No, Stephanie, I was being sarcastic."

"All of that aside, I just wanted to tell you that I'm here for you if you need me. You know how indebted I am to you, so if there's anything I can do to help you through these difficult times, don't hesitate to ask."

"Fine, although I can't think of what that would possibly—"

"I know! A spaghetti casserole! Don't say another word. I have a marvelous recipe, and I'll bring it to you, steaming hot."

"The recipe or the meal?"

"You are such a kidder, Molly."

She hung up. I went back to petting the dog. "A visit from Stephanie. Oh, joy, BC. This will top off a truly marvelous morning."

Stephanie Saunders had been my nemesis from the moment she transferred into my eighth-grade class at Carlton Central School. When we first met, she might as well have announced: "Aha. So you're the class clown. You must be covering up a whole slew of insecurities. Let's explore them together, so that I can forever help you to feel bad about yourself, shall we?"

However, Stephanie would be here all too soon, and there was no point in spoiling the time that I now had to myself by thinking about her. I grabbed my yellow pages and started to look through each listing for private investigators. There were twenty or so, and none of the names rang a bell. The name of the investigator at the meeting had been mentioned only in passing last night, and I couldn't recall it. Sam . . . something-to-do-with-tires. Sam . . . Michelin? Radial? Retread? I paged to the section of tire advertisements and remembered the name: Dunlap. Sam Dunlap.

There was no "Dunlap Investigators" heading, so I started calling each listing, beginning with the first one: "AAA Investigations—All Ya Want To Know," which should have been AYWTK by my book but that was probably less eye-catching—and asked for Sam Dunlap. At the fourth number I dialed, "Information Retrieval Services," the man who answered said, "That's me. What can I do for you?"

"My name is Molly Masters. I'm—"

"I know who you are," he said, cutting me off. "What do you want?"

Though somewhat taken aback at his gruff manner, I mustered some self-assurance and answered, "I'm worried about this information you uncovered about my father. I very much doubt you've gotten the full picture. Innocent people are going to get hurt."

"Hey, Ms. Masters, if any 'innocents' get hurt, it won't be 'cuz of anything I've done."

"Is it true that Sylvia Greene hired you as a private investigator?"

"Yeah. But that's nobody's business but mine."

Though he was obviously intent on being as uncooperative as possible, I had to press on for my father's sake. "Would you be willing to speak with me about the incidents of the last couple of days? I'm very worried about my father. He's under a lot of stress. Anything you could tell me that could reassure him would be extremely helpful."

"No can do. The work I did for Ms. Greene is confidential. Even though she's dead."

"Okay. But could you just tell me which other board member, besides my father, Sylvia had asked you to investigate?"

"Lady, I already told you as much as I'm gonna say. I'm in more than enough hot water with the police. I don't need to add you and your big nose to my troubles."

He hung up.

I stood still, listening to the dial tone while replaying the conversation in my head. Me and my "big nose"—and thank you so much for the compliment, Mr. *Retread*!—smelled a rat.

Chapter 5

We Be Goin' in Circles

I did some serious pacing, trying to figure out how to get information out of Sam Dunlap. He'd apparently managed to dredge up something from both my Dad's and a second board member's past. Maybe Sylvia had taken a scattershot approach to the problem—had hired Sam Dunlap to investigate the backgrounds of all the board members at once.

Maybe I could hire him to perform the same search that he'd recently made for Sylvia. Minus whatever he'd turned up regarding my father, that is, because I didn't wish to learn about my father's past from Sam or from any other private investigator.

Why, though, would somebody kill Sylvia to keep a secret hidden? The gig was already up, so to speak. The investigator also knew this person's secret, and he'd gotten the information from someplace. The killer couldn't hope to root out all traces of his or her past merely by getting rid of Sylvia.

I called Information Retrieval Services a second time, thinking as I did so that Sam Dunlap—and any coworkers—had probably chosen the name carefully. He could get away with saying he was from the IRS, which would put a nice scare into the other party. I recognized Sam Dunlap's voice as he stated his company's name.

"This is Molly Masters calling again. Mr. Dunlap, I just wanted to ask you—"

"Ms. Masters, as I already told you, the information that—"

"You already told me you have to stick to your confidentiality. But I'm wondering if I could hire you to run a second background search on the board members."

My suggestion gave him considerable pause. Finally, he said, "I can't do that."

"You *can't*, or you *won't*?"

"Works out the same either way. Ms. Masters, I suggest you stick to whatever it is you think you do best and forget about Sylvia Greene's death."

Frankly, I wasn't sure what it was that I "do best," but come to think of it, harassing people into answering my questions was probably right up there at the top of the list of my talents. "Believe me, Mr. Dunlap, nothing would make me happier than to do just that. But my father has been accused of a crime he didn't commit. Someone could have killed Sylvia to prevent her from publicly divulging the information that you gave her. Hasn't it occurred to you that you could be next?"

"Yeah, of course it has. I'm not an idiot. A woman died in front of me, thanks to—" He broke off. "Hang on a sec." When he got back on the line, his voice was calmer, though sarcastic. "Thanks for your concern, but I can take care of myself."

I pictured him, as best I could remember, from the night before. Though a young man, he looked more like a high school teacher than an investigator—slight build, thick glasses, curly light-brown hair. He certainly didn't strike me as the physical bruiser sort who truly could "take care of himself" in most instances.

"Don't you think you have a civic duty to share your report with the police?" I asked pointedly.

"I already did. Hey, listen, lady. I'm getting back to work now. I suggest you do the same. And don't call me again. You got that?"

On that less-than-pleasant note, he hung up.

"Well, that was no fun whatsoever," I said to Betty, who wagged her stubby tail in response.

While pondering my situation, I gave the dog her breakfast, a half a cup of kibble. Ever hopeful that I was just about to drop a T-bone steak into her bowl, she waited expectantly until I said, "Okay," then she began to eat.

I wasn't at all sure that Sam Dunlap was telling the truth about his having gone to the police, but that was something that could be easily double-checked. I made a mental note to tell Tommy about my conversation with Sam the next time the opportunity arose. That meant risking Tommy's chewing me out for meddling in his investigation, but I was willing to pay that price rather than withhold any information that could vindicate my father.

Like Lauren with her baking, I find solace in my work, creating humorous—at least, one hopes "humorous" is the adjective that leaps to mind—cartoons for my business. Sadly, the already small market for personalized faxable greeting cards seemed to be steadily declining in the past couple of years. Though I still had a couple of clients at office-product stores who used my cartoons to demonstrate their merchandise, individuals weren't about to pay me to design personalized cover sheets and so forth when they could send a free electronic greeting over the Internet. However, I also augmented my meager earnings by doing freelance greeting cards.

I had been working on a nonoccasion card for women (90 percent of card purchases are made by women). The card now seemed painfully appropriate. It showed a couple walking along a circular path totally enclosed by a brick wall. They were literally in a rut formed by their own footprints. The man is saying to the woman, "Now, where were we?" as the woman wears a forlorn expression on her face. The caption for the cartoon reads: *Do you ever get the feeling that we're going in circles?*

The doorbell rang. Hoping it was my parents, I swung open the door without looking through the peephole. Though naive of me, I wasn't prepared for the disheartening sight of Stephanie Saunders, holding a casserole dish.

"Hello, Stephanie." I glanced at my watch and verified that it had only been an hour or so since we spoke. When the woman decides to cook for someone, she doesn't mess around.

"Molly, you poor thing."

Michael, her four-year-old with perpetually tousled blond hair and an engaging smile, stepped out from behind her. Not particularly wanting to think of myself as a "poor thing," I focused my energy on him and said, "Hi there, big guy!"

"Hi. I got new shoes on!" he announced, grabbing onto his mother's black skirt to lift one foot up and show me its sole.

"Hey, those are cool! Do they make you jump fast and run high?"

"No!" He giggled, rolling his eyes. "I *run* fast. And I *jump* high."

Stephanie broke the pleasant mood by thrusting the casserole dish at me, which I had no choice but to accept, along with her pot holders. "Here you go, dear. Again, I am so deeply, deeply wounded on your behalf."

I regarded her for a moment, unable to meet her eyes because of the sunglasses she wore, which topped off her black knit dress with matching black jacket. Perhaps she was in full mourning on my behalf, as well as being "deeply, deeply wounded."

"Really, Steph. You make it sound as if you've flung yourself into my line of fire and taken a round of shrapnel for me. But thanks for the casserole." I couldn't think of anything else at all pleasant to say, so I opted to return my attention to her son. "How are you today, Michael?"

"I go potty!"

"Good for you. I do, too, sometimes."

"Want to see?"

Not especially, I thought, but before I could suitably frame my response, Stephanie interjected, "He thinks he needs to use your bathroom. We're . . . still in the process of potty training."

"Oh, I see." I kept my vision on her son, who, in spite of his genes, was adorable. "That's a noble pursuit, young man. Let me put your mom's handiwork in the 'fridge, and I'll show you where my bathroom is."

We started to walk away, Michael eagerly trotting beside me, but Stephanie said firmly, "I need those pot holders back right away, Molly. In fact, would you mind terribly transferring the entire meal to another dish? That's handcrafted terra-cotta earthenware you're holding. It's terribly expensive and one of a kind, and, well, I'd hate to have anything happen to it."

I forced a smile and turned around. "My goodness. Of course I'll transfer it right away. Terra cottage, did you say? I'm so impressed. It must be worrisome to put such a piece of . . . art into your oven."

She removed her dark glasses and raised a perfectly plucked eyebrow, no doubt realizing I was being sarcastic but unwilling to call me on it. "I'll take Mikey to the bathroom while you're transferring containers."

Stephanie really brought out the worst in me. Here she'd gone through the trouble of cooking a meal for me, and all I could do was be cutting and sarcastic toward her. When her husband had died, shortly before her son's birth, I'd helped her in other ways, but never thought to bring her food. Why couldn't I be a little kinder to her?

While silently trying to instruct myself not to let her get my goat, I spooned her spaghetti-based supper into my pseudo-Corningware dish and washed out her One-of-a-kind-aren't-I-oh-so-cultured-terra-whatchamacallit-thingee. Her dish plus her personally-cross-stitched-by-Georgia-O'Keeffe pot holders were ready to go home with her by the time she and her son emerged from the bathroom.

It occurred to me that I was not doing a stellar job at putting myself into a kindhearted frame of mind.

"False alarm," Stephanie said, smiling as she met my eyes.

I winked at Michael, who was clinging to her skirt, and then held out the dish and pot holders to his mother. "It's all dutifully transferred to another container. Thanks again."

"I go potty now, Mommy," Michael said proudly, and promptly began to do so, wetting the front of his pants. Stephanie's jaw dropped and she let out a little moan, but grabbed him under the armpits and raced back into the bathroom.

Trying hard not to laugh, I called after her, "Stephanie, I'll go look in my son's closet and see if I have any hand-me-downs that are small enough to fit him."

"Thank you," she said in a choked voice.

I knew how much it hurt her to say that to me, and I would dearly hate it if our positions were reversed. I went off in search of outgrown children's wear and, again, tried to search my soul for more generosity. She had jet-setted around and lived the bachelorette's life since she'd been widowed, and yet she managed to be PTA president, year after year. Surely they awarded a special place in heaven for PTA volunteers.

Maybe that was why this particular PTA president was so intent to give me a hell on earth.

After changing her son's clothes—and remarking snidely that she'd "never even heard" of the brand name of my son's outgrown pants, which was because they were from a low-end department store she'd never visited, Stephanie and son left. I made and enjoyed a quiet lunch by myself.

A couple of hours later, the children, upon arriving home on their respective school buses, greeted me with their customary short-term memory loss when I asked them what they did in school that day.

Determined to drag at least one recollection out of them, I focused my efforts on Karen, knowing she was my best hope. "Did you have any pop quizzes or anything?"

She furrowed her pretty brow, but said only, "Nope."

"Did anything make you laugh today?"

"No, but Mom? I need new shoes. I hate my sneakers. Everyone else's are way cooler than mine."

"But yours are brand new! We just bought them two months ago, and you thought they were cool enough then." Here was a disadvantage of teenagers when compared to four-year-olds: they don't appreciate their shoes as much.

Karen shrugged and started running up the stairs for the phone in the master bedroom. "Can I go call Rachel?"

"Sure," I yelled after her, not seeing the point in mentioning that Rachel was the person she'd left only five minutes earlier, and yet she'd had nothing to say to the mother she hadn't seen in seven hours. Karen, for all of her extraordinary qualities, was on the verge of teendom—more accurately spelled "teen-dumb." My own experiences as an adolescent were permanently etched into my memory, which was scary now that I was on the parenting side of the equation. However, I could take heart in the knowledge that ten years or so from now, she would realize her mother was both incredibly wise and a wonderful conversationalist.

I sighed and turned my attention to my son. It was time for him to go to soccer practice, where I often saw Gillian Sweet. We never spoke to each other, both remaining entrenched in our own thoughts on the sidelines, but under the circumstances, maybe she would shed some light on the board's turmoil. "Get your shin guards and cleats on, Nathan."

He stared at me with a blank expression on his face.

"You've got soccer practice in fifteen minutes."

"I do?"

He had soccer practice after school every Tuesday and Thursday but had selective memory lapses that allowed him to (a) forget to bring his gear to school in the morning, (b) forget to stay for practice and instead come home on the bus, and (c) plead ignorance of the above twice a week.

"I'll meet you in the car."

A minute or two later, Nathan stormed toward the car where, as promised, I was waiting. He flung open the door to the backseat and hurled his ball into the car with so much force that he had to duck as it ricocheted back toward him.

"Is something wrong?" I asked, being attuned to these subtle nuances.

"I don't want to go to soccer practice! Why can't I just play in the games without having to practice all the time?"

"You can't play in the games unless you go to practice. That's the team rules. Do you want to play this weekend?"

"Yes! But I barely had time to start my homework!"

"I'll give you a hand with your schoolwork when we get back."

"I'll never get it finished! I'm gonna flunk fifth grade. I'm never going to get to college, or get a good job, or get any friends. Nobody's gonna want to marry me. I'm going to live in a small apartment and have a lonely little life!"

"Nathan, please, sweetie, let's remember that you're ten years old. Let's just get you through soccer practice and tonight's homework, and we'll stave off your midlife crisis for a later decade, all right? Please?"

He slumped further back into his seat. His thin arms were crossed on his slender chest. His cheeks blazed beneath the constellation of brown freckles.

My heart felt a pang for him, but if there was anything helpful to say to him, I didn't know what that was. Heaven knows I'd tried enough variations of aphorisms, to no avail. My son had inherited my pessimism, and was compulsively neat, which, if the latter was also inherited, had skipped a generation. Last month, intending to give him an uplifting lesson about optimism and hope, I had set half a glass of water on the counter and, when he entered the room, asked him whether the glass was half empty or half full. He swept up the glass without answering, stacked it in the sink, and demanded to know why "someone's always leaving their dirty dishes around the place!"

We arrived at the soccer fields behind the redbrick elementary school. Gillian Sweet had brought one of those handy short-legged folding lawn chairs that I'd often admired, but never seemed to remember to search for when I was at an appropriate store. Realistically, though, even if I were ever to buy one, I would forget to bring it with me.

I headed down the sidelines and took a seat on the grass beside her.

"Hello, Gillian. Our sons are on the same soccer team, I see."

That was about as lame an opening comment as I could possibly make, especially since they'd been on the team together for almost two months now. She merely said, "Yes."

"That was quite an experience at the board meeting last night."

"Yes. I still can't believe it all really happened. School board meetings tend to be draining, but not literally."

Surprised at her nonchalance, which bordered on flippancy, I said, "I'm sure it was upsetting for you. I mean, your friend died and everything."

"That's not—" She stopped. Then gave a little laugh and said, "Funny thing, I just can't seem to remember what I meant to say to you."

"Oh?" I was having a truly hard time figuring out what was going on with her. For a moment, I even had the fleeting thought that she was acting somewhat drugged out, but wrote it off as paranoia on my part.

She stared out into the distance, where the fifteen or so team members were running sprints. "Ironic, isn't it, that your son and mine are on a sports team together? They'll probably want to stay on teams in junior high and high school. That's one of the things your father's vote would put an end to."

"Whenever you revote, that is."

"Yes. We'll have to appoint a replacement. I'm almost surprised you haven't considered running yourself."

"For the board? No offense, Gillian, but I'd sooner swallow broken glass."

Gillian nodded, the wrinkles in her forehead making her look old. I hid my own forehead wrinkles behind my bangs. "That's wise of you, Molly. There are times when I have to admit, I've realized I've taken the more torturous route."

We stopped talking for a while and watched the practice. The boys were doing various calisthenics, which they finished up, then started running passing-and-shooting drills.

All the while, my nerves were starting to give out. An article revealing a family secret was about to hit next morning's papers, and I had no idea what it would contain. "Gillian, I need to ask you something. Has Sylvia ever revealed to the rest of the board what this supposed secret of my father's was?"

She looked at me and asked sadly, "Your father didn't tell you?"

I instantly regretted that, of all of the board members, I'd chosen to ask the one I liked the very least. This was not the person I would have wanted to deliver bad news of a personal nature to me. "I'm just asking for a yes or no here, Gillian."

She ignored my last comment and said, "I'm really not at liberty to say what went on in private discussions of the board. Even if I were I'm, frankly, not comfortable discussing this with you. You need to ask your father. It's his . . . secret, after all."

"But my father doesn't even know *what* Sylvia was threatening to divulge."

"That's not true."

"*What's* not true?" My pulse raced at the thought that I was about to hear something I didn't wish to hear about my father.

She looked around. There was nobody within hearing distance, and yet she said under her breath, "Why don't you follow me to my car so that we can speak privately?"

"Fine." I gritted my teeth and got to my feet. I was too committed to stop now, but this was horrid enough without my having to play Secret Agent games with her.

Neither of us spoke another word until we were in the front seat of her minivan. Gillian fidgeted for a while, then finally met my eyes. "Molly, I'm afraid that your father knows very well what it was that Sylvia had uncovered about him. She told us all what it was a full week ago, during a conference call that she set up. I just wish that you didn't have to learn that from me, Molly. He should have told you himself."

Dad knew a week ago? And yet he'd insisted as we were driving to the board last night that he was utterly in the dark. "I don't believe you. If this was in a conference call, maybe . . ." My mind raced to come up with some plausible explanation. "Maybe his phone had disconnected before your conversation was completed. I've known my father my whole life. He wouldn't lie to me."

"Molly, there were also half a dozen witnesses to an argument Sylvia and Charlie got into in the back room. She told him again exactly what she was going to announce if he didn't resign. If you don't believe me, talk to any of the other board members. Or, worse, you can wait to read about it in the papers. You can trust me to keep quiet, but the same can't be said for some of my less-scrupulous associates."

"Some . . . scandalous newspaper article, quoting the board members, wouldn't convince me of anything. You could all have compared notes after leaving the hospital. This could be a conspiracy—you, Michelle, Carol, Stuart, and Kent, all could have been working together to kill Sylvia and to frame my father."

Gillian's eyes flashed in anger and her cheeks reddened. "Molly. Come on, now. Are you listening to yourself? Do you honestly believe the five of us could have cooked up something like this?"

No, in fact, I didn't believe that. The five of them couldn't possibly work together well enough to accomplish even the simplest of changes in district policy, let alone pull off a murder together. Nevertheless, I answered honestly, "I would sooner believe that than believe that my father lied to my mother and me."

"Suit yourself. You can believe whatever fairy tale you wish to. Or you can check with Sam Dunlap, who isn't a board member."

I deliberately chose to play innocent, wanting to see how familiar with this private investigator Gillian really was. "The man Sylvia had brought into the back room with all of you?"

"That's right. He's a private investigator, as I recall your father telling you last night in the hospital waiting room. Surely you don't think a professional investigator conspired with the rest of us to do in poor Sylvia?"

The last shred of denial that I'd been clinging to so desperately deserted me. I leaned back against the headrest and stared straight ahead, unwilling and unable now to look at her. "You've made your point, Gillian. So just tell me. What was it? What was this terrible secret that Sylvia had discovered?"

After a long pause she answered, "Your father's criminal record."

Chapter 6

You Rearranged the Furniture Again?

Gillian had been unwilling to elaborate. We maintained distant posts on the sidelines during the remainder of practice. I was still in a daze as I drove Nathan home. He was chattering to me, but I couldn't listen, and I answered him with no idea of what I might be agreeing to. It must have been something about watching TV, for he went straight to snatch up the remote control the moment we arrived, and immediately answered my objections with "But you said I could!"

This caused Karen, a much more avid television viewer than her brother, to desert the textbooks she'd spread onto the kitchen table and run to join us in the family room. She was seated on the couch, underneath Betty's blanket, with Betty on her lap before I could figure out how to phrase my Yes-but-Mommy-wasn't-listening-at-the-time response to Nathan.

I decided that I had too much emotional investment in being a daughter at the moment to worry about being a mother, so I grabbed the portable phone. I sat down on the living room stairs, out of earshot from the children, and called my parents.

Their machine answered with a new message in my mom's voice: "You have reached the Petersons. If you are someone you wouldn't wish to talk to if you were in our place, please hang up the phone. Anyone else, please leave a message."

Which category would I fit into? I couldn't decide quickly enough and hung up. Immediately afterward, I realized that I was being silly. Of course my parents wanted to speak with me. We were family. I dialed again, listened through the message a second time, and said, "Mom? Dad? Are you home?"

After a brief pause, my father picked up the phone. "Molly. How are you? Is everything all right?"

"Dad, I need to know what's going on. I just finished talking to Gillian Sweet, and she tells me that Sylvia revealed you had a criminal record."

He said nothing for a moment, which seemed to last for several minutes. "Did she say what kind of a criminal record?" His voice carried a heaviness in tone that imparted to me no surprise or resentment to indicate that Gillian had made up the story.

"No. She didn't elaborate, but I'm hoping that *you* will."

"I see."

I waited, but he said nothing more. "But I don't! I don't 'see' at all!"

"Your mother and I will be over in a few minutes."

"Okay. I'll be here." I hung up.

Now my emotions were in such turmoil that I felt nauseated. Dad hadn't told me not to worry or to calm down, or anything to refute what I'd just learned. This could only mean that Dad did, indeed, have a criminal record, which he'd kept secret. And now he was a murder suspect, and his previous "record" was about to make tomorrow's headlines. I looked up toward the heavens. *Somebody up there, throw me a life preserver!*

To prevent myself from doing what I desperately wanted to do—which was to grab my keys, drive to the Albany airport, and get on the next departing flight regardless of its destination—I snatched up my drawing pad, dropped into what we call "the big chair" in the living room, and started drawing.

Overwhelmed by the feeling that my very existence was about to be turned on its head, I conceptualized that emotion. I drew a room in which all of the furniture is crudely nailed to the ceiling. A haggard-looking man carrying a briefcase peers at the ceiling mournfully, while a woman with clasped hands smiles at him as he says, "You've been rearranging the furniture again, haven't you, dear?"

The doorbell rang, and my heart seemed to leap to my throat. This was silly. My fear was running roughshod over my sensibilities. What could he possibly tell me? That "Charlie Peterson" was an alias for Chuck the Knife—some serial killer from years gone by? That my sister and I were black-market babies? That he was the youngest living Nazi war criminal on record?

Well, okay, all of those possibilities were pretty darned unsettling, but they were also undoubtedly way off the mark. Enough of this self-torture, I scolded myself while making my way to the door. Meanwhile, Karen and Nathan ran into the room. Their television show must have been on a commercial break.

"Who's at the door?" Karen asked.

"It's just Gramma and Grampa. What happened to your television show?"

"Stupid repeat," Nathan said sadly.

"Cool!" Karen said simultaneously, in response to my answer about our visitors. "I want to show Gramma my penny collection."

"There won't be time for that." The doorbell rang a second time. "Just a moment," I called, intent now to get the children out of the room or this agonized waiting would likely never end. "They're coming over to discuss taxes and insurance policies. Do you want to stay and listen? Otherwise, there are some coins in a green metal box on the bottom shelf of the laundry room that you can go through and add to your collections."

"Come on, Nathan. Let's go look at Mom's money. Maybe we'll find an Indian-head nickel!"

That was about as underhanded a ploy as I'd ever used to get my children out of the room. I'd sunk to an all-new low. I should have been ashamed of myself, but I was too busy feeling relieved that it had worked. I knew that all those coins I'd collected from various pockets while doing laundry would come in handy someday.

Mom and Dad were standing side by side as I opened the door. Dad's posture was so stooped over that Mom seemed to tower above him. He gave me a small smile. Mom looked embarrassed and gave my hand a squeeze as they stepped through the door. She had to know what Dad was going to say.

In testimony to how awkward and uncomfortable this felt, I found myself treating my parents as I would regular house-guests and asking them if I could get anything from the kitchen. They both murmured, "No thanks," and took seats on the couch. I closed my drawing pad and sat down, facing them on the big chair.

Dad cast a nervous glance at my mother, who patted his knee and said to me, "Molly, this isn't nearly as bad as what you must think."

I nodded, already a bit relieved. Mom was at least as pessimistic as Nathan and me combined, so if anyone could surmise what I "must think," it would be she.

"You see, Molly," Dad began, "after all of this first came up with Sylvia, and I had a couple of days to think about it, I went to see a lawyer. He told me not to tell anybody anything. Not even your mom." He gave Mom a sheepish smile, then mumbled, "It all dates back to your Uncle Ted."

Uncle Ted, my dad's older brother, had died of leukemia some forty-five years ago, at the age of twenty-two.

"Go on," I said, because Dad was now sitting there with this look of befuddlement on his features as if he'd already lost his train of thought.

"Charlie, for heaven's sake," my mom said. "Forget what that idiot lawyer said. It's all right. Just tell her."

Mom was wringing her hands. Dad was looking pale again. It was as if he hadn't been eating well for the last couple of weeks, too. He looked like a scarecrow, his shirt seeming to hang off his bony shoulders.

"It was just a youthful indiscretion on my brother's part, really," Dad went on. "He and his buddy had been drinking. At the time they were . . . I don't know. All of eighteen, I guess. Legally adults. I was fifteen. Still a minor, you see.

Plus, he was in the Marines, and he was looking at the possibility of a dishonorable discharge for getting caught. And so I . . . took the rap for him."

"What rap?"

Dad was working his way slowly around to what these "criminal" charges were, presenting the explanations and excuses before the actual event itself. I struggled to be patient, beginning to relax a little as the ages involved negated some of the most egregious offenses that I'd imagined in my head.

"Disorderly conduct. Reckless endangerment." He shrugged. "Ted and his best friend were launching potatoes at cars with this souped-up catapult they'd built. One of the potatoes . . . it hit this elderly lady's car window."

Potatoes? Here I'd been thinking that my father might have been some kind of war criminal. This was all about pitching some potatoes at a car when he was a teenager?

"So you claimed you were the one who'd fired the potatoes?" I prompted.

"Yes. Though it wasn't true. I was only a witness. In fact, I told them not to do it. Your uncle claimed it was my yelling at him suddenly that . . . startled him, and he wound up misfiring. The woman driver was so scared, she lost control of her car and caused a terrible accident."

"But, even if it's on your permanent record, you were a minor then. Surely nobody would care about some childish prank that happened . . . what? Fifty years ago?"

"There's more to it than that. You see, the woman . . . swerved. She drove into the opposite traffic lane, and it caused a head-on collision. She died from her injuries. A little child, a poor little five-year-old, was also badly injured, though I heard he was eventually fine. There was a court case. My brother and his buddy compounded everything. They perjured themselves, testifying that I had done it."

"How awful. But still. This was so long ago." I looked at my mother, whose gaze on my father was unwavering.

"It set up a web of lies and deceits that never ended."

"What was your sentence? They didn't actually force you to serve time as a juvenile offender, did they?"

He shook his head. "Community service, mostly. They weren't going to put a fifteen-year-old kid into jail for hurling a potato at someone. So that would have all blown over, eventually. It should have been the end of the story." Dad let out a heavy sigh and sat staring at his knees. "Only . . . unfortunately, my brother felt that he owed me. The day I was to take a college entrance exam, I got really ill. Ted volunteered to go to the test administrators and plead my case to schedule a retake. Only, he posed as me and took the test instead. He got caught. It went on both of our records, but he didn't have any prior offenses and I did, so I was the one left holding the bag a second time."

"The thing is that your uncle wanted to be a lawyer," Mom said, a bit testily. She made it clear by the tone of her voice how much she resented Dad's brother for this. "He felt that he couldn't get his license if he'd had a criminal record."

My father was still looking horridly uncomfortable, but said nothing to my mother. "So, Uncle Ted didn't suffer any consequences for taking your test for you?"

"He explained that he was only trying to help his sick brother. He got into a bit of trouble, having to apologize and everything, and he did get a reprimand. We both claimed it was my idea. They made me take a test at a different time, under close supervision, but like I said, that went on my record, too."

"But . . . I still don't understand. Why didn't you tell me and Mom about this years ago?"

"Ted found out about his having leukemia just a few months after the cheating incident. He asked me then if I'd keep his role a secret. I gave him my word that, no matter what happened, I would never tell anyone. Ever. I'd been able to keep that promise until the mess with the board came up. I honestly never believed anyone would uncover it. I made my amends long ago. I never tried to hide any of it, except my brother's role, and it never stopped me from being hired at the university. I thought the whole incident was behind me."

"But Sylvia thought that this made you unsuitable for the school board?"

"She insisted that I was unsuitable to serve as a representative of the schools with a history of having cheated on an exam."

"When did she say that? During the meeting, just before she died?"

"No. Earlier. I'm afraid that . . . I've known for more than a week now that Sylvia knew about the charges leveled against me as a teenager. At last night's meeting she and I got into an argument about her publicly revealing my past, and the rest of the time was spent with the whole board arguing over whether or not Sylvia had the right to call a private meeting and invite a nonmember. All the private investigator ever got around to saying was his name and that Sylvia had hired him to look into all of our backgrounds."

"So Sylvia really brought him into the room to frighten the other board member into resigning . . . the board member whose secret was so much worse than yours that she'd abandoned the prospect of making you her target."

My parents exchanged glances. They seemed to be quite dumbfounded by this suggestion. Apparently they weren't in the habit of analyzing devious behavior, the way I was.

"The whole thing backfired, apparently," I continued, "and Sylvia wound up dead."

Dad said slowly, "But how could the killer know in advance to bring the poison?"

"Sylvia probably warned the person earlier, not realizing how desperate he or she truly was."

"That seems out of character, Molly," Mom said. "From what I've seen of Sylvia Greene, that would have meant that she'd been decent enough not to tell the other board members the secret the moment she discovered it herself."

Dad said quietly, "Must've been one hell of a secret for her to have been that discreet."

Or, as someone had postulated last night, this secret, unlike my father's, concerned one of her two supporters, Kent or Gillian. "Regardless of whatever else you do, Dad, you've got to call that Mr. Johnson guy at the paper. Explain what really happened with Uncle Ted and everything. People will understand, once they have the full story."

He was already shaking his head. "No! I refuse to be-smirch my brother's memory. I made my decision years ago to take my lumps for this, and that's what I intend to do. I worked hard to try to convince Sylvia Greene not to proceed. My biggest fear isn't what might happen to me. It's that, even after all these years, if this thing gets into the papers, there's the chance that my brother's deceit will surface because of some fool hoping to vindicate me."

"But Dad . . ." I let my voice trail away. He had risen and was already heading for the door. I suddenly felt as though I didn't know my own father.

Mom looked at me, her expression glum. "I'm sorry we lied to you." She spoke quietly, looking over her shoulder to test Dad's reaction. He headed outside without turning. "I didn't know the truth myself until last night."

"Even if it comes out that Dad shot a potato at someone that led to a fatal accident and cheated on an entrance exam, that was so long ago. No one would hold that against him."

She nodded. "I think you're right. But it all depends on how the story is written up in the paper."

She shuffled out the door after my father.

I could only hope that the press would be fair. Unfortunately, though, the journalist in question would be the man who'd quoted me out of context and whom I'd antagonized this morning.

Feeling hopeless, I headed toward the laundry room to check on the kids' progress with the coins and to ask that they redirect their energies back toward homework.

My suggestions were met with the usual grumblings. I decided to hide out in my office for a while, hoping to get my thoughts together. I glanced at my fax machine and noticed that there was a sheet in the tray. Someone must have faxed me while I was out this morning, or I'd have probably heard the machine ring.

I picked up the paper and read:

Molly—You and your family are in danger. Tell your father that he must resign if he wants you all to stay safe.
This won't stop until a terrible price has been paid.
                                        A Concerned Citizen

Chapter 7

If It Weren't for Bad Luck . . .

The tag line on the fax merely showed that it was from a local self-service copy shop. Because the fax had been sent hours ago, there was no point in my calling the store now to try to see if anyone remembered the sender. The note might literally be from a "concerned" if unstable person who'd been in attendance last night when Sylvia died.

In any case, I quickly decided, there was nothing to be done. I was not about to "tell" my father to resign, even if his doing so might get me and mine out of the killer's cross hairs.

I tried to forget about the warning as best I could, and we settled into our typical family evening routine. Jim was late, which was often the case. I was growing more and more anxious waiting for him, which was a pretty obvious clue that my concern over the fax wasn't buried nearly deeply enough.

After feeding BC, the kids and I ate our dinner, courtesy of Stephanie, which was truly delicious—drat it all—then Nathan got out his guinea pig, which continually ran away while BC tried to sniff him. The two animals had grown up together, and BC wouldn't hurt Spots, or vice versa. Racing around the table in this manner was the one way that both of them got some exercise, not unlike a hamster wheel. Nathan found these chases comical and periodically helped Spots by providing a moving human obstacle for BC.

Our pets' behavior struck me as no more foolish nor repetitive than my current emotional state. Here I sat, growing ever more resentful toward Jim for not being home with us at a time when I was most worried about my family's safety. This, in turn, would lead to my snapping at Jim, and to his pointing

out how unpleasant coming home to someone who'd snapped
at him was, which gave him no motivation for rushing home.
I resolved that I would do my utmost to stop the cycle, to be
sweet and loving to Jim when he came home.

Karen, meanwhile, was not interested in getting her guinea
pig out as well. She was occupying herself by shrieking in
frustration at her inability to press coins into the slots of
her newest collector's packet. That everyone else, including
her younger brother, had no problem pushing the pennies
into place was making her ready to lash out at the next person
or beast to cross her path. At last, I heard the sounds of
Jim driving into the garage, and reminded myself not to be
snippy.

"Dad-eeeeee!" Karen whined the minute he stepped in the
door. "I can't do this!"

Jim, who looked exhausted, sighed and glanced in my direction for support. "Don't look at me," I said. "That's a tone
of voice daughters reserve for their fathers because they
know full well it doesn't work on their mothers."

Jim patiently showed Karen how to angle the coin into
place and then push down with her thumb. This had to be
at least the fifteenth time he'd shown her, judging by the
number of coins in place minus the ones Nathan and I had
inserted.

"Karen's a weanie," Nathan said.

"I am not! You are a weanie wussy!"

"You're a weanie wussy midget!"

"Enough with the name-calling! Karen just has delicate
thumbs," I said on her behalf. "Karen, why don't you get
something to help you? Use a rock or something."

"I don't have any rocks!" She was being surly and nothing
I could say would meet with her approval.

My pulse rate was increasing with my rising agitation.
This was not a good sign. Forcing my voice to stay even, I
replied, "Experiment till you can find something that you can
use to push the coin. And Nathan, it's time to put Spots back
in his cage."

Once the kids had left the room, Jim dropped down in the

chair at the dining room table, giving himself a neck massage. He met my eyes. "How did everything go today with your father? Did he finally tell you about his dilemma?"

My internal warning flags went up. I hadn't given Jim any notice that my father was supposed to come over today and explain things to me. "Uh, yeah. He did. What made you ask me that?"

"I dunno. No reason." There was a slight hesitation in his voice, as if he knew he was backing himself into a corner.

"How did you know he had a dilemma in the first place?"

"I . . . didn't know he did. I just assumed." His cheeks colored slightly and he averted his eyes.

"You're not the type to assume anything about anybody. That's what *I'm* always doing, and it drives you nuts. Did my father already talk to you about this?"

Jim cleared his throat and got to his feet. He went into the kitchen and dished up some food for himself, then sat down with his plate of food. I followed him, but he was avoiding my eyes.

"Yum," he said, still chewing. "This is delicious."

"You already knew. My father already told you and not me, or my sister, or my mom!"

Jim furrowed his brow. "Don't get mad at me, Molly. It's not as if I dragged it out of him and all the while chose to keep his secret from you. He visited me at my office last week, out of the blue. He . . . told me he had to talk to someone he could trust."

"Meaning he didn't trust *me*. I can keep a secret with the best of them!"

Jim frowned and darted a glance in my direction. "No, you can't, Molly. You tell Lauren practically anything and everything."

"That's just because women . . . talk. We socialize. You men can spend three hours watching a game together and never say one meaningful word."

"Exactly. And your dad didn't want to be the topic of your next 'meaningful' conversation."

"But I wouldn't have told even Lauren anything that he didn't want me to repeat."

"Not verbatim, maybe. You'd have just given her enough hints that she could fill in the missing pieces."

"So when my father came to you and told you all about him and his brother, it didn't even bother you that you were keeping a secret from your wife?"

"Not especially, no."

"So now we're keeping secrets from each other? Don't you realize that that undermines the very foundation of trust upon which marriages are based?" I stomped my foot. "Oh, damn it all, Jim! I didn't want to get into an argument with you. We might as well have run around the table, trying to sniff each other's butts!"

"How's that again?"

"Never mind," I growled.

"I'm not violating some . . . We're not talking about my cheating on you or something important. It was his secret, not mine."

"And it was my father, not yours. And furthermore, he's suspected of murder. And yet you can't even be bothered to get home on time."

Jim returned to his meal and resumed eating with a vengeance.

"I'm going to the grocery store. You can get the kids to bed, for once."

I stormed out of the house, but my anger had changed to despair before I could start up the car. This was the time for me and my family to draw together, not to be fighting, and yet I was taking my frustrations out on Jim. I'd long ago accepted the fact that he and I handle things differently, by virtue of our vastly different personalities. Which didn't mean that one of us was fundamentally wrong and the other right.

My father had made the decision to keep his brother's transgressions a secret and had held onto the decision through forty years of marriage. My parents' marriage had held up just fine. So who knows? Maybe this "foundation of trust" thing was overrated.

Before even one street or piece of scenery mentally registered, I found myself in the parking lot of the grocery store. Surely if I'd run over anything, I'd have noticed. Time to stock up on food items that we didn't especially need.

Somewhere along the frozen-food aisle, out of the corner of my eye, I saw someone start to enter the row, then quickly reverse directions. I got the impression that this was someone who didn't wish to see me just now. Naturally, I gave up on my purchase and hurried down that direction.

I recognized the long-legged woman at the far end of the aisle: Michelle Lacy. "Michelle," I called out.

She turned and feigned happy surprise at the sight of me. "Molly. How's your father doing? I know he must be under even more pressure than my family and I are."

"Yes, but he's doing all right."

"Good. I'm glad to hear that."

I searched her pretty features and realized that, while I didn't know her well at all, we often tended to agree on school issues, and I felt a sudden need for an ally on that board. Just to test her reaction, I said, "I talked to Sam Dunlap."

"Did you?"

"Yes. He told me that he was investigating another board member other than my father."

"I never doubted that."

"Oh, good. So you realize that there was more than one person on the school board with a reason to want Sylvia out of the picture."

"Molly, you needn't worry about securing my support for your father. I'm certain he's innocent."

"You are?"

She nodded. "Charlie wasn't going to gain anything by Sylvia's death, and yet its timing made him look guilty."

"Exactly. So who do you think did it?"

"I don't know. Only that it wasn't me or Charlie. That leaves Carol, Stuart, Kent, or Gillian."

She gave a glance at the items on the nearest shelf, then began to search for something in earnest. It was nice to know that she at least was willing to proclaim my father's innocence.

"Sugar cubes?" I said as she put a large box in her cart. I hadn't realized that they were even available anymore. I'd assumed that in the bureaucratic backward way of handling things, sugar cubes would have been banned in the seventies as a way to stop people from dropping acid.

"My horse loves them."

"You have a horse? You're so lucky. I used to ride a lot when I was a kid." My parents had paid for my sister and me to take riding lessons throughout most of our teen years. The classes stopped when the instructor started to give us repeated lessons on how to clean his horses' stalls, and my parents realized we were being taken advantage of.

Michelle's eyes lit up. "That's a nice coincidence. Kent and I are going riding tomorrow. Sylvia was going to come, too. You should join us. We prefer to have a third person along. Makes it look less like something illicit is going on between Kent and me." She gave me a conspiratorial wink. "I know you've found out firsthand how unpleasant the press can be."

Unappealing as it was to serve as the spoiler for press photo opportunities, this horse ride might give me the opportunity to find out what two of the board members were really like. "All right. I will."

"Our horses are stabled at a ranch less than a mile from the Saratoga Battlefields. You can meet us at the stables, and I'm sure I can pull in some cards and get a free ride for you."

"That's nice of you. And I'm certainly never one to argue with receiving a free ride."

Michelle didn't crack a smile. "Shall we say ten A.M.?"

"Sure. We can say that. You'll need to tell me the name of this stable and the address, of course."

She took a step back and scanned me at length, as if mentally measuring whether I'd make a suitable third wheel. "The stables are English-riding only, so wear your jodhpurs. And a riding helmet is a strict requirement."

Jodhpurs? Me? Was she serious? "My jodhpurs are worn

out from overuse, and I haven't had the time to restock my closet."

Again she didn't smile or even bat an eye, so I sighed and said honestly, "I've always rode western-style. Would it be okay if I just wear jeans?"

"I'm afraid that our riding stable is rather, well, image conscious, Molly." She held my gaze for a long moment, probably noting the way my face was blanching. "There's a strict dress code. Do you have boots?"

"Not exactly. I've got some red rubber galoshes, though."

"A riding helmet?"

"Yes. Although mine was designed for bicycles." She was giving me such a look of disgust that I added, "It's got snazzy racing stripes, at least."

"Tell you what. We can get around the dress code, so long as you don't come to the stables. Wear whatever you wish, and Kent and I will simply pick up the horse for you and meet you at the Battlefields themselves, where we'll ride. The west entrance."

"Fine. I'm not good on directions, but I think I can figure out where the west entrance is."

"And what an appropriate setting this will be," she said under her breath.

"You mean because this is the battlefields, and you and Kent disagree on school issues?"

She gave me an enigmatic smile. "See you tomorrow, Molly."

I shopped for some of my family's typical staples: macaroni and cheese, chops, marinated chicken breasts, frozen ravioli, string cheese, ice cream. Then I grabbed two bags of prepared salad greens and headed for the checkout line. When that particular product had first been introduced, I'd wondered who on earth could be so lazy as to not want to tear up their own lettuce. Ironically, a few months later it turned out that the answer was: Me. In spades!

While waiting at the checkout line, I had a bizarre thought and ran back to grab a box of sugar cubes myself. What if Michelle was lying about her horse being the one that went for sugar cubes? Maybe Sylvia had had some bizarre habit of sucking on sugar cubes at the meetings—heaven knows that she was caustic enough that she could have used a little sweetening. If so, Michelle—or someone else—could have poisoned the cubes. . . .

Alone in my car on the way home, my thoughts soon returned to my conversations with my parents and then with Jim. For all of my bad luck, meeting Jim Masters and having him fall in love with me had forever tipped the balance toward the good side. Add to that the fact that we'd been blessed with two healthy, amazing children. Maybe it was only fair, then, that there were some serious obstacles for us to overcome now.

Unlike last night, Jim was awake when I got home, and he put away the groceries while I went upstairs to say good night to the kids. Karen was in bed, her room lights out and her alarm already set.

"Are you asleep?" I asked quietly.

"No. 'Night, Mom."

"Good night, world's greatest daughter." We gave each other a hug, then I went to Nathan's room.

Nathan was nowhere to be found—not in his room, my room, or the bathrooms. I went back into his room to double-check the closets, and when he wasn't there either and Jim said that, no, he hadn't come downstairs while I was in Karen's room, I had that momentary panic I so hate.

"Nathan?" I called, and sighed audibly when he giggled and answered, "Down here, Mom."

I knelt and looked under his bed, where he was lying atop his sleeping bag, his flashlight beam trained on some magazine he was reading.

I fought off a slight irritation at his having tricked me. "Are you all ready for bed? Teeth brushed and all of that?"

He didn't answer, but asked, "Mom? Did you know that there's only one atom in each centimeter of outer space? And if you're in outer space without a space suit, your blood boils and you explode?"

"No, I didn't. But did you know that it's well past your bedtime?"

"But I'm not sleepy."

"That's unfortunate, but I'm too grouchy to accept that as an excuse." I took his flashlight away from him and set it on his dresser. "Are you sleeping on top of your bed or underneath it tonight?"

He got out from under his bed, giving me the silent treatment, climbed into it, and pulled up his covers.

"Good night." I kissed his cheek, which was cool and soft.

He pulled the covers over his face. "You're no fun."

"It's the result of all this gravity, sweet boy. See you in the morning."

Again, he wouldn't respond to his mean ol' mother, so I turned out the light, closed the door, and headed down the stairs.

Jim had finished putting away the groceries and was seated at the kitchen table, watching me. "I'm sorry I was late getting home tonight. Are you still angry at me?" he asked.

"No. And I was more angry at my father and myself than at you, but you were the only one I could yell at."

"Are you going to play Molly Masters, Super Sleuth again? Try to rescue your father?"

I sighed. "I should give you a big song and dance about how I've learned my lesson and will sit quietly and wait for the real killer to be revealed and my father to be cleared. Can we just say that I know as well as you do that that's what I should do, and leave it at that?"

"I suppose I have no choice. Let's go to bed."

"I'm going horseback riding tomorrow morning. I'm even getting a free mount."

He laughed, gave me a kiss on the cheek, and said suggestively into my ear, "Sounds good to me. But how much is your horse going to cost?"

This is one of the many reasons why I love my husband. Not only can he still make my heart go pitter-pat after all of these years, plus tolerate and understand me at my worst, but he—unlike certain school board members—has a sense of humor.

Early the next morning, before the sun had a chance to rise, I rushed outside in my slippers and robe and grabbed the newspaper. Frost had crisped the lawn, giving everything an ethereal glow. I shivered uncontrollably as I padded back up the driveway—probably due more to my nerves than to the chill.

Betty was whining as I shut the heavy door behind me with a noisy thud. She wanted to get out of her kennel, but I needed to see the article on my father before doing anything else.

I unfolded the paper and stood on the tile entranceway. Biting my lower lip, I held my breath as I opened it to the front page.

There was a file photograph of my father, a studio portrait showing his strong jawline and piercing eyes beneath the wire-rims, the semicircle of white hair on his otherwise bald head not looking quite as unkempt as it often did in person. The headline of the article was: BOARD MEMBER'S HIDDEN PAST.

I muttered a string of curse words under my breath and gave the article a quick read to assess the damage. It was shorter than I'd envisioned, only four paragraphs, in fact. The opening one was slanted so as to catch the reader's attention:

Confirmed sources have revealed that, as a young man, school board member Charles Peterson was convicted of felonious mischief, which resulted in a woman's death. Peterson was also caught cheating on a college entrance exam.

In the second paragraph, the story went on to mention that he was a minor at the time and that the "conviction" was in regard to a traffic accident. There was little revealed in the article that my father hadn't told me yesterday, with, of course, the notable exception of his brother's role.

In a particularly shoddy job, the reporter had not interviewed other board members to get their reactions, and only a one-sentence mention was made that "Peterson could not be reached for comment."

It was impossible for me to judge how I'd feel if I weren't his daughter or didn't know him personally. Except for the splashy headline, it was a reasonably fair presentation.

I set down the paper and went to the kitchen. As I made myself a cup of tea, I glanced out the window. The early morning sun cast a reddish hue on the whispers of clouds. The first line of a verse my father had taught me as a child came back to me: *Red sky in morning, sailors take warning.* I said to myself under my breath, "Good thing I'm going horseback riding and not sailing, hey, Dad?"

Chapter 8

Taking It All in Stride

Later that morning, after sending my children off on the school bus, I drove to the appointed rendezvous point within Saratoga Battlefields. The air was crisp, the sky cloudless. The leaves were their splendid array of fall colors, yellows to reds and every possible shade in between. I had to admit that this was the one season in which, in my opinion, upstate New York had my beloved Colorado beat in terms of beauty.

Kent Graham and Michelle Lacy were, indeed, in jodhpurs. This was the only kind of clothing that I could think of that deliberately ballooned around one's thighs and yet was considered classy-looking.

The two of them were, in fact, a striking couple. They stood in front of the three horses, whose reins were tied to a gate. Michelle cut an especially dashing figure, her short hair tucked behind her ears. She was almost as tall as Kent. He had a mixture of white hair amid the once sandy-brown. Somewhat to my surprise, he looked equally at ease in his black felt British riding hat as he did wearing a coach's baseball cap. In fact, Kent looked smashingly British in his red jacket, black riding helmet, and matching black knee-high boots. Michelle wore a soft, slightly fuzzy brown jacket with dark elbow patches and a white blouse.

In contrast, I was wearing loafers (not at all good footwear for horseback riding but I wasn't expecting horseback riding to become a habit), blue jeans, a cotton blouse, and my bicycle helmet. Though Michelle wore an inscrutable expression, Kent blanched slightly at the sight of me, his gaze lingering on my helmet.

"Hi, Kent. Michelle."

"Molly," he said as if he were saying the word *Maggot*.

"Good morning, Molly," Michelle said with considerably more warmth than Kent was displaying.

Opting to confront his attitude directly, I said, "You know, your skull truly doesn't care how classy your helmet looks before smashing into a rock."

"That might be. I'm just afraid you'll spook the horses. You look like you're wearing a big white bucket on your head."

"And I would have, too, but there'd have been no place to store our mop in the meantime."

Attempting to change the subject, Michelle blurted out, "Molly, we were just discussing how irresponsible the press has been to run such a one-sided story on your father. They should have gotten the whole story before they printed anything at all."

"The whole story?" I repeated, wondering if my father had talked to his fellow board members already. Maybe he'd told them about his brother's role.

"The reporters never even tried to contact either of us for our opinions, and they should have made every effort to get your father's response."

Of course, they did try to get my father's response, but I wasn't about to defend the press. "They're probably saving all of that for future exposés," I said. "They'll put him on trial via the press and the court of public opinion over the next few days."

"Exactly," Michelle said, holding my gaze. "It's terribly unfair."

"Yeah," Kent said irritably. "It stinks. All this yakking isn't accomplishing anything, though. Can we get going?"

I turned my attention to the horses. Michelle quickly untied the reins of a gorgeous palomino. Kent's horse was a chestnut—black mane, red-brown body—with white hooves. At a short distance was the third horse, a whitish colored mare, reins secured around a post.

"By all means. And thanks again for inviting me to join

you." I walked up to my horse. She seemed to be half asleep. "Using my considerable mathematical skills, I'm figuring that this horse here is mine?"

"You got it," Kent answered. "Her name is Nellie."

"As in 'Whoa, Nellie?' "

"You shouldn't have much trouble trying to stop her," Michelle said reassuringly. "She's pretty calm."

"Seemingly so. I think she's nodded off right where she's standing."

"All this talking probably bored her to death," Kent grumbled. "Can't say as I blame her, either."

For the sake of my father's future relationship with this duo, I knew that I should try to make nice, but Kent's crabbiness was getting on my nerves. "For such a man of action, it's surprising to me that you would choose to serve on a school board. Don't you find that you have to talk and, occasionally, listen to others?"

"Yeah. That's why I like horses." He patted his mount's withers. "Blaze here ain't no damned Mr. Ed."

"Too bad. I bet I'd find his opinions—" I broke off and managed to stop myself from saying "more enlightening than yours" and instead said only, "interesting."

My attention was soon fully captured by my horse. Only the tethering of Nellie's reins was preventing her from lying down. "She's not on her last legs, is she?"

"Heavens no," Michelle replied. "She's not dying. She's just mellow."

"She did seem to be a little gaseous earlier," Kent added, climbing effortlessly into the saddle of his tall, elegant horse. "On the way over here, she did more farting than trotting."

"Kent!" Michelle said.

"What? I'm just being honest. Molly will be above it, though, so she shouldn't be affected."

"Except that hot air rises," I muttered as I got onto my saddle, "and from the looks of this particular horse, I doubt we'll be moving fast enough to keep ahead of her . . . posterior emissions."

I looked into Nellie's eyes and read pure boredom; not

unlike the way my children's eyes glaze over when I lecture them. I untied her reins, wondering now if I'd still have the coordination to get into a saddle without the use of a stepladder.

"Let me check your stirrups," Michelle said. "I've guessed that you're five-six or so . . . five inches shorter than me, so I set them accordingly."

"Thanks."

I gathered both reins in one hand and held them taut against the front of the saddle. Nellie stayed perfectly still until the moment I got my left foot in the stirrup. Then she started walking forward, leaving me to hop along with her on my right foot, silently cursing my inability to do the splits, until I managed to boost my leg up and over her rump. Already this horseback riding was ten times harder than when I was younger and my body was, well, younger.

Once I'd gotten both feet in the stirrups, Nellie stopped. I stood up in the stirrups and then sat back down so that Michelle could check the adjustment.

"That looks good," Michelle said. "How does it feel?"

"As if my knees are way up in the air when I'm seated," I answered honestly.

"That's just the difference between the English style and the western, to which you're accustomed."

"I think too much time has passed to call myself 'accustomed' to any kind of horseback riding." That was an understatement, in fact. When we were teenagers, my sister and I used to laugh at some of the actors in TV westerns that obviously were awkward-looking in the saddle. Back then, I'd felt like a centaur, as though my body were melded with my horse's. Now Nellie seemed as big and wide as an elephant, and I instantly felt a hundred years old.

"Ah, don't sweat it," Kent said. "It's just like riding a bike. It'll all come back to you."

The only thing I was currently expecting to perhaps come back to me was last night's dinner. "Maybe so, Kent, but it feels as though I'm on one of those old-fashioned bikes with the enormous front wheel and with pedals that are way too short."

"Ready?" Kent asked as Michelle gracefully mounted her horse.

"Let's just make sure Molly is comfortable," she replied. "Molly, take Nellie around in a quick circle."

I had already established that my own aim would be set not on feeling "comfortable," but on not injuring myself. I'd never been in an English saddle, and the riding techniques are quite different. There is much more knee action in the English technique. The rider stands up and sits down according to the horse's gait. In contrast, my western instructor used to holler, "No daylight, Molly!" because he didn't want to see any space between my body and the saddle. Also the reins are held more taut in English, one in each hand. There was no way I could easily adjust to that. I was too used to having both reins in my right hand, steering with leg pressure on the respective side and with both reins at once.

I urged Nellie forward, having to resort to a couple of light kicks when my "Giddyup" and knee pressure didn't do the trick. She picked up speed and got into a slow trot as I circled the small open area surrounding the entrance to the path. Michelle's horse, in the meantime, was acting up quite a bit, snorting and backing up, clearly much more spirited than Nellie. "Oh, boy. This is going to take some getting used to," I said.

"You'll manage," Kent said. "Let's get going before the sun sets on us." Quite a smooth-talker, that man.

The dirt path was wide enough for two horses to ride abreast, but not all three. Within minutes, Kent was riding well ahead of us, setting the pace as, seemingly, all men do when they're in the company of women. Michelle was keeping a tight rein on her horse to make her stay back with me. The horse was still shaking her head and straining to break into a faster gait. Nellie, on the other hand, obviously wished she were asleep right about now.

"I don't know what's gotten into Sugar," Michelle said

under her breath, almost as if she were talking to the horse instead of to me. "She's skittish today, for some reason."

"Maybe she woke up on the wrong side of the stall."

Michelle gave me a disapproving glance. "We rode up from the stables. We were thinking that we could take the horses back in another two hours. Nellie is on loan from someone whom I've let Sugar out to for companion rides many times, so there's no great rush."

"Good. I have a feeling *lethargia* is more on Nellie's agenda than rushing is."

"Seemingly so," Michelle said, reining in Sugar as she looked wistfully toward Kent up ahead of us.

It occurred to me that if I hoped to share any conversation with Kent and Michelle, which was the major reason I'd decided to come riding, I'd better do so early, before Nellie got too far behind. "I've never ridden here, Michelle. If you don't mind, I'm going to try to urge Nellie into catching up with Kent."

She raised an eyebrow and smiled. "Give it your best shot."

I had to both kick Nellie and give her a smack with the end of one rein, but I eventually got her to pick up the pace enough to pull at least within a length of Kent's horse. "So, Kent," I called, "you both used to go riding with Sylvia?"

"Yep," Kent said over his shoulder. "Couple times a month."

That was surprising, since Michelle didn't cast her vote with Kent and Sylvia. "It's nice to see that the three of you could get along, despite not always being allies on the school board."

"Yeah, well . . ."

He let his voice fade, so I prompted, "Didn't you ever argue?"

"Naw. Not while we were riding."

"That's so hard to believe. I've been to most of the board meetings in the last couple of years, you know."

He shrugged and gave a glance over his shoulder at Michelle. "We had a rule not to discuss school issues while riding. We'd argue quite a bit about whose horse was faster or the better jumper. That type of thing."

He ducked beneath a branch, then gestured ahead of him, "Path really opens up here. Our horses are used to cantering. How 'bout we wait for you when we're back among the trees?" The trees that he indicated were way, way off in the distance.

Without awaiting my reply, he took off on his horse, and an instant later, Michelle on Sugar whisked past me. I tried to urge Nellie to keep up. "Where's your competitive spirit, Nellie?" It was hopeless. I decided to let Nellie continue at her own pace—a reasonably quick trot—while I tried to get my bearings.

The Saratoga Battlefield has always been one of my favorite parks. It has a winding, circuitous route that visitors can drive along, with designated stops. A short walk at each stop leads you to displays with recorded information about what transpired in each place, and forest rangers in authentic revolutionary costume sometimes reenact scenes at these locations. It is also a richly beautiful hillside, especially in the fall, though any season is nice.

From my current vantage point, I looked down on the fields below and imagined them full of soldiers behind their barracks. It must have seemed utterly devoid of beauty then, to those soldiers fearing for their very lives. Sitting on horseback centuries later, I would have loved to race down the fields to where the cannons still stood.

Kent and Michelle were way ahead of me by now. I couldn't get in sync with Nellie's pace. It felt as though I were riding on a mini–roller coaster, my insides getting jostled. My struggle to match my own movements with Nellie's gait gave me an idea for a cartoon. A character, badly bruised all over his body, is shown lying on the ground, obviously having tripped over the object behind him, and he's talking into a cellular phone, saying, "I *am* 'taking this in stride.' It's just that my stride happens to include falling flat on my face."

Several minutes later, we'd crossed the small field. As

promised, Kent and Michelle were waiting at the next trail-head for me and my plodding horse.

"Not to be downright paranoid, but I'm beginning to wonder how you went about selecting this particular . . . steed of mine."

"Nellie was the only horse available," Kent replied.

"Ah. That would explain it."

"She's getting a bit up there in years."

"Well, so am I, but I do a better job keeping up with those of my own species. If Sylvia were here instead of me, would this have been her horse?"

"Hell, no," Kent said. "She used to ride Firestorm. The biggest, fastest horse in the stable. She'd insist. Always got the feeling that if she were to find herself on the slowest horse, she'd get off the saddle and outrun us on her own two feet, if that's what it took."

Michelle laughed. "No kidding. That Sylvia was one competitive lady."

"Unlike Nellie," I muttered.

Once again, Kent and steed led the way down the path and were soon ahead by quite a bit. Michelle slowed her horse until we were stride for stride. "You write greeting cards, don't you, Molly?"

"Yes. I have a business called Friendly Fax and create personalized faxes for customers—though that business has been dwindling of late. I do freelance greeting cards for the standard companies, as well."

"Do you use the same kind of . . . humor in your cards that you use in real life?"

"Yes," I answered proudly.

"I see. Well. I don't think I would like them very much."

I gritted my teeth and said, "I guess that means I won't count you as one of my future customers."

"No." She pursed her lips and looked thoughtful for a moment. "I suppose I should tell you about my new sentiments regarding this school-budget vote. Things won't go the way you and your father are expecting them to."

"They won't?"

"You should warn your father that he's no longer in the majority."

This truly was surprising and unsettling news. Even though the school-financing vote was the least of my concerns at this point, it was the only thing that had been going well of late. Dad would be crushed. "You've changed your mind?"

She nodded.

Still hopeful that I was misunderstanding her, I asked, "You're going to vote to fund sports and phys ed instead of arts, music, and drama?"

"That's right."

"You haven't voted with Sylvia's block in the past two-plus years! Now that she's dead, you're going to support her?"

"Don't make it sound as if Sylvia's death has been cause-and-effect. Our budget now is spread as thin as a Kleenex tissue. The school's insurance rates have skyrocketed and eaten into the budget ever since they had that fire a couple of years ago. I've simply decided that, in the long run, we'd be doing greater damage to our school district by not funding sports."

"But the public at large will pass whatever bond elections they need to pass to reinstate their precious team sports! They're not going to notice the loss of the orchestra, dramatic productions, or art shows till it's too late!"

"Nevertheless, that's what I've decided." She glared straight ahead and set her lips in a firm thin line.

I reined in Nellie to get away from Michelle before the temptation to gouge her eyes out became too powerful to overcome. Michelle raised an eyebrow in surprise. Through my clenched jaw, I explained, "I think my horse just farted."

"I'll ride on up ahead with Kent. But don't worry. We'll wait for you."

I tried to calm down. There was no point in my getting this angry. Surely if she'd changed her mind once, she could change it back again. Alienating her, though, was not going to further my cause.

My wits—such as they were—fully collected, I kicked Nellie back into action and we started off in the same direction as the other two had gone. They were completely out of sight, but I soon found the two sets of hoofprints and followed their path.

Our course led alongside the beginnings of a brook, more like a steady dribble where the water no doubt joined up with something more appreciable farther downhill. Nellie had gotten midstream when I realized with a start that either the earth was rising all around us or Nellie and I were sinking. Quickly.

"Kent? Michelle?"

How had they gotten this far ahead of me? It wasn't especially sporting of them to bring me here and then desert me in the woods.

"We seem to be sinking. Is anyone there?"

Silence. Nellie was already either on her knees or sunk down into something up to her knees, and I needed to take action.

If we'd just crossed over quicksand, I reasoned, it wasn't going to be that long until I was sucked down, even if I was in a saddle. I leapt off the horse, who immediately lay on her side. I realized then that she was just intent on resting for a bit, and had chosen to get me off the saddle by rolling if she had to.

I pulled her reins in front of her, gave her a minute, then coaxed her back onto her feet. I wondered how far away my two "companions" were by now. If Michelle had truly invited me to serve as a chaperone of sorts, she probably did have a legitimate concern about the two of them not being seen alone together. There was a chemistry between them that was so strong, I wouldn't have been at all surprised if I came across them necking. Since they were both married to other people, that would not be good for either of their reputations.

It was also interesting, though, that I felt such a forceful attraction between them, yet they'd been diametrically opposed on every single issue facing the board since day one. Could they have been doing that deliberately to hide their relationship?

I got back on Nellie and we started off. There were still no signs of my riding companions. "Kent? Michelle?" I called.

"Molly," Kent yelled to me from some location up ahead, "I'm racing Michelle down to Boot Hill and back. We'll meet you at the crest of the field in a few minutes."

"Okay," I called back, blindly. There were too many branches here blocking my view. Come to think of it, I didn't even know where this "field" was that they were speaking of, let alone its "crest."

Boot Hill. I hoped Nellie would have the energy to take me to see it. I'd been there many times during field trips and visits with my parents and had brought Karen and Nathan to see it several times during past summers. The area had been named for the monument to Benedict Arnold. Or, more accurately, to the leg he lost in these battlefields when he was on the American side. His name was never even mentioned specifically on the monument itself. It consisted of a granite marker with a brass plaque inscribed to something like his "bravery and sacrifice." Ironic, perhaps, that this should come up, when I was feeling rather betrayed myself, first by my father and now by Michelle.

I came to a fork in the road. My horse kept going as if she knew exactly where her buddies had gone.

I let Nellie lead me, trusting her animal instincts and painfully aware of my own penchant for getting lost. However, just a few yards down the road, I realized that the hoof-prints we'd been following were gone.

I turned Nellie around and headed back.

Though I soon corrected for my mistake and found that they had indeed turned the other way down the fork in the road, their decision to ride by themselves, as well as to invite me in the first place, struck me as fishy.

Maybe they knew about my atrocious sense of direction. Maybe they'd deliberately given me a horse with an equally bad inner compass and were trying to give me the slip. They'd chosen Nellie because they knew she was a tired old nag, which is exactly what I was feeling like myself.

Just then, I heard a woman scream.

"Michelle?" I called at the top of my lungs.

"Sugar! Whoa!" Kent cried to Michelle's horse.

I whacked Nellie with both reins, and to my surprise, she responded. We tore off in the direction of the sound, which took us up an incline. We reached the top. In the distance, I saw Sugar in full gallop, tearing down the hillside, Michelle holding on for dear life.

Chapter 9

If Wishes Were Horses . . .

Instead of continuing her canter, Nellie broke into a full gallop, all four of her legs pumping hard. Just getting her to canter had been a significant accomplishment, but having her gallop downhill was frightening. At this angle, it was far too conceivable that Nellie might buck and send me up over her head and then trample me. Darned ironic if, while trying to assist Michelle, I wound up being the one to be badly injured.

To spare my tailbone further trauma, I stood in the stirrups while leaning low against the horse, as close to a jockey's form as I could emulate. However, I doubted that jockeys' teeth chattered like this, or that tears ran down their cheeks while they raced.

Kent was still way ahead of me, chasing after Michelle and trying to pull alongside her horse, but Nellie was no longer losing ground.

Michelle let out a second scream as Sugar raced toward a narrow path in the forest. She would never be able to stay in her saddle at this speed while being whipped by branches.

Just as she reached the trees, her horse reared and then bucked, sending Michelle flying. I pulled Nellie's reins, and, thankfully, she slowed to her usual lumbering trot.

Meanwhile, Kent had stopped his horse and dismounted in one rapid, athletic motion. He raced to Michelle's side and knelt beside her. From my jostling-and-rattling vantage point, I could tell that he was speaking to her and that she seemed to be answering. I'm sure he was asking if she was all right, but I couldn't hear their words over the sound of Nellie's hoofbeats and my bouncing body parts.

Michelle had done something of a somersault on her landing and was now sitting upright, facing away from me. "I think so," I heard her say as I reached them.

With Kent closely supervising, Michelle was slowly tilting her head to one shoulder then the other, as if checking herself for serious injury. She seemed to be fine, though, looking almost unruffled despite her fall.

Kent said to her, "Good thing you're in such good physical condition. You managed to control your fall. Otherwise, you could have gotten badly hurt."

Kent helped her to her feet, and I turned my attention to her horse. Sugar was still in the immediate area, with her reins dangling, and seemed traumatized—snorting, whipping her head around, pawing at the ground.

I wished I had some treat to offer her so that I wouldn't frighten her. I'd forgotten my sugar cubes, so I held out my empty palm as if it carried an invisible horsey treat and said soothingly, "Hey, Sugar. That's a good girl," as I approached.

Sugar was still shaking her head and pawing nervously, watching me with the whites of her eyes showing. She started to move away, making it clear that she didn't know me and didn't trust me. I stood my ground, but gasped at what I saw when she turned sideways.

"Look! Sugar's bleeding from underneath the stirrup on her left side!"

Though it was a preposterous thought, I immediately looked back at Michelle's boots to see if she was wearing spurs.

"Oh, my God," Michelle said. "My poor baby." With only a slight limp, she strode toward her horse.

Michelle collected her horse's reins and then hugged Sugar's large neck, while Kent and I rounded the animal to inspect the injuries. Her right side was fine, but her left side was bleeding substantially. Kent lifted the stirrup, then snorted in disgust. "There's a small nail in the leather of the stirrup straps. Sugar must've been in agony the whole time we were riding."

"I can't believe I didn't see that while I was saddling . . ."

She let her voice fade, then turned an accusing glare onto
Kent. "You were the one who put the saddle on Sugar for me,
while I was getting Nellie ready to ride."

"The nail must have already been there, but I didn't see it,"
Kent retorted. "Sorry."

"How could you have missed something like that? And
who else but you could have done this?"

Kent crossed his sturdy arms across his chest. "Come on,
Michelle. You know me better than that! I'd never hurt a
horse. I swear to you on bended knee, I did not put the nail in
Sugar's stirrup strap!"

Kent looked at both of us, though not from "bended knee."
"Ladies, I ask you. If I were trying to set Michelle up to take a
fall like this, would I be so stupid to do so in front of a witness?" He pointed at me.

"Probably not," I answered, "unless you put the nail there
yesterday, before you found out that I was joining the two of
you."

"That's a crappy thing to say!" Kent said, the muscles in
his jaws tight with anger.

"You posed the question."

He glared at me, then focused on Michelle, who was strok-
ing her horse's nose and soothing her. "Again, Michelle, I did
not put that tack in your horse's saddle. Come on. We've
known each other for years. I'd never do something like this
to you!"

"I . . ." She paused and sighed. "You're right. I was just so
upset at seeing my poor Sugar." She clicked her tongue. "I
can't believe anyone would do something like this! Who was
it?" Michelle demanded again.

"I don't know. It could have been anyone who knows
where you keep your horse and saddle. Maybe it's been there
for days now."

She shook her head vigorously. "I went riding by myself
just this past Sunday. It was not there then. I'm certain of that
much."

"Maybe it was Molly," Kent said, indicating me with a jerk
of his head. "She could have pushed the nail into your saddle

while she was supposedly inspecting the three horses when she first arrived."

Michelle whirled around to focus on me.

"Oh, please. I haven't gone anywhere near Sugar's saddle this whole trip. I never had the opportunity to shove a nail into the stirrup, let alone the motive."

"I'm not so sure about that," Kent grumbled. "One thing we can all be sure about is that I'm the one who risked his neck rescuing you. Just keep that much in mind, all right?"

"Thank you for helping me," Michelle replied, but without much feeling.

"You're welcome." Kent managed to pull out the nail, then took a white handkerchief from his pocket and helped Michelle to wedge it between the pieces of leather in Sugar's saddle, providing a little makeshift padding over the wound. In the meantime, Nellie lay down, and I decided to join her, knowing that a third pair of hands working on Sugar's saddle would not be helpful.

After a while, Kent boosted Michelle into the saddle. Sugar seemed fine, and Kent got back onto his horse.

"This experience has all been shot to hell," he said. "Let's just get the horses back to the stables and call it a day. All right?"

"Fine," Michelle said. She was still in very low spirits. She gave me a long look. "Somebody boobytraps my saddle so that I'll get thrown, right after Sylvia gets murdered. Maybe I'm next on the killer's hit list."

I was too busy trying to coax Nellie back onto all fours to offer a comment. By standing directly in front of her and pulling on her reins, I finally got her off her side.

At length, I realized that they were both watching me. Apparently it was either my turn to deny that I'd done it, or they'd never seen a rider trying to get her horse to stand up before. I climbed into Nellie's saddle quickly—though not effortlessly—before she could change her mind. "Michelle, would anyone else on the school board know enough about your horse as to be able to identify—and tamper with—your saddle?"

She raised her eyebrows. "I'm not sure. I mean, virtually everybody who knows me knows that I own a horse. I mention her often enough. And I've probably even mentioned the name of the stables where she's boarded." She looked over at Kent.

Kent paused and furrowed his brow. "Maybe. I can't swear to it either way."

I could ask my father, I thought, whether or not the riding stable that Michelle used was common knowledge among board members.

We trotted toward our original meeting place. The joy that I'd once experienced from horseback riding had definitely been lost for me somewhere during the space of the last couple of decades. My stomach muscles and, in fact, the entire lower half of my body were aching like mad. All I could think of under the circumstances was a distortion of the old saying: If wishes were horses, beggars would *really* be out of luck.

I went home and took two aspirin plus two ibuprofen tablets. Betty Cocker was going nuts sniffing at me, trying to identify my new Eau de Horse. My rear end and thighs seemed to have become swollen in the past couple of hours.

While whimpering louder than Betty ever did at her very worst stage of doggie desperation, I eventually managed to peel my jeans off. I got into the shower and drained the hot-water tank in my efforts to de-horsify myself.

During my shower and while I gingerly dressed afterward, I couldn't get past the thought that, if Michelle changed her vote, Dad's cause could be annihilated. Sylvia had been murdered. Michelle had narrowly averted serious injury. Put in this light, it seemed prudent to heed that fax warning about the danger that Dad and my family were in.

Could someone on the pro-arts contingent be so obsessed with winning that he or she was wiping out the competition? With Michelle switching sides, the only pro-arts supporters, other than my dad, were Stuart Ackleman and Carol Barr.

I mulled over the events at the murder scene once again

and limped into the kitchen, my muscles aching as though I'd recently given birth. I decided that it was quite possible that the poison Sylvia had ingested had been in her otherwise-empty water glass right from the start. Sylvia could easily have poured water into her glass, not noticing a small quantity of poisonous liquid already present.

This theory meant that I needed to track down the elderly woman who'd carried Sylvia's coat and set up the glasses at the start of the meeting.

I called Lauren, who'd worked as a secretary in the school long enough to know many of the employees at the Ed Center. When she answered, I immediately said, "Lauren, what can you tell me about the woman who was setting up the dais Monday night?"

"Agnes Rockman," Lauren said quietly. Her coworkers must have been in the vicinity. "She used to be the super-intendent's personal secretary, but now she works for the school board. She's retiring at the end of this year. I'm sure that working for the board was less demanding an assignment for her."

"So that means that this Agnes worked directly for Sylvia?"

"For the school board, yes."

"Here's my theory, Lauren. Sylvia might have treated her employee as badly as she did those who disagreed with her. Maybe Sylvia was making her life miserable and Agnes seized the opportunity to get rid of her."

After a pause, Lauren said, "You've . . . never met Agnes, have you?"

From the sound of Lauren's voice, it was obvious that she doubted my scenario. "No, why? Are you certain she's innocent, or something?"

"Let's just say it would be highly unlikely that she'd . . . do what you're suggesting. Unless something truly extraordinary occurred, very recently. I have her number in my employee handbook. Hang on a moment."

While I was waiting, I remembered that the secretary had become so completely overwrought when Sylvia collapsed that the superintendent had been forced to take her out of the room. This must be what Lauren was referring to when she'd been so skeptical about my theory.

Lauren came back on the line with the information and gave me Agnes's work and home phone numbers. I thanked her, disconnected, then immediately dialed Agnes's office number. The woman who answered told me that she was filling in because Agnes had "suffered a personal loss recently" and was not going to be in the office until tomorrow. I asked if this "personal loss" was Sylvia Greene, and the woman said, "Yes, she and Agnes were close friends."

The moment I called Agnes at home and introduced myself as Charlie Peterson's daughter, she launched into an emotion-laden speech about how misunderstood and wonderful Sylvia had been. When I asked if I could speak to her about Sylvia's death, Agnes immediately invited me to her home and even gave me directions. That was surprising, but I'd gotten the impression that she desperately wanted someone to reminisce with about Sylvia. Though I was hardly a Sylvia fan, I was horrified and angered by her murder and decided it was reasonably honest of me to accept the invitation.

Agnes lived in an old restored farmhouse, set back from the main road. The siding was painted red with white trim. Each of the rooms had faded wallpaper. The interior featured wide floorboards, which were uneven but neatly varnished. The house was furnished in antiques that struck me as being nice enough but more valuable in terms of memories than in monetary worth.

She was an elderly and, frankly, physically unattractive woman with wide, almost mongoloid features. My first impression, though, was that she was a sweet, caring person. We sat in rather uncomfortable Shaker-style chairs in her dining room, and I listened and nodded as she told me what a wonderful person Sylvia Greene had been in private, despite her more ornery public persona.

"How could anyone have done this to her?" she sobbed to

me for at least the fifth time. "She was a little . . . intimidating, the way she'd be so in-your-face and using the Latin all of the time. But that was just because she was secretly holding such a low opinion of herself. Ms. Greene was like a daughter to me. Or a younger sister, anyway. But a beloved younger sister. I would have done anything for that woman. Anything. Absolutely."

With such a strong bond between the two women, it was strange that Agnes kept referring to her as "Ms. Greene," and never Sylvia. "I'm curious about the water glasses. Do you usually pour the water itself, or do you just set out the glasses for them to fill?"

She sniffled a little, then answered, "I'm always too busy before meetings to fill their glasses. I just set them out."

"Do you carry the glasses in from some other location and set them down at random? I mean, the board members don't each have their own labeled water glasses or anything, do they?"

"We keep the glasses in a small kitchenette within the building, and all of the glasses are exactly the same." She dabbed at her bloodshot eyes. "I've heard that she was poisoned, but I don't see how, unless someone slipped something into her glass of water and then handed it to her. Which reminds me. Can I get you anything to drink?"

"No, thanks," I said, a bit too quickly, perhaps. I was not going to be eating or drinking anything handled by one of the board members or by Agnes.

"It's all over the radio talk shows that someone on the board must have done it. Poisoned her."

"Do you believe that theory?"

"Why, yes. I don't believe all the callers, of course. There have been several who've accused Mr. Peterson of being the one. That I don't believe."

"I'm glad to hear that you realize my father is innocent."

"Of murder," she said pointedly.

"You knew what Sylvia was about to divulge, then, I take it?"

"I do. And, I suppose, now that it has hit the front page of the newspaper, so does everyone else. But don't worry, dear. I don't think the less of you for being his offspring. You don't blame the acorns for the tree, I always say."

Bristling, I said pointedly, "I happen to really respect and admire my tree. Speaking as an acorn, I mean."

The phone rang, and Agnes went to answer. After saying hello, she launched into a series of questions: "Are you serious? But doesn't he realize that this is too soon? He did? But why?" None of the answers were meeting with her approval, and she was clearly distressed when she hung up.

"Is something wrong?" I asked.

"Molly, I'm afraid I've got to get myself together and go to the Ed Center."

I promptly got to my feet. "What's wrong? Is there anything I can do?"

"No. It's just that," she grimaced and said through clenched teeth, "Stuart Ackleman. As vice president of the school board, he has called a meeting of the board to announce their decision on who is going to take Ms. Greene's place."

"*Their* decision? Won't they hold a new election?"

She shook her head. "It takes far too much time and resources to schedule a new general election. This chosen replacement will merely serve on the board until the next regularly scheduled election. Which is next fall."

"Okay. I guess I can see that. But why are they doing this so soon? Out of respect to Sylvia if nothing else, they should have waited at least a week. This is outrageous!"

She nodded. "I know. That's Stuart Ackleman for you. Apparently, under his insistence, they have already reviewed a slate of candidates, voted, and are set to make an announcement in half an hour. I can't believe this! I'm the board's secretary, and no one even thought to notify me sooner."

I was very concerned about how my father had held up during this meeting. He had to still be reeling after this morning's newspaper article on him. A couple of hours later, he'd had to vote on his slain fellow board member's replacement.

"The meeting's at the Ed Center?" I asked rhetorically,

finding this utterly distasteful, considering that a woman had died there not two days ago. "Can people from the general public attend?"

She nodded. "It's not a closed meeting and Stuart will have alerted the media." She folded her arms and plopped back down on her chair. "But I've changed my mind. I'm not going. They can ask Superintendent Collins's secretary to fill in for me. At least one of us has to show poor Ms. Greene a measure of respect."

"I'm going to go, though. I need to support my father." I collected my purse. Agnes was watching me, squinting from her myopic eyes, literally or figuratively. "Thanks for your graciousness in inviting me to your home and speaking with me."

"Well, Ms. Masters, all I can say is I hope the police figure out who killed Ms. Greene. I'd have done anything for that woman." Her lips trembled and her eyes welled with tears.

Her obviously sincere sorrow gave me a new theory. Maybe she hadn't meant the poison for Sylvia. Could she have slipped poison into someone else's glass for Sylvia's sake? A glass which could have accidentally wound up with Sylvia?

By the time I arrived at the Ed Center, I'd all but dismissed that notion. If Agnes had wanted to poison one of the board members, she would have filled that one person's glass with water, lessening the chances of the tainted glass going to the wrong person. Otherwise, with just the empty glasses and water pitcher, it would have been far too common for the person nearest the pitcher to pour two or three glasses and hand them out at random. No, Agnes Rockman most likely was completely innocent.

I glanced at my watch. The children should be home from school by now, but Karen had her own key. Nevertheless, I didn't want to leave them home alone for long. I arrived early at the small auditorium, now the scene of the crime. Carol Barr was seated in her appointed spot. Stuart was there, but my father wasn't, nor was Kent or Michelle. As usual, though, Stuart was biding his time, waiting to be the last to be seated.

Several members of the press arrived, including my much-detested Mr. Johnson. He saw me, but averted his eyes, and I decided to avoid a confrontation.

Kent and Michelle appeared within moments of each other. It occurred to me as I sat watching the people arrive that the board's new appointee might be easy to spot out of such a small group.

My father arrived, accompanied by my ever-supportive mother. I got up and made my way across the room to greet them.

"Hi, Dad. Who's the new board member?"

The muscles in his jaw were working. "Stuart's grandstanding and asked us all not to tell anyone. I'm sorry." Dad had averted his eyes. "Better get this over with," he murmured, then left Mom's side to go to the dais.

"How did you know to come here?" Mom asked me. "I was under the impression that this was all put together in a hurry."

"I happened to be speaking to someone from the Ed Center."

She nodded. "Let's just hope that the new board member is someone sensible that your father can work with."

"Yes."

"Bet it won't be, though," Mom said, ever the optimist.

I kept an eye on the back door while the board members took their seats. I dropped into my seat in shock as I recognized the person who entered. "No," I said to myself in a quiet whisper. "This can't be happening!" There had to be another reason for her to be at this meeting.

"Let's begin," Stuart said, banging on the gavel with obvious relish. He smiled at his fellow board members, then said, "As the new president of this board, it is my privilege to announce our newest board member. We know that our decision to find a replacement for our fallen comrade might have seemed too swift for some. However, alacrity is something this board has never been accused of to date." He paused and smiled, as if expecting the audience to laugh. No one did. Stuart cleared his throat. "As we all know, no one could truly replace Sylvia Greene; however, we were fortunate to have a candidate so obviously qualified and devoted to this school district that there was no reason to delay our decision. The person we've chosen has been PTA president for as long as any of us can remember."

"No," I said, still whispering, but it was loud enough this time for my mother to elbow me.

Stuart scanned the audience.

As I'd feared but couldn't quite accept, my all-time arch-rival, Stephanie Saunders, stepped forward.

Chapter 10

They Said It Couldn't Be Done (They Were Right)

Stephanie, her smile beaming as bright as a spotlight, made her way to the front of the room and shook Stuart's hand. "I'm honored to serve on the board in this capacity, as tragic as the circumstances may be." The realization that her facial expression was not registering those "tragic circumstances" seemed to hit her a moment too late, for her cheeks grew pink as she lowered her eyes.

"Thank you. We all know that you'll do an excellent job." Stuart nodded at those of us making up the small audience.

Moments later, the meeting was adjourned, and I sat there in a state of shock. Mom patted me on the knee, then got up and made her way to the dais so that she could walk out with my father. Stephanie of course assumed that my mother was there to greet *her* and stepped between my parents.

"Mrs. Peterson, I'm so honored to be on the board with your husband. How is Molly?"

At the moment, trying hard to swallow her tongue and asphyxiate herself, I silently answered.

"I stopped by yesterday to bring her a hot meal, but she hasn't told me what she thought of it yet. Did she happen to mention anything about it to you?"

Her obvious ploy for praise rankled me. Granted, I should have called to thank her or written her a note, but only a day had passed, and who's to say I wouldn't have gotten around to doing so? Eventually. In any case, she didn't have to let my *mother* know of my bad manners, and it was very hard to believe that Stephanie hadn't already spotted me amid the many empty chairs.

"Molly's quite capable of speaking for herself." Mom glanced back at me, and Stephanie followed her gaze.

"Oh, there she is. Hi, Molly."

I raised my chin in acknowledgment, the best I could do against the tide of anxiety that was threatening to engulf me. Michelle had warned me that she would vote to fund sports. We would now need Stephanie's vote to ensure that the arts were sufficiently funded.

Stephanie glided down the steps toward me and gave my arm a squeeze. "I'm so looking forward to working on this board with your father."

"I had no idea you were even interested in serving on the school board."

"Oh, I wasn't especially, until I saw how seriously you and your family seem to take all of this school stuff. It's finally given me the opportunity to even things out between us."

" 'Even things out?' " I was very confused. Did Stephanie even care how I felt about her? If so, that was news to me. "How could your serving on the board possibly even things out between us? You already gave me a casserole. Which was delicious, by the way. Thank you very much, Stephanie." I said the last loudly enough so that my mother, who was passing by, could overhear. Mom was oblivious, though, holding onto my father's arm without a glance in our direction. She'd seemed almost numb during the meeting. All of this trauma focused on my father must have thrown her off balance.

"Oh, I'm so glad you enjoyed the meal. I meant to warn you before you took it out of my dish to be careful not to ruin the cross-hatching of the spaghetti. But what I meant was . . ." she paused and gave me a big smile, "we can work together, just like the old days on the school paper."

"I hated those days."

She raised her eyebrows and studied my face for a moment. "Oh, that's right. You did, didn't you? And yet those are some of my fondest memories from high school. Just goes to show you. It's crazy, the directions life takes us in, isn't it?"

"Yes, this is definitely crazy, all right."

Stephanie returned to the dais to effervesce with the remaining of her newfound peers, and I left, grinding my teeth.

The next morning, after sending Karen and Nathan safely
off to school, I went down to my basement office to get some
work done. There was a fax in my receiving tray. This one
came from the Carlton School District's general fax number
with no additional identification. It read:

Sam Dunlap is not who you think he is.
He has his own secret past he's hiding.
Check into his family.
Especially his sister.
You might want to read the obituaries.

I read the message three times, trying to get a handle on it.
The words appeared to have been typed and printed from a
computer printer, a dot matrix of some sort, which I hadn't
seen used in a long time now that laser printers and ink jets
had become so affordable.

Who was sending me these faxes? Maybe it was someone
on the school board who was sympathetic to my family's
plight; a friend of my father's, perhaps. But if that was the
case, why give me the information? Why not give an anonymous tip to the police? The fax had to have come from the
same person who'd sent the earlier fax urging my father to resign. My hunch, having met the woman, was that both faxes
were from Agnes Rockman.

I checked yesterday's obituaries, but though Sylvia's was
there, I found nothing in it that struck me as significant. The
cause of death was not mentioned, and memorial services
were scheduled for the following week. The fax must be referring to an obituary that ran a while ago.

I needed to ask my father about who might have sent me
the fax. I copied it, then called my parents, listened through
Mom's now irritating message to hang up if you weren't a

good guy, then said, "Dad, if you're there, can you pick up the phone?"

A moment later, he picked up. "Molly?" he asked, sounding so sad that I was instantly worried.

"I was just checking to see if you were home. I'd like to show you something. Are you going to be there for a while?"

"Just reading the paper. Come on over."

A few minutes later, my father let me in and told me that Mom was out grocery shopping. After a brief explanation, I handed him the fax, and he dropped into his official "reading chair" where his temporarily deserted newspaper lay at the ready.

While he read the fax, I perched on the edge of Mom's chair nearby. "I need to know who on the board might have access to a dot matrix printer and to the school district's fax machine."

"Anyone on the board has access to a dot matrix and a fax machine. They're both in a small office that we all share at the Ed Center."

"If no one from the board itself happens to be using it, is it deserted?"

"No, it's Agnes Rockman's office. She's our secretary."

"I'll bet this is from her," I muttered while watching him read it a second time.

He shook his head and handed the fax back to me. "This is probably a prank. Somebody read the article in the morning's paper identifying Mr. Dunlap, knows who you are, and is playing a nasty trick. Things like this happen all the time. Don't let it get to you."

"I got another one yesterday. It wasn't printed on a dot matrix, though. It warned that your life was in danger and that you should resign." Actually, the fax had implied that his *family's* lives were endangered, but there was no sense in alarming Dad.

He sighed and ran his palm over his bald pate. "Can't say that I'm surprised. I'm just sorry that you had to deal with it, instead of me."

"Has anyone given you a similar message?"

"No, not quite. But we were getting all sorts of prank phone calls and hang-ups. That's why your mom changed the greeting on our answering machine."

"This is such a nightmare. Are you holding up all right?"

He nodded. "We called your sister last night. Told her everything that's going on." He shifted his vision and stared out the window for a long moment, a forlorn expression on his face. "I should have done something. The seeds of this had to have been planted some time ago. I should have seen it coming."

"You know that wasn't possible. No one could have predicted Sylvia would be murdered."

He didn't even acknowledge that he'd heard me. I silently weighed the board members as suspects against one another and found myself mulling over Dad's and my earlier conversation, when he first told me about the accident his brother's potato-launching had caused. He'd said that a five-year-old had been injured. "Dad? Is there any chance that the boy who was badly injured in that accident your brother caused grew up to be Stuart or Kent? Somebody on the board?"

Dad let out a startled laugh. "No, Molly. That's just . . . too farfetched. He was ten years younger than me, so he'd be . . . fifty-eight now. That's too old for Kent and too young for Stuart."

I nodded, relieved that the past hadn't come back to haunt my father to an even greater degree than it already had. "Do you think that Mom's doing all right?"

"Of course. You know your mom. She's fine."

I *did* know my mom, possibly better than he did when it came to understanding her emotions. "I was just wondering if maybe she felt a little hurt that you hadn't told her sooner about Uncle Ted."

"I was just following my lawyer's advice," Dad retorted through a tight jaw, facing me once again, now with his arms tightly crossed against his chest. "She understands."

"Good." I felt myself bristle at Dad's defensive attitude. Regardless of the legal issues, it was obviously horrible advice from the family's perspective. Why couldn't Dad have seen that? Before I could stop myself, I blurted out, "I'm not sure that I do, though."

He furrowed his brow. "We didn't raise you to hold on to hurts and disappointments, Molly. I felt that the promise I'd made to my dying brother was more important than a confession to you or to your mother. I told you I'd done nothing wrong. That was the truth."

"But it wasn't the truth when you said during our drive to the Ed Center that you had no skeletons in your closet. You already knew what Sylvia's upheaval was all about at the time. You'd told Jim a few days earlier. Why didn't you just tell all of us and ask us to keep it in the family?"

Dad rose and turned his back on me to face the window. "I had paid an expert good money to advise me, and he told me not to."

"If it were me, as soon as Sylvia first let on that I was under suspicion, I would have warned my family of the likely disclosure, while keeping my brother's name out of it. And if my lawyer told me to do otherwise, I'd have found another lawyer."

The muscles in Dad's jaw were working. "I did the best I could, Molly. I'm sorry if that wasn't good enough for you."

His reaction surprised me. Though I deeply regretted bringing up my hurt feelings when he was obviously low, the fact that I felt them at all struck me as justifiable. And I didn't know how *not* to "hold on to hurts and disappointments" except to examine them openly. "This isn't about you . . . disappointing me, Dad." My throat was tightening and my voice came out strained. "It's about me trying to understand why you made the choices you made regarding me."

He said nothing, his back still turned.

Feeling about as miserable as possible, I left. It was unrealistic of me to have expected Dad to ignore his lawyer's advice; he was of a generation unlikely to question advice given to him by a doctor, a lawyer, or even an auto mechanic.

There was a time when I believed that my personal heroes, such as my father, were made from stronger, purer stuff than the rest of us. I'd long since discovered that people generally try to do the right thing, but the lines between heroes and cowards are forever shifting, drawn according to the given set of circumstances and one's personal vantage point.

I made it home, accompanied only by the sensation that I'd lost something during my short walk—my sense of humor, perhaps. The truth is, I cared so deeply about the people in my life that I had to hide my feelings behind laughter as a means to skirt around the pain.

I cuddled my dog until I managed to shed the vestiges of self-pity, then forced myself to set my mind to examining just what this anonymous fax really meant regarding Sam Dunlap.

More than twenty-four hours had passed since I'd last butted heads with Tommy. If I were to call him to ask what he knew about Sam Dunlap, he wouldn't answer the question, but I'd feel obligated to tell him about the fax, and he'd tell me to stay out of this, and so on. I decided to forestall that tiresome duet for now.

Determined to find this information the only way I could think of, I went to the Carlton library and started in on our microfiche roll of old newspapers. I worked backward from the present, which meant possibly going through a month's worth of papers, but at least the obituary listings were short and located on pretty much the same page of every edition. An hour and a half later, I had gone through eight-plus months' worth of obituaries. I had developed motion sickness as well as a distinct dislike of the color blue from staring at the blue screen.

Just as I was about to admit that my father had been right— that the fax had just been a sick joke—a photograph in the obituary section struck me, because the woman was so pretty and young. Half the time, families had the papers run some reprint of the deceased that was taken forty or fifty years earlier, but this time the dates matched. The woman had been only thirty-six.

The woman's name was Mary Jacobsen Greene. Was this "Greene" as in Sylvia Greene?

My heartbeat increased when I read the names of the bereaved: Husband, Aaron Greene. Samuel Jacobsen, brother. The fax had stated that Sam Dunlap wasn't who he claimed to be; could this "Samuel Jacobsen" and Sam Dunlap be one in the same? And was this Aaron Greene possibly Sylvia's ex-husband?

There was no mention of cause of death, and the donations in lieu of flowers gave no clue. This was unusual and struck me as a deliberate omission, which might indicate that the cause of death was not something the family wished to reveal.

I scrolled back to the front page of that edition and discovered a headline: WOMAN'S DEATH RULED SUICIDE. A phrase leapt out, *"was despondent over her recent separation from her husband. . . ."*

The fax had warned me to look for Sam Dunlap's sister and to look in the obituaries. Now here was the suicide of a woman with the same last name as Sylvia and with a brother named Sam. This was too big a coincidence for me to swallow. There had to be some connection.

How could I find out? Hire a second private investigator to check out PI Sam Dunlap's real name and personal history? If my doing so allowed me to ferret out who was threatening my family, it would be worthwhile.

I pondered the matter for a few minutes and developed such an outlandish theory that I felt compelled to run it past someone else and dispel the whole notion. Using a pay phone at the library, I called my husband at work. His voice sounded cheerful when he answered.

"Hi, Jim. I want to bounce something off of you."

"Go ahead, so long as it's not a brick."

He was stealing my lines these days, but I decided not to object. "If you were out to get somebody, and you wanted to make them look bad, could you pass yourself off as a private investigator and feed them a batch of libelous nonsense about their peers?"

"I don't follow. What good would that do?"

"The person you were out to get would make public knowledge of all of the libelous malarkey you concocted,

112 — Leslie O'Kane

thereby discrediting themselves and setting themselves up for a winnable lawsuit."

"But why would I do that? Why be that circuitous about everything? The information that this PI fed to Sylvia about your father was accurate, as far as anyone but your father himself knew."

"True, but that might be exactly why it was the perfect lead-in for the PI. You get one true story to give to the person you're setting up. Now the person believes everything you tell them, even when they're bald-faced lies. Only what you don't realize is that there is someone with a horrible secret. Someone willing to commit murder to keep it hidden."

"But, Molly, why wouldn't I just confront the person directly and . . . punch him in the nose?"

"Because it's a woman, and you wouldn't feel good about punching a woman in the nose."

"So I'm a guy, right?"

"Right, but the person you want to punish is a woman."

"So, if I'm a guy, why am I acting like a woman? Why am I acting underhanded and devious instead of going the direct route—taking direct action?"

"Men can be just as underhanded and devious as women, you know."

"Yeah, but not as a rule." He added under his breath, "I hope nobody from the office has been listening to my end of this conversation, or I'll never live it down. What's this about, anyway?"

"I got a fax today about Sam Dunlap, that private investigator, and I'm beginning to suspect that he bore a big grudge against Sylvia Greene."

"Molly, what are—" There was a voice in the background and Jim replied, "Just a minute." He got back on the phone and said irritably, "Do us both a favor and keep Sergeant Newton fully informed. Give him the fax and let him handle it. I've got to get back to work."

We said our good-byes and hung up. I put a couple of quarters into the microfiche machine and printed out the page from the newspaper, retrieved both of the faxes from my house, and brought them to Tommy, whom I found in his minuscule office at the police station.

After he'd read over the items I'd given him, I said, "I'm not especially worried about the faxes. I'm choosing to believe that whoever's sending them is doing so because she— or he—thinks they're helping me. What I don't understand, though, is how could someone else have known about Sam's identity, and yet Sylvia didn't know herself?"

Tommy drummed his fingers on his desk and, not meeting my eyes, grumbled, "Maybe she did know. And didn't care. Figured he wouldn't hold anything against her for the past. Meantime, you've gone and inserted yourself smack in the middle of another one of my investigations."

"Not intentionally, Tommy. It's just that my father's an innocent suspect. Would you mind calling the guy and asking if he'd meet with us?"

"Us?" Tommy sighed and pushed back from his desk, eyeing me. "The way I see it, there are two ways you can go about this, Moll. You can keep stirrin' up trouble, which is, I know, always your first inclination. Or, you can try doin' things the legal, sane way that anyone in their right mind would choose. You can stay home, keep your mind occupied on other things, and let me and my men solve this murder."

"You make it sound as if I'm just getting in your way. You never give me any credit for the valuable information I give to you."

"Uh-huh." Tommy combed his fingers through his hair, then leaned forward, his elbows on his desk. "I'm glad you brought the subject up. There's a reason for that. See, the information you just gave me here?" He lifted up the papers that I'd brought him. "I've already got this in my file."

"Oh. Well, if that's true," I said so pointedly, because of course, it *wasn't* true with regard to the faxes, "I'm sorry to have wasted your time." My cheeks blazed and my voice was tight. "How close are you to arresting Sylvia's killer and vindicating my dad?"

"We're ... making progress. The investigation is right where it should be."

"That's bull and we both know it! Do you mean to tell me that you don't think you should have already arrested the killer by now?"

"Sure. But then we got extenuating circumstances. Such as you messin' up our evidence."

As far as I knew, I hadn't "messed up" any evidence whatsoever, but I didn't want to call Tommy on it, for fear that he'd have some example at his disposal that he could humiliate me with. Instead, I leveled a glare at Tommy and said, "Well, pardon me for caring!" I headed for the door, which was so close by I merely needed to rise from my seat and pivot.

"You're pardoned, just quit doin' it."

Incensed at him for lousing up my exit, I marched out to my car, closed myself inside, and gripped the steering wheel. Somehow, someway, I was going to see to it that this killer was brought to justice. Even if I had to do so single-handedly.

Chapter 11

Just a Little Greene

To my considerable curiosity, Carol Barr was waiting in her large silver-colored sedan in my cul-de-sac when I returned from the police station. Surely she didn't have cause to chew me out for something, too, but the way my life had been of late, it struck me as unlikely that she'd come here out of mere courtesy.

I rolled down my window and called to her, "Are you waiting to see me?"

She poked her head out and gave me a smile. "Yes, Molly. Do you have a minute?"

"Sure." I was "having" lots of minutes lately, but few of them were turning out to be either fruitful or enjoyable. And I was surprised that Carol had come to my house like this.

Before my father had been voted onto the school board, Carol Barr used to strike me as the one sane voice of reason on that board. Stuart Ackleman and Michelle Lacy always voted in kind, but it was only Carol who struck me as ready and able to push politics aside and put the children's interests first. Quite a concept for a school board member during these contentious times. Whenever I'd made citizens' presentations to the board—which I'd done on occasion prior to Dad's winning a seat on the board but not since—I'd sensed in Carol a bit of admiration. Among the others, I'd gotten the feeling that they'd allowed me to speak only because they had to, and weren't actually listening.

I put the car in the garage and came out to join Carol at her car. She wore a purple sweatshirt and black stretch pants, which did not look flattering on her short, rotund form. But then, I was hardly a fashion plate myself. Unless a broken plate counted.

She sized me up with her brown eyes. "Hello, Molly. I hope I'm not interfering with your lunch plans."

"No, not at all." Though, now that she mentioned it, I was pretty hungry.

"I was at your parents' place. Just dropped in on them for a few minutes to see how your father is doing."

"And how is he?"

"He insists that he's fine. Typical male. Not saying much, I'm afraid. I'd hoped he would be a little more willing to discuss our situation."

"Situation?"

"We appointed Stephanie Saunders, as you know, to take Sylvia's place until another representative can be chosen in the next election."

"Yes. I know Stephanie quite well." Unfortunately. "We went to school together."

"That's what your dad said. We're trying to get a read on how she's going to vote on the budget issue."

"Who is 'we'?"

"The board members. Stuart and your dad and I are of course hoping she'll be more in line with those of us who recognize the importance of the fine arts. I don't know if you've heard, but, well, Michelle is wavering on the issue now, and we might really need Stephanie's vote."

"Yes, but I would think that Sylvia's replacement would reflect her views, right? Much as I disagreed with them personally, those wrongheaded opinions of hers were what got her elected."

"Please." Carol rolled her eyes. "What got her elected was the big bucks she put into her campaign. She sunk tens of thousands of her own money into the signs alone. Remember 'Put a little Greene into your school board'?"

I chuckled. "Now that you mention it. I'm surprised Sylvia ever put up with being called 'a little Greene.' If anyone were ever to have called Sylvia that to her face, she would have demanded the person's head on a platter."

"Anyway, I've hoped to enlist your help. Could we speak inside? Not that this is top secret, or anything, but I'd feel more comfortable."

"Sure. Come on in." We headed up the walkway together. As I unlocked the front door for her, leaving my garage door open, my thoughts raced toward the condition of the house before I left. This would hardly be the first time that I'd invited someone to come into my natural habitat—a total mess.

Fortunately, Nathan had tidied the place up a bit before leaving for the bus this morning. Betty Cocker was thrilled to see me, though she barked some at Carol, who acted uncomfortable at the dog's less-than-friendly greeting. I got BC to behave and offered Carol a seat on the couch, which she accepted, and sat down on the big chair myself, with BC pushed up against my feet.

"I hope you're not thinking that I have any inside knowledge of the workings of Stephanie Saunders's brain. That woman has perplexed me since day one. I remember a time she and I happened to be walking next to each other while changing classes during our junior year in high school. Out of the blue, she said to me, 'Molly, don't you just love to brush your teeth? I think it's such a treat to be able to do something for yourself that makes you look better.' That's a remark which, twenty-plus years later, I still have no response to."

Carol laughed and said, "You have no idea which way she'll vote?"

"No, I don't."

"I called Stephanie myself after the de facto board meeting yesterday." She paused, then murmured, "My God. I just used Latin. I do hope the Ghost of Sylvia hasn't . . . Anyway, Stephanie told me that she hadn't made up her mind yet."

I went to cross my legs, forgetting for the moment how close the dog was, who'd nodded off, and how sore my leg muscles were. I wound up inadvertently kicking the dog, which hurt me more than it did her. The accompanying unexpected pain caused me to let out a small groan.

Carol raised her eyebrows in surprise. "Are you all right, Molly?"

"More or less. My legs are killing me. I went horseback riding for the first time in years yesterday."

"With Kent and Michelle?"

"Yes. How did you guess?"

"Sylvia used to make a point of chaperoning that pair's little outing."

"Did Sylvia herself used to refer to her riding with them as 'chaperoning'?"

Carol gave me a sly smile. "Michelle and Kent have been . . . strange bedfellows for years now, dating back before either of them made it onto the board."

So they *were* having an affair. That didn't surprise me, but it did make me wonder why Michelle had invited me to join them. Maybe they'd broken it off and she'd wanted to make certain she wasn't alone with him. "How does that affect their voting?"

She shrugged. "I'm sure they feel that it has no effect. Nobody's come straight out and asked them. It's a secret, of course. Just happens to be the worst-kept one since Clinton's tryst in the Oval Office."

"Not even Sylvia has asked them? That sounds completely contrary to everything I know about her."

"Oh, of course she asked them. During one of our closed-session meetings. I meant that I personally have never asked them about it, nor has anyone else asked them publicly. Michelle confessed as much to me one night. But when Sylvia confronted them at the private board meeting, Michelle denied that they're having an affair. Furthermore, she told Sylvia that if she pushed things, she'd be committing professional suicide, since the charges were untrue."

"Even if they're not . . . lovers . . . they do spend a lot of time together, so I can't see how Michelle could get terribly offended at the accusation. What does she say about their horseback riding?"

"That they've known each other from the stable where they have both boarded their horses for the past ten years.

That they can be friendly, despite their opposite views on what's right for the schools."

"Hmm," I muttered, keeping my opinions to myself. Kent and Michelle's behavior was confusing to me. Even if I had a purely platonic relationship with a man, I personally would find a way to include the spouses often enough in our get-togethers, out of respect for Jim's feelings. Though we know we can trust each other completely, there's much to be said for avoiding even the appearance of impropriety. That must explain why the two took such care to invite Sylvia and then me to join them. Which reminded me: This was a fine opportunity to learn how much others knew about the particulars of Michelle's horse. "What's the name of the stable that they use? I meant to ask them but forgot."

"I wouldn't know. I'm sure there can't be more than one or two right by the Battlefields, though. Why do you ask? Are you planning on getting a horse yourself?"

"No, just riding lessons for my daughter," I lied. Come to think of it, Carol was far too intelligent to admit to me that she knew this information, if she had actually been the one to put that nail in Michelle's saddle. A tack in the horse's tack, as it were.

The wordplay had distracted me. Carol had started to say something, then she coughed and held a hand to her throat. "Could I trouble you for a glass of water?"

"Of course. I've probably got juice or soda, if you'd prefer."

She shook her head. "Just water. With ice, please. If you don't mind."

Betty raced me into the kitchen, ever hopeful for treats, while I fetched Carol's water, mulling things over as I did so. I couldn't imagine that there was anything in the regulations strictly prohibiting board members from becoming lovers. Which was not to say that, if there had been, Kent and Michelle's reaction would have been, "But wait! Regulation Ten-Fifty-Two-A specifically states: No smooching. Why, we're not *allowed* to fall in love!"

When I came back into the living room, Carol was

standing by the rolltop desk. I wasn't sure if it was my imagination or not, but she seemed to be a little disconcerted, as if I'd startled her.

She made a slight stutter-step as if she were off balance as she reached for the glass, bumping into and shutting one of the drawers in process. Carol blushed from ear to ear. Was her visit here a ploy to search through my personal papers? If so, how utterly bizarre.

"Carol. You look like I caught you at something. Did something in my desk attract your attention?"

"No, no." She gave me a sheepish smile. "I was just admiring your desk, that's all."

"I hope you didn't open the rolltop. That's where we hide our smaller messes. It's a junk drawer of sorts, only we've had to devote the entire top of the desk to that task." Plus the garage and two rooms in the basement, but no sense in being too candid.

She accepted the glass of water from me and took a couple of sips. "The more I think about it, the more I realize that I'm probably wasting your time with this visit. I was going to ask whether or not you thought you could exert some influence over Stephanie's decision."

"Not a positive influence, no. Though it's possible that if I were to tell her I wanted her to vote to fully fund the sports budget, she'd do exactly the opposite."

Carol handed back her mostly untouched glass of water. "I'd be more than happy to see you give that a try. This is a serious matter, Molly. The future of the children in this district depends on keeping our arts and music programs fully funded. It is the single most important issue facing our society today."

I nodded, thinking that, while I agreed with her, I half expected to hear a soundtrack of "My Country 'Tis of Thee" in the background. "All right. I'll talk to Stephanie. But I can't make any promises."

"Nor am I asking for any. I'm just hoping you'll feel her out, give me your best guess as to which way the wind is blowing for her."

Straight in one ear and out the other, I thought, but managed to hold my tongue. "I'll call her after you leave."

She reached into her small purse and handed me her business card. "Let me know how you think she's going to vote."

"I will if I can, though it might have to be merely my best guess. We were on a debate team together for a short time during high school. She could argue both positions on any given issue with equal passion." I'd concluded that Stephanie was a skilled actress, but that she truly didn't care about anything that wasn't directly affecting her life at the moment.

"All right then. Thank you. I can't tell you how much this means to the children."

"You're welcome, though, again, I doubt this is going to do much good."

With Betty trotting alongside my feet, I escorted Carol to the door and watched while she got into her car and drove away.

What a strange visit, I thought. Why wait for me to arrive home for such a simple request? Why not simply call, or enlist my father's help in asking that I poll Stephanie?

The moment Carol was out of sight, I went through my desk drawers, searching for anything that might relate to my father or that might be hideously embarrassing, not counting their appalling state of disorder, or something that didn't belong and which she could have planted. Nothing caught my eye. She'd had the sense not to straighten the papers, if she had indeed gone through them in the first place.

But why on earth would she go through my papers? It wasn't as though she could hope to find anything germane to herself or to the school board.

These days, there seemed to be more questions than answers to just about everything. Now I had to contact Stephanie, of all people. I knelt and rubbed my cocker spaniel's tummy. "That's a good dog, Betty. Yes, that's right, I'm stalling. I don't want to be an adult. Too many of us are mean and nasty." Which was not even the worst of what could be said about Stephanie Saunders. Actually, she was easiest to deal with when she was revealing her nasty side; it was her relentless showboating and surface chumminess that tended to wear me down.

And yet, considering that Michelle Lacy's vote was now up for grabs, it probably really *would* help my father and the pro-arts cause if I could speak to Stephanie and find out how she was inclined to vote.

Gag me.

I dialed and Stephanie answered.

"Stephanie, hi. It's Molly. I was expecting to get your machine."

"Molly. How are you, dear? How's your family holding up?"

"Oh, we're all every bit as perky as ever. I was wondering if you've had a chance to decide how you feel about the budget allocation."

"Not really. Why?"

"Frankly, I'd like to know whether or not you're supporting arts and music funding in the school district."

"Oh. That. I haven't decided yet. I fail to see why anyone cares much about my position."

Her attitude instantly annoyed me, although I suspected that I was playing directly into her hand. How dare she suggest that it made no difference? What kind of an attitude was that for a new appointee? "It's the single most important issue you'll be asked to help determine while you're on the board!" I was quoting Carol and probably sounded even more gung-ho than she had, but didn't care.

"Molly, please don't raise your voice. I'm flirting with a headache."

Flirting with one? I hoped the headache fell in love with her and married her for life.

"All I meant," she went on, "was that my vote won't matter in the least. Your father, Carol, Stuart, and Michelle are voting to put the money into the arts and music programs, so they have their majority regardless of my vote."

"That's not necessarily the case. Michelle Lacy indicated yesterday that she might be changing her vote toward funding athletic programs."

"Oh. I see." She sounded surprised. "In that case, I'd better pay a little more attention to this whole thing." She sighed. "Honestly. You would think with all of the money in this community, we could fund both arts and sports, wouldn't you?"

"No kidding. But we can't, according to the budget analysis that the district spent a small fortune to have done for them."

"Well, they'd better shape up if they expect me to let my son attend their school."

I rolled my eyes. Her high schooler, Tiffany, had attended school in this district for twelve years now. The thought of her not enrolling Michael in kindergarten class was surely going to bring the district to its collective knees, all right. "You're on the school board now, Stephanie. You're one of the few people who can actually help improve the school district."

"Yes, I am. You're absolutely right." Her voice carried enthusiasm. "Enough of playing cheerleader. I'm one of the star players myself now!"

"Rah."

"Thanks, Molly. You've put this all into perspective for me."

Still needing to give an answer to Carol Barr, I asked, "And how do things look from your perspective?" A frightening question if there ever was one, but I truly wanted to be able to get Carol Barr the answer that she'd seemingly put so much effort into obtaining.

"Pretty shabby, frankly. You know what, Molly? You and I are going to march right into Superintendent Collins's office right now and demand that he go through this budget and find the necessary funding."

"We are?"

"Absolutely. We can carpool, even though your place is a little out of the way for me. I'll drive. Your little Toyota is just too small for my taste."

"I'm aware that your taste needs a lot of space. But I'm not sure this is such a good idea. Karen and Nathan are getting home from school in two hours and—"

"As the saying goes, Molly, there's no time like now. I'll pick you up in a few minutes. Actually, make that twenty or thirty. I've just got to do something about my nails before I appear in public."

I doubted that there was a disclaimer on that particular cliché to the effect, "There's no time like now . . . provided one's nails are properly manicured," but Stephanie hung up without awaiting further comment from me.

I glanced at my ever-faithful, ever-present little dog who'd fallen asleep but quickly awoke when I petted her. A trip to the school superintendent's office with Stephanie Saunders. This was worse than being sent to the principal's office. I stared into the black pools of my dog's eyes. "Want to trade places with me, Betty?" I asked.

That would make it two female dogs going together to the superintendent's office, I thought.

Chapter 12

Beauty and the Mommy-beast

Half an hour later, which had given me more than enough time for lunch, Stephanie rang my doorbell with one of her nicely painted nails, which I somehow managed to resist envying. She was wearing autumnlike clothing—a suede skirt with matching jacket over her cream-colored silk blouse, and a silk scarf with a pattern of brown- and yellow-colored leaves.

"Ready to go, Molly?" she asked, which didn't seem worth responding to since I'd answered the door with my house keys in hand.

I locked up and we headed together down my walkway toward her BMW, which the vanity plates identified as "Steffy." I'd once remarked what a neat coincidence it was that she and her car had such similar names, but she was not amused.

"You didn't have any trouble getting us an appointment with Mr. Collins on such short notice?"

"An appointment?" she repeated derisively, scanning my face as if she expected me to shrink in embarrassment. "You are so naive, Molly. The reason my interior decorating business was such a success prior to my early retirement, as opposed to how badly your own . . ." She stopped, no doubt having noticed that my jaw and fists were now clenched. "Well, let's face it, Molly. 'Friendly Fax' is hardly a *Fortune* Five-hundred Company, now is it? Making advanced appointments allows the other party to gain the upper hand. One should only make appointments if doing so is to one's own benefit."

"And *one* doesn't feel that checking to see if Mr. Collins is even going to be in his office before *one* drags me out of my house would have been to *one's* benefit?"

"He'll be there. Honestly, Molly, you are such a pessimist."

This seemed to have become my personal motif of late—people calling me pessimistic. Hearing it from Stephanie was hard to take, though. I got into the front seat and said hello to little Mike seated behind me, who was his typical happy self.

"I got a truck!" he announced and showed me his Matchbox-size blue pickup.

"Hey, that's really a nice truck, Mike. It's missing its wheels, though."

"I removed those for his safety," Stephanie informed me as she fastened her seatbelt. "Mikey could have pulled them off and swallowed them."

"Bet his truck doesn't go as fast that way."

"Didn't you pull the tires off of your son's toy vehicles?"

"No, but then, he was never much of a swallower. A chew-'em-up-and-spit-'em-outter, maybe."

She frowned as she pulled out of my subdevelopment. "Let's listen to some music," Stephanie said and, to my delight, put on the radio too loud for us to have to speak. Normally, I'm not a fan of blaring radios, but then, I'm normally not in the company of someone I dislike.

The drive to the Education Center was every bit as unpleasant now as the time I'd ridden there with my parents. Stephanie pulled into the handicap space by the front door.

"You can't park here. It's handicap parking, Stephanie."

She ignored me and got out, opened the back door, and started to unfasten her son's car-seat belt.

"We're in a handicap space, Steph."

"I'm pushing forty and have a rambunctious four-year-old. What's your point?"

"That you still have feet and legs that work! That if you don't move this car, I'll borrow the receptionist's phone and call the parking authorities myself and have you ticketed and towed!" *You toad!* I silently added.

Stephanie lowered her sunglasses enough to shoot me a

glare over the top of the frames, but then smiled at her son. "Mikey? Take my grouchy friend's hand and wait for me while I move the car."

Too indignant to feel any sense of glory over my minor victory, I got out of the car and took Mike's very sticky hand. He never could have swallowed anything coming from these fingers, anyway. Those little toy wheels that had been so carefully removed would have just stuck to his skin. We waited on the sidewalk and watched as Stephanie all but burned rubber as she backed up and pulled into a different space.

Uncomfortable at harboring so much resentment toward the mother of my sticky-handed little friend, I smiled at him and asked, "How's preschool going for you?"

"Good."

"Do you like your teachers?"

"Yes."

"You sound just like my children. They give one-word answers, too, when I ask them about school."

"Oh."

As Stephanie made her way across the asphalt toward us, the slight breeze ruffled the ends of her scarf and her long blond hair. She pushed it back behind her ear and smiled winningly at her son. She truly was a gorgeous woman, and I'd have been much more appreciative if only I'd been granted the opportunity to worship her strictly from afar.

She rummaged through her purse, saying, "Well, Molly, now that we're politically correct, let's go see what Superintendent Collins has to say for himself." She spread a tissue across her palm, then said, "Take Mommy's hand, Mikey." With the tissue forming a buffer between their hands—and her pretty nails—she led the way into the lobby.

We quickly spotted a sign that directed us to the superintendent's office and entered his private waiting room. There sat Agnes Rockwell, who looked surprised to see us. She appeared to stiffen a little as she looked at Stephanie, who was currently occupied as she picked tissue lint from her son's fingers. Agnes was no doubt quite familiar with Stephanie from her former post as PTA president for life, as well as her new role as board member.

We walked up to her desk. "Agnes, hi," I said. "I'm surprised to see you here. I assumed you had your own office as secretary for the school board."

"That's correct. Normally I'm in the office next door. Just filling in for someone who's home sick today." I glanced at the second doorway she'd indicated, wondering if there was any evidence in that room regarding the identity of my mystery faxer, though I still strongly suspected one and the same was sitting right in front of me. Agnes pressed a couple of keys and glanced at her computer screen. "You aren't here to see Mr. Collins, are you? There's no mention of his having an appointment with you today. Or with you, either, Ms. Saunders."

"That is so typical," Stephanie said, deserting Mike's messy hand to put her own hands on her hips in mock disgust. "I must have set this appointment two weeks ago!"

Agnes gave up scanning the computer screen and pulled out the center drawer in the desk and paged through an appointment book. "I'm sorry, Ms. Saunders, but there's just nothing here, and Superintendent Collins is completely booked today."

"That is just not acceptable. Let me remind you that I'm on the school board. If Reggie has any interest in keeping his job, I suggest he find five minutes to speak with us."

Agnes narrowed her eyes and set her chin. "Mr. Collins does wish to keep his job. He might accommodate your ploy of pretending you had an appointment today, which you, in fact, didn't have the common courtesy to make. I, however, am retiring in a few months. You have no power over me, Ms. Saunders."

My opinion of Agnes instantly skyrocketed, and I wanted to applaud. Stephanie crossed her arms and fixed a long stare at Agnes. "Would you please tell Reggie that I'm here?"

Agnes crossed her own arms, pursed her lips, and said, "Today I work for Superintendent Collins and not for you. If you wish to see him, you'll have to wait until he happens to come out here."

Stephanie smirked at her, then grabbed her son's fuzzy hand. "Come on, Mikey. We need to take matters into our own hands." She headed toward the door of the superintendent's office and opened it.

Agnes started to push her chair back from her desk as if to block Stephanie's path, but then must have seen the futility and, instead, shot an accusing glare at me.

"Coming here wasn't my idea. I assumed she'd made an appointment."

"Sorry to barge in on you, gentlemen, ladies," Stephanie was saying as she entered the other room. "If I could just trouble you for two minutes of your time, Mr. Collins, I'd be forever grateful. I can speak to you in your lobby, if that would be convenient."

"I'll be there in a minute or two," came a deep voice.

"Thank you so much," Stephanie cooed.

Agnes, her red face providing a strong contrast with her white hair, put both hands on her desktop and rose from her chair. "Pardon me, Ms. Masters," she said evenly. "I'm going to find a plant or two to water someplace else in the building. It was good to see you again."

Agnes stormed out of the lobby, while a triumphant-looking Stephanie returned and took a seat, pulling Mike onto her lap. "You see that, Molly? What it takes to succeed in the business world is self-confidence and a willingness to walk through whatever obstacles are put in front of you."

"Maybe so, Stephanie, but do you like yourself?"

She didn't answer. After a short, uncomfortable silence, Reginald Collins emerged from his office, looking rather rumpled in his rolled-up shirtsleeves and with his tie askew. He was a tall, pudgy, bespectacled man who seemed to sport a five-o'clock shadow at all hours. He gave Stephanie a toothy smile and held out his hand, as if to shake hers. She gave a little wave, indicating with her eyes how very full her hands were with Mike sitting peacefully on her lap.

"Ms. Saunders. I'm glad you stopped by. I only wish I had more time."

"That's quite all right, Mr. Collins. This is Molly Masters, whose father is on the school board."

"Nice to meet you." He shook my hand, then bent down and offered his hand to Mike. "Good to meet you too, sir. You and your mom are very important people."

Mike gave him his solemn attention. "Hi. I'm four years old."

"That's a good age to be." He straightened and said, "What can I do for you, Ms. Saunders?"

"You need to find enough money in the budget to fully fund both the sports and the fine arts programs."

"Nothing would please me more than to do just that, but it's simply not possible. We've squeezed all the blood from this turnip of a budget, and until voters can approve a bond issue in the next election, some serious cuts have to be made."

While he spoke, Stephanie calmly took out her wallet and grabbed a business card from an inner compartment. She handed the card to him, then rose, setting Mike on his feet. "This is the name of my accountant. He's very familiar with school budgets, and even used to do contract work for this district until a few years ago. Give him a call and have him set up an appointment to look at this bloodless budget of yours. Tell him that I will pay for his time while he assists you. He's the very best that there is. If he tells me that there is no money in the budget, I will support you at the school board in whatever course of action you deem appropriate. Until then, I intend to stonewall and block you at every turn. Have a good afternoon, Mr. Collins. I'll let you get back to your little meeting now."

Taking Mike with her, she left without a backward glance.

I could feel my own cheeks growing warm, and Mr. Collins had a splotch of color that was rising from his neck as he watched Stephanie leave. For the sake of the school budget, I was thrilled that Stephanie was not only sharing the name of her crack accountant, but paying for his services. On the other hand, I was appalled at her tactics and embarrassed on the superintendent's behalf. I cleared my throat and muttered, "I'm really not a friend of hers."

Mr. Collins said under his breath, "I miss Sylvia Greene. Never thought I'd say that."

Stephanie was apparently feeling as frosty toward me as I was toward her. We drove back to my house in silence. She dropped me off at the head of the driveway and continued on her way.

I still had almost an hour until my children's bus would arrive. I decided to pay a visit to Sam Dunlap and address the business mentioned in this morning's fax head-on. Though, ironically, this meant employing Stephanie's methods in arriving with no appointment. I had butterflies in my stomach as I drove out to his office. If he truly had done what I'd suspected—lied about the board member's backgrounds just to set Sylvia up for a fall—he was unfathomably ruthless.

He was on the phone when I arrived at his small, cluttered office. He seemed to be in the midst of packing. I had to make my way through an obstacle course of cardboard cartons. He held up his index finger when he saw me out of the corner of his eye, not recognizing me, which was good. I didn't want him to have the time to formulate precisely what he wanted to say to me before we spoke.

He hung up, rotated in his swivel-style desk chair, then said, "Sorry about that. Can I help you?"

I studied him, thinking how far Sam Dunlap was from a Sam Spade type of character. He was quiet and slight, a bookish sort, easily overlooked in crowds. "I'm Molly Masters. We spoke on the phone the other day."

"Oh. Yes." He looked surprised and a bit disconcerted.

"I'm not sure you understand how serious this situation is. My father has been accused of murder. He's innocent. His so-called criminal record can be easily explained."

"Listen, ma'am. I don't—"

"Please don't call me ma'am. I prefer Molly or Ms. Masters."

"What happened to Sylvia Greene had nothing to do with me. And I'm sorry about your father, but I only told Ms. Greene the truth about him."

" 'About *him*,' you say. What about the background checks you did on the others? Did you tell her the truth about those, too?"

He grimaced a little, then rotated in his chair and pulled the phone closer as if he was eager to place some calls. "I'm real busy here. Like I said, I'm sorry about your dad, but I was just doing my job. The only reason he was singled out was because I couldn't uncover anything about any of the others."

He was being much gentler than he'd been on the phone. He looked so nonthreatening that I was having a hard time reconciling the gruff image that he presented on the phone with the genteel one in person.

"That's not what Sylvia told my father. She told him that you'd discovered something really ugly regarding someone else, so she was going to ask that person to resign instead."

He shook his head. "You've been misinformed. There was no information to be had on the other board members. She just wanted me there at the private meeting to make everyone nervous enough to vote her way."

"I see," I said, though I didn't believe him. He was telling me this just to get me off his back.

"I told the police that as well. I'm sorry. I wish I could be of more help, but I can't."

"Someone sent me a fax about you." I riffled through my purse and then showed him the copy of my fax. He furrowed his brow, lowered his glasses on his nose, and read silently over his frames.

Sam looked up at me. "Where did you get this?"

"It was faxed anonymously to me."

"I have no idea what it means." He thrust it back to me, rocking on his chair to affect a persona of someone who hadn't a care in the world. The act was unconvincing.

I took a deep breath, realizing I wasn't going to get anywhere with this man unless I went on the offensive. "I think you do. I did some homework. I found out about your sister's suicide. And her marriage to Sylvia Greene's ex-husband." I was bluffing, of course. The woman who'd committed suicide bore a different maiden name from Dunlap, and I hadn't been able to verify that she and Sam had been siblings.

Sam studied my face for a moment, then looked away, the muscles in his jaw working. "So, then, you also know I'm the last person who would have sent you that fax."

"But you're certainly not the last person who would gain from Sylvia's death." He glared at me, and I demanded, "Are you." A verification, not a question.

"What's your point, lady?" His voice was taking on the toughness I'd experienced earlier. "First you suggest I might be next on some . . . scholastic suburbanite's hit list. Now you're telling me you think *I* killed her?"

"Did you?"

"No, and I don't know who did, either." His every muscle seemed to be tense, and I was prepared to run for the door if he made one move toward me. "Truth is, much as I tried to dig up dirt on everyone, especially Ms. Greene, the bitch herself, nothing panned out."

"How could she hire you, knowing your relationship with her ex-husband's late wife? She had to know how much you hated her."

"She *didn't* know I was Mary's brother. Hell, to know that, she'd have to have come to the funeral. She couldn't be bothered."

"You mean to say that she hired you by pure coincidence?" I asked incredulously.

He shook his head. "I approached her. I've been a private investigator for an insurance company in Delaware for years now. I took a leave of absence, then set up shop here under an assumed name so she wouldn't know who I was. Then I took it upon myself to check the backgrounds of the board members so I'd have some way to lure her in. Told her I'd uncovered something that she'd want to know about her fellow board member."

"You made up stories on the other board members and fed them to her." I was right! I'd have to work an "I told you so" into a future conversation with Jim.

He rose, his face an angry mask. "I loved my sister. She was one of the finest people anyone would ever want to meet. But she was fragile. Sylvia could sense that in her. She wouldn't let her ex-husband have that kind of happiness, so she attacked him at his weak point—his new wife, my sister. Sylvia was relentless. She even accused Mary of breaking up their marriage and claimed that Mary caused their grown daughter's car accident. Mary hadn't even *met* Aaron Greene before the accident. Sylvia knew that, but she didn't care. She got Mary to question everything about herself, and she just couldn't take it. She killed herself. But Sylvia might as well have pulled the trigger."

"You fabricated stories that discredited her opponents on the board to make Sylvia look like a fool when she falsely accused them."

He smirked. "Every time someone was squeaky clean, I doctored a batch of evidence to make it look like the guy was the business equivalent of Charles Manson. If they were corrupt, I told Sylvia that they were Snow White. The only accurate information I gave that bitch was the stuff I had to use to bait her with—your father's misspent youth. I had to give her something true so she'd believe my lies about the other board members."

"So you set out to hurt Sylvia by destroying the lives of other innocent people? And you think your actions are justified?"

He crossed his arms on his chest and regarded me with a furrowed brow. "Hey, I took that into account. They all would have been fine. I was going to turn the tables on Sylvia the moment she publicly stuck her foot in her mouth. I'd've vindicated the party she wrongfully accused and exposed Sylvia as the villainous bitch that she was. I know it would have cost me my own career, but I would gladly have paid that price. Only, she ruined it for me."

"How?"

"By dying."

"That was hardly her choice."

He lowered himself into his chair with a faraway look in his eyes. "Wasn't mine, either. If it had been me, she'd have first been hit in the only place where it could have hurt—she'd have been publicly humiliated. And she would have gone with as much anguish as she caused my sister."

His rancor seemed to soak the room and me by virtue of his proximity. I wished I could just beam myself back home where I could curl up in the fetal position underneath my bedcovers.

"Why did you tell me all this?"

He scoffed and met my eyes. "What good does knowing any of it do you? If you tell the police, I'll just deny it. Tell 'em I was playing a joke on you and you fell for it. I've already destroyed any corroborating evidence. Even if they believe you, like I said, I didn't kill her. All I did was spread some malicious rumors to my client, who's now deceased."

"How can you do this, Mr. Dunlap? How can you treat people this way?"

"The name's Jacobsen, as you already figured out." Through clenched teeth, he stared at me and answered, "I did what I had to do. Sylvia Greene destroyed my sister's life. This was the only way I could stop her from doing that to somebody else."

As much as I'd grown to dislike Sylvia Greene, Sam Dunlap-cum-Jacobsen's revenge at any cost—the price paid by others—struck me as worse. I leaned on his desk and stared into his face until he met my eyes.

"Somebody knows about you, Mr. Jacobsen—the person who sent me this fax. I'm pretty sure that she was a good friend of Sylvia Greene's. That means Sylvia probably *also* found out about your scam before she died." I swept my arms back to indicate his office. "You did all of this in vain."

He sat there, slack-jawed, and said nothing.

Chapter 13

Mom on Megawatts

To my surprise, my father was waiting by my mailbox when I arrived home after leaving Sam's office. His hands were sunk deep into the pockets of his tan, zippered jacket, and his features were crestfallen. He was wearing his old fishing hat, which had long since seen better days, but it gave him the appearance of having a full head of hair.

My nervous system instantly went into full alert for fear that he'd come to tell me more bad news. And yet, he never thought to wear a hat without a direct reminder from Mom, so she'd been home when he left the house. Therefore, surely nothing too catastrophic could have occurred to spur his decision to see me.

Despite my worry, I rolled down the window and smiled. "Hi, Dad. Have you been waiting long?"

"Just a few minutes. Got to get back home soon, though." His voice was a little lower and his speech a bit slower than normal. Could Tommy have told him that his arrest was imminent?

Feigning a lightness I was far from feeling, I asked, "Want to hitch a ride into the garage with me?"

He shook his head, his eyes slightly averted from mine. "We need to talk. Want to walk me halfway back, by way of the park?"

"Sure. Let me just put the car away."

Dad rarely suggested that we "talk" and so I wasn't about to stall, but a glance at my watch reminded me that Karen's junior high school bus would be here in another five or ten minutes, and Nathan's soon after. The kids would be fine home alone for a few minutes if I didn't get back before they did.

The park was a playground in the center of Sherwood Forest, our subdivision. Though both were in the same general direction, the park was actually farther away than my parents' house, but it was my father's favorite haunt during times when he was mulling over some big decision.

We walked side by side for a couple of blocks without speaking. He was deep in concentration, his hands still steadfast in his pockets, shoulders stooped.

"What's up, Dad?" I finally prompted.

"A few grasshoppers. Not much else."

His forced attempt at levity was all the more reason for my concern. We headed down the park's path between two houses. "You wanted to talk?"

He sighed. "I owe the family an apology. I've been thinking a lot about our conversation earlier. Once I had a chance to look at it objectively, I realized I was wrong. I shouldn't have kept your Uncle Ted's secret. He was still a kid when he died, too immature to realize that hiding from the truth only makes things worse for all concerned. Whereas I'm certainly old enough to know better. I never should have listened to that lawyer and kept quiet about what Sylvia was about to reveal. I never should have lied to you or your mother. I kept hoping I could convince Sylvia not to go forth with her claims against me. Guess it's true what they say: Be careful what you wish for."

"I understand why you felt you needed to keep your promise to your brother."

He furrowed his brow. "Don't make it sound admirable, 'keeping a promise.' It made me feel noble, shouldering the blame, even after he was gone. Now I think about you and your sister. I think about what would happen if Bethany asked you to do something like that for her. Or vice versa."

He paused reflectively and shook his head as he glanced at the playground equipment, currently deserted. Over the last couple of years, the metal swings and slides and teeter-totters of my childhood had been replaced by the more natural look of weatherproofed logs and railroad ties and recycled truck tires. "The things we think are so terrible when we're young, they're never half as bad as all the damage we do in trying to keep them hidden."

"True, but you know, we get a second chance as parents. And you and Mom have been outstanding role models and teachers to your children. Think of how many lives you've touched at the university, too. If your brother had lived, he'd have been proud of you."

We weren't an overtly emotional family. Quite the opposite. My father was clearly both surprised and touched by my words. He put his arm around my shoulders, smiled, and said, "Thanks. I'm sure proud of the daughters your mother and I have raised."

"Why . . . that would be me and Bethany, wouldn't it?" I asked, feigning surprise.

He smiled, but it faded quickly and his mood darkened as we made our way around the jogging path that circled the playground and basketball courts. "I've spent my whole life involved in the field of education, one way or the other. All this has made me realize that I should have quit while I was still under some delusion of being ahead."

"You're not thinking of quitting the school board now, are you?" I asked anxiously.

"It's not fair to you and your mother to put you through this kind of public scrutiny. Even once they catch Sylvia's killer, some folks will still be insisting that I had a hand in it. That's human nature. It'd be best for all concerned if I got out of the public eye, once and for all."

"Dad, if you're asking my opinion, you should stay and fight this for all you're worth. You can't worry about what others might think and say about you. Isn't that what you'd tell me right now if our positions were reversed?"

Dad stopped walking and stared at the ground, as if lost in contemplation. He finally nodded. "Yes, it is." He sighed. "Guess this means I'm going to have to stick it out." He met my eyes and smiled. "Thanks, Molly. You're going to make yourself one heck of a wise old lady someday."

Dad said that he "really should be getting home now," gave me a quick hug, and we parted ways. I was tickled at the idea of myself as a "wise old lady" someday. I'd often hoped that my current eccentricities would be more excusable when I was much older.

Karen's bus pulled away from the stop as I rounded the corner. I hurried my pace. The short period before Nathan got home was one of the few opportunities I got to spend some time alone with Karen. Though we rarely discussed it, I think we'd both accepted the fact that Nathan's personality was forever going to designate him as the squeaky wheel in the family.

"Karen!" I called, making a megaphone of my hands.

She waved and waited for me. In defiance of the cool temperature, her lilac-colored jacket was tucked partway into her backpack, which looked as though it outweighed her—and probably did, she was so petite. She was wearing a maroon, long-sleeved, knit blouse and her elephant-leg jeans, which could fit both Karen, Nathan, and two of their closest friends at the same time. I hate the style so much I'd told her she had to use her own money to buy them, which is exactly what she'd done.

We went inside the house together and fawned over Betty for a while, who was thrilled to get both of us at once.

After giving many hugs and kisses to the dog, Karen asked, "Guess what, Mom?"

"What?"

"I've decided that I'm going to be a veterinarian when I grow up."

"That's great, sweet pea. You'll be a wonderful veterinarian. Though you might have to teach yourself not to scream and leave the room at the sight of a spider."

"Why? It's not like I'll have to treat anyone's pet spider, Mom."

"No, but what would you do if someone brought in their pet tarantula?"

She made a face and shrugged out of her fifty-pound backpack. "I'd get my assistant to take care of it."

"Ah. So you're going to be not only a fine veterinarian, but a popular boss. 'Go take the tarantula's temperature, Jeeves, or you're fired!' "

Karen rewarded my silliness with her infectious laughter, then went into the kitchen in search of soda pop and soda crackers.

"How was school today?" I called after her.

"Fine."

"Did anything interesting happen?"

"No."

Determined at least to get her to listen to the question before firing off a one-word response, I followed her into the kitchen and asked, "Okay, Karen, answer me this. Let's say you and Rachel are in the cafeteria and there's a terrible flood. You two are safe on top of a real high cabinet. There's only room for you to save one more person, and your only choice is one of the boys in your school. Who would you choose?"

"Ricky Morgan," she answered immediately, then stuffed a cracker into her mouth.

This was a name that I didn't recognize at all. "Why would you save him?"

With a few cracker crumbs flying from her lips, she answered, "'Cause he's the best swimmer in the school, and he can get help so we won't have to hang out the whole day on top of a cabinet. I'm gonna go call Rachel, okay?"

So much for our quality mother-daughter time.

Left to my own thoughts for a couple of minutes, I instantly began to worry about whether or not I'd done the right thing in encouraging Dad to stick with the board. What if he was right and his good name was forever to be sullied by suspicion?

Nathan barged through the front door, and we went through the same exercise in futility that I'd just experienced with his sister. Karen reappeared; expressly, it seemed to me, so that she and her brother could get into their usual after-school quarrel.

Soon they were toe-to-toe on some life-shattering issue regarding the cap on the bottle of ginger ale. I moved to a different room, but they soon followed me, now arguing about who owned a particular pencil. Nathan triumphantly snapped the pencil in two and handed her the shorter, no-eraser piece, which caused Karen to erupt. It occurred to me that what I really needed was a personal microphone hooked up to an enormous amplifier so that I could drown them out when I scolded them.

That gave me an idea for a cartoon. A woman is sitting in her kitchen, the newspaper spread on the table before her, and she holds a cup of coffee in one hand, a microphone in the other. She is smiling as she says into the microphone, "Bobby, stop picking on your sister! Sally, just ignore him." In the next room, two children cringe as her amplified voice booms over the loudspeaker fastened to the ceiling. The caption reads: *Elsie Flattenbush loves her new "Make Mommy Loud!" home audio system from Acme.*

Meanwhile, Karen stormed off to her room and Nathan launched into his tirade of complaints about the torturous concept of homework. I was delighted when the phone rang, allowing me to escape for a while.

I grabbed the portable phone in the kitchen. The caller was Carol Barr. She said, "An ad hoc committee is throwing a pro-arts rally tomorrow night. They've asked all of the school board members to attend, and of course I'm going to be there, since this is so near and dear to my heart. Can you make it?"

I glanced at my calendar. "I think so, but why such short notice?"

"They managed to rent out Proctor's Theater in Schenectady. It was the only time the theater was available."

That explanation tripled my interest. Proctor's Theater meant a lot to me personally. Back when Carlton was considered the sticks, so much so that we didn't have any movie theaters closer than Schenectady, my family would go to Proctor's. When I was sitting in my best dress in the red velvet seats, my parents wouldn't have to tell me to be on my best behavior. I was too busy feeling like a grownup, waiting for the magic of the movie—or, on some truly priceless occasion, a live play or performance—to begin. There was no better place imaginable for a pro-arts rally; from its famous sign and all of its light bulbs to the enormous gold-colored Wurlitzer organ and embossed-fabric walls, this was both art and history at its best.

"They've asked members of the Honor Society at the high school to call ten families apiece and tell them about the rally and ask them to call a couple of their friends in turn. They're hoping to have at least a couple hundred people, and they'll play up the fact that they didn't have any opportunity to advertise, et cetera, to full advantage."

"Great. I'll be there and I'm sure Mom and I can notify people in our neighborhood."

"That would be wonderful. Actually, we also need a little help setting things up. Could you possibly get there half an hour early? At seven-thirty?"

"I'd be happy to." For once, volunteering was going to be a treat. I would love the chance to explore behind the scenes of that old theater, in its hallowed halls where some of the greats performed during vaudeville's heyday.

While hanging up the phone, I remembered that this was Thursday, another soccer-practice day, and we were already late. Nathan greeted this news with his usual grace and announced that he was "having a miserable life!" At the moment, I could only say, "So am I," which made him launch into his apologies for being such "a terrible son" to cause "everyone around to be miserable."

The joys of motherhood.

The next day, my parents and I concentrated our energies to notify people about the rally. I printed up some fliers, using a cartoon drawing of Shakespeare on a stage, saying, "To be or not to be." The caption underneath read: "That truly is the question. So join together and insist that we will not allow our children to be culturally and artistically deprived!"

Lauren helped us, and we divided Sherwood Forest into quarters and knocked on each door in our section, leaving fliers or handing them to the homeowners.

Jim said that he would have to work late and would just

meet us at Proctor's as soon as he could get there. Tommy's teenage sons had a basketball game that night and would be of no help watching the younger kids. Unsure of how late we'd be and uncomfortable with the concept of leaving our children alone at night, Lauren and I decided to hire a joint baby-sitter at my house.

Tiffany Saunders was the only one available on such short notice, though I questioned the wisdom of paying someone less mature than my own daughter to baby-sit. She arrived on time, in all of her green-hairedness, beating Lauren and her daughter to my house. The green hair was now the only thing that stopped her from being the very image of her mother at this age, so I actually didn't find the unusual hue objectionable.

Karen was too polite to say anything, though her eyes widened as she stared at Tiffany's head. Nathan, on the other hand, instantly broke out laughing at the sight of her.

"What?" she asked.

"Is your hair lime flavored?" he asked.

Tiffany's cheeks colored, giving her a bit of a Christmaslike appearance. "I like the way it looks. So do my friends."

"Why?"

She clicked her tongue and said, "You're too young to understand."

Rachel threw open the front door, froze at the sight of Tiffany's hair, then backed out the door again, saying, "I gotta go ask my mother if it's all right for me to be baby-sat by someone with green hair."

"As if!" Tiffany grumbled, clicking her tongue.

I had no idea what Tiffany was referring to, but collected my coat and purse, knowing that Lauren would have already seen Tiffany in her green-haired splendor at the high school. Rachel ducked back inside a moment later, saying, "Mom says it's okay."

Scowling, Tiffany clicked her tongue again and thrust her hand on one hip. "Like, I'm so relieved."

"If we put colored sprinkles in your hair, it'll look just like a Christmas tree," Nathan said and giggled, still finding this hilarious.

Tiffany rolled her eyes and looked at me. "If he makes one more joke about my hair, I'm charging you double."

"Nathan, that'll come out of your allowance."

He put his hand over his mouth and called a muffled, "Bye, Mom," at me.

The four of us—my parents, Lauren, and I—drove out to the theater and found a parking space. My parents seemed to be in no hurry, moving slower and slower these days. I lingered with them as they made their way down one of the aisles. Lauren rushed to the stage to ask what needed to be done to set up the room. Amazingly, I could hear her conversation even from my position in the center of the auditorium.

That struck me as so extraordinary, it brought out some childlike glee in me. "Lauren," I called, waving to her. "Come up here. Let me show you something."

She obliged, trudging up the steps to me.

"The acoustics of this place are unbelievable. You wait here." I trotted down to the stage and waved at her. "To be or not to be," I said in a normal speaking voice. "That is the question."

I trotted part of the way up the aisle again. "Did you hear that?"

"Perfectly," she said appreciatively.

"That's without microphones or shouting. Do you want to try it?"

"My one chance on stage, hey?" Lauren trotted down the steps. Granted, we should be setting up as promised, but there seemed to be no chief to boss us around, so why not have fun?

Lauren stood on stage facing me and said in lilting tones, "Oh, Romeo, Romeo. Wherefore art thou Romeo?"

I laughed and started to head back to the stage to join her. Just as I was about to do my "light from yonder window" speech, I heard a derisive laugh and turned to see who it was. Stephanie.

"I thought this was going to be a rally, not amateur night," Stephanie grumbled as she made her way onto the stage.

"We were just having a little fun, Stephanie," Lauren snapped at her. For a whole host of good reasons, Lauren and Stephanie get along even less well than Stephanie and I do.

"In front of the entire school board, I see," Stephanie added under her breath. I scanned the seats and saw that, indeed, all of the board members had not only shown up, but arrived a good twenty minutes before the rally was supposed to begin.

"I wonder why even the pro-sports people are here," I muttered.

"Stuart called all of us personally and suggested we come."

Carol Barr came up to us on the stage. "Molly, Lauren, thanks for coming."

"Stephanie was just pointing out to us how all of you board members are here. Are you going to help us set up?"

Carol shook her head. "No, if we helped set things up that would make it look like we had a conflict of interest—board members running a funding rally."

"If only I could convince my husband that my cooking dinner every night represented a conflict of interest for me."

Someone was playing around with the lighting, and I found myself with an overwhelming urge to run into the spotlight and do a dance of some sort. "Stephanie, I'll bet you took tap dancing lessons at some point."

"Yes, I did. How did you know that?"

I pointed at the spot downstage from where we were standing. "Here's your chance to hoof it."

She smiled, but said, "Molly, this is not the time nor the place. Nor the shoes," she added, indicating her stilettos.

"We need to ask one of the stagehands where the folding chairs are kept," the woman that Lauren had been talking to earlier said, furrowing her brow at our shenanigans. Drat! A chief!

On second thought, a chair hunt would allow me to see

some of the hidden parts of the theater. "I'll take care of that."
Meanwhile, Lauren rejoined the woman to discuss some
more of the particulars of setting up the stage.

In one of the wings, I located a man who had enough keys
hanging off his belt to lock up the world. I asked him where
spare chairs were kept, and he gave me directions that included several doorways and turns off some hallway. Unfortunately, I have no sense of direction whatsoever and also
can't keep directions in my head for more than two seconds. I
have too much pride to admit this to strangers, so I headed off
into the workings of the backstage area, unassisted by a map
or compass. Seeing the "hidden parts of the theater," indeed.
I'd be lucky not to be spending the rest of my life lost in the
building like the Phantom of Proctor's.

I climbed a back staircase off the stage and soon found myself in a hallway of dressing rooms. I went into the nearest
one, which wasn't as large or fancy as I'd envisioned. It was
fairly austere, even, with plain, wood-paneled walls painted
white, a makeup counter and mirror surrounded by light
bulbs. Had George Burns, Red Skelton, or Al Jolson once
looked into this very same mirror?

Maybe there were larger dressing rooms farther down the
hall that boasted pictures or autographs of their famous pa-
trons. I poked my head into the next dressing room, which
was essentially identical to the first one. Maybe the largest
dressing room would be at one end of the hallway to give the
star of the show some separation.

Just as I was about to enter the last room off the hallway, I
heard someone arguing.

"There's no way I'm going to play along!" a woman was
saying in an angry whisper. "I've had it with keeping your secret! We're all under a shroud of suspicion now, and it's high
time—"

"You said you loved me," a male voice replied. "How can
you desert me now?"

"I'm sorry. I have no choice. It's over between us. My husband deserves better than this."

The voices seemed to be coming from the bottom of the

staircase I'd recently climbed. The only people here were a couple of Proctor's employees, the three or four of us women who'd come early to help set up, plus the board members. Could this be Michelle and Kent arguing? If so, the quarrel could be related to the murder.

As I tried to double back to see if I could find out who was speaking, Lauren poked her head around the corner. Before I could shush her, she called to me, "I think I found the folding chairs."

The voices immediately fell silent.

A moment later, there was a metallic click, then the lights went out.

"Oh, fine," I muttered, not moving while I gave my eyes the chance to adjust to the sudden darkness. "The lights *would* have to go out right when we're in a windowless hallway. With stairs."

"Don't panic, anybody," a male voice called out. "It's probably a minor power outage. We'll get the back-up power going momentarily."

"What is it about that phrase—*don't panic*—that strikes such terror in my heart?" I asked Lauren.

"Maybe because it's so often said when there's good reason to panic."

"My eyes don't seem to be adjusting at all."

"That's because there's no light whatsoever to adjust to," Lauren replied. "There are no windows on this entire floor."

I managed to press my palms against the wall and slowly start to feel my way toward Lauren. "Did you hear about the ghost in this place? Proctor's is supposed to be haunted. Some old vaudevillian actor or something, who haunts the dressing rooms." Realizing that we were currently in the very same hallway of said dressing rooms, I added, "Uh oh."

"Molly, do me a favor," Lauren said. "Skip the ghost talk when I'm standing here in pitch blackness."

Just then a woman let out a piercing scream.

Chapter 14

To Be or . . . Could You Repeat the Question?

"Don't panic, everybody," that same male voice cried a second time in answer to the scream.

"Who was that?" I cried. "Lauren? Are you all right?"

"I'm fine," she said, and I managed to do a Frankenstein's monster walk till I literally bumped into her. "I think it was someone on the stage. Are *you* all right?"

"Yeah. Lauren, just before the lights went out, I heard some voices down this hall. A couple, arguing. The woman might even have been the one who screamed. Did you see who they were?"

"No, I . . ."

The lights came on. After a second or two of squinting, I got my bearing.

"You okay?" a gruff male voice around the corner asked some unseen person.

"Who the hell threw the circuit breaker?" a second male voice called from somewhere above us in the stage area.

"This way," Lauren said unnecessarily, for I was already following her.

We climbed the steps. Stephanie Saunders was surrounded by the half dozen board members and a pair of male Proctor's employees. She was sitting on the center of the stage, whimpering and sputtering to anyone who would listen about how "horrible" her experience had been. She probably walked face first into a spider's web and would require months of therapy to recuperate.

"Somebody tried to strangle me!" she cried.

I was skeptical, but when I joined the others, I could see

148

that there were red marks on her neck. They were in the shape of fingerprints, as if someone had grabbed her from behind.

"Oh, Steph," I said, instantly feeling guilty for having doubted her. "Are you all right?"

Hearing my voice seemed to jolt her out of her state of distress. Stephanie rose and slowly turned a full three-hundred-and-sixty degrees, looking at all of us on the stage. In cartoon format, she'd have had daggers shooting from her eyes and steam coming out of her head. I'd never seen her this angry.

Still eyeing each of us slowly, she said, "One of you people tried to kill me. My youngest child is only four years old! Make no mistake. I *will not* allow myself to be killed!" Stephanie raised her fists and, in a dramatic motion worthy of Vivian Leigh, cried, "As God is my witness, I will find out who you are! And I will make you pay!"

There was a moment of silence as we all stared at her. I scanned her rapt audience surreptitiously. Agnes Rockman had arrived and was near Stephanie. The same board members were here now that had been suspects in Sylvia's murder, including, unfortunately, my father. My mother, too, was on stage. Nobody spoke, but I realized that everyone was doing the same thing I was—taking stock of who else was present and might have tried to choke Stephanie. Meanwhile, we all seemed to share the same inability to come up with anything appropriate to say to her.

"Umm, I, uh, found the folding chairs," Lauren announced.

Never before had so many adults gone to the task of setting up folding chairs, leaving Stephanie to make her own way back into the flow of the evening and out of her soliloquy. Suddenly none of the board members seemed to consider the act of carrying a chair at a school funding rally to be a conflict of interest.

While we arranged the newly found folding chairs on the stage, Stephanie watched from the front row of the theater, glowering. Once we clearly had more than enough chairs in place for the presenters, I got off the stage and joined her.

"I'm so sorry that this happened to you, Stephanie. Is your throat all right?"

"Fine. I'm fine. You might want to tell your other little worker ants up there that they're doing this for nothing. We're canceling tonight's rally. I've already put a call in to Sergeant Newton. He's going to interview each suspect, and that takes priority over some stupid rally."

"But, Stephanie, why cancel the rally? Tommy can just talk to the . . . suspects individually while it's taking place, or right afterwards. It's not as if whoever did this is going to run away or take everyone hostage."

"Molly, somebody just tried to kill me! I'd say that that's a damned bit more important than saving some kindergartner's finger-painting class!"

Though I could understand her reaction, the words still rankled. "You need to tell Stuart you've canceled the rally. He's the school board president, after all. Are you going to tell him, or do you want me to?"

"You do it. I'm not speaking to him or anyone else on this board till my assaulter is behind bars."

"That's going to make working with your fellow school board members really difficult, isn't it?"

"Actually, it will be business as usual. Half of those people haven't spoken to the other half in years. They won't even notice."

I went over to Stuart, who was talking to a Proctor's employee. I interrupted their discussion of stage lighting and said, "Stuart, I need to tell you something important. I was just speaking with Stephanie, and—"

"Is she all right?"

"She's called the police and she wants the rally to be canceled."

"But . . . but . . . people will have driven all this way to get here! We won't be able to notify them first. This will do irreparable harm to our efforts!"

"Be that as it may, she wants to have the police conduct their investigation right away, and she does have a point."

"Which is?"

"Which is that someone tried to strangle her. We can't just ignore it."

"No, but we don't have to sacrifice the entire cause either!"

"Please, Stuart, I'm the proverbial messenger here. Why don't you take this up with Stephanie? She's sitting in the front row and has probably overheard every word we've said anyway."

"She couldn't have heard us," he said in a whisper.

"Sound carries unbelievably well here."

"Evidently so," he muttered under his breath as he headed off the stage toward Stephanie.

Now that I thought about it, the male voice that I'd overheard backstage had sounded an awful lot like his.

The next morning was Saturday. That meant Nathan's soccer game. School board members could be murdered or nearly strangled, but soccer marches ever onward. Karen refused to come with us, and we wound up dropping her and BC off at the house of a friend who also owns a cocker spaniel. Jim and I, on the other hand, try to never miss one of Nathan's games. Now it was a particularly much-needed release.

Stuart had somehow managed to persuade Stephanie into letting the rally take place last night, on the condition that all of the people who'd been in the vicinity at the time of the assault were held for questioning during and after the rally.

Because Lauren and I hadn't been in the immediate area and so weren't suspects, we were told to stay in the audience, while Tommy and two of his officers took the board members' statements in separate dressing rooms, as I learned later from my father. Meanwhile, Carol Barr's and Stuart's planned speeches had to be scrapped. The teachers and experts that spoke did an excellent job, though attendance was not what we'd hoped—less than a hundred, which was almost as depressing as the maelstrom surrounding the board itself.

In contrast, Nathan's game started out well, with Nathan's team leading three to nothing at the end of the half. Gillian was there, sans husband, watching and rooting for the team. She shot me an extralong gaze—borderline see-how-important-sports-are? stare—when her son scored one of the goals.

During halftime, with Jim sitting in on the team meeting with most of the dads but none of the moms, Gillian came up to me. Seeing her in direct sunlight made her look older than normal, the lines around her eyes and on her forehead clearly visible. Perhaps the same was true for me—an unpleasant thought. "They're playing well today, aren't they?" she asked.

"Yes. That was a nice goal Peter made."

She beamed. "Yes, it was. Thanks. I hope he'll get the opportunity to develop his game as he gets into junior high in a couple of years."

I had to resist rolling my eyes, knowing she just couldn't keep from digging it in about the sports-versus-arts thing. "Gillian, doesn't it ever strike you how shameful all of this underfunding is? How our parents put us baby boomers through school, giving us every conceivable opportunity? Don't you remember how it felt when we were in high school ourselves? We were going to make this world a better place as soon as we were old enough to vote and be in power. Yet here we are, with a higher income bracket than our parents had, bickering about which opportunities we're going to deny our children."

Gillian's face fell. "You're right, Molly. Of course. It is shameful. But when the only choice available is the lesser of two evils, you have to hold your chin up and choose one."

"Is that truly what this has come down to . . . the lesser of evils? Or has somebody made horrible, wasteful spending decisions that we're all paying for now?"

While I was speaking, somebody stepped up from behind me. I turned to see that my parents had arrived late to watch the game. "Mom. Dad. Hi."

Dad, however, merely gave me a somber nod, then said to Gillian, "I wonder if that's what Sylvia's killer thought he or she was doing. Choosing the lesser evil by committing such a reprehensible crime."

"We may never know," Gillian said, then sighed and forced a smile. "On the bright side, the boys are up by three goals." The referee blew his whistle, signifying the start of the second half. "Excuse me while I reclaim my spot on the sidelines."

Gillian walked off just as Jim called out, "It's time to go over your rotations." This was Jim's quasi-coaching role on the team. He made sure the boys knew who was supposed to be playing which position. There were four rotations—or line-ups—in each half. Nathan and Peter were both sitting out this first rotation of the second half. Not being friends, they ignored each other and watched the game.

Our current lineup was a disaster. My parents and I rooted loudly, but it was one of those times in sports where you can almost swear that you see the field tilting so that your team is forever required to go uphill. By the time the whistle had blown for the new players, the opposing team had scored two goals, whereas our team had not taken a single shot. The next rotation was at least evenly matched. Neither team scored. Nathan's team had only to keep the other team from scoring for two more rotations and they would win.

The third rotation, too, seemed to be evenly matched, with Nathan again sitting this one out. My father must have decided to extend the olive branch to Gillian and was now sitting beside her. As time was expiring, Jim came over to Nathan and crouched in front of him to be at eye level. "Nathan, you're going to be in at goalie for the last rotation."

"No! I hate playing goalie!"

"It's going to be fine, Nathan," Jim said. "You do well at goalie, and the team needs you."

"But I—"

Just then the other team kicked a rocketing shot. The ball hit the goalie on the shoulder and rebounded to the other team's center forward, who kicked it easily into the goal, tying the score.

Nathan gasped and the parents on our side groaned. The referee blew his whistle, which I thought was in honor of the goal, but he cried, "Last rotation."

Our goalie dropped to the ground. Cries of "Are you all right?" went up from us mothers. The assistant coach from behind the goal helped him up. He was sobbing. The coach had to half carry him to the sidelines.

"Are you hurt?" one of the dads asked.

"No, but I blew the save," he cried as he flopped on the ground right next to Nathan and me.

Nathan grabbed my jacket sleeves with both fists and looked into my eyes, his face pale. "Mom. Please don't make me be goalie."

"You have to, sweet boy. You can do it."

My mother stepped beside me to help with the cause. "You're going to be great, Nathan," my mom said, pumping her fist.

"Nathan!" Jim swung his arm, emphatically gesturing at Nathan to get onto the field. "Go! They're waiting for you!"

My son wouldn't loosen his grip on my clothing. "We'll all still love you even if you let them get a dozen goals, Nathan," I said desperately. "Just do your best and have fun out there."

"I can't." He shook his head.

"Nathan! What's wrong with you?" the coach hollered.

I dropped onto both knees to force Nathan to look at me despite his lowered chin. "Nathan, listen to me. There will be a thousand moments in your life like this one when you have to do something that you're afraid you're going to fail at. You need to do this for yourself. You need to go out there and try your hardest and realize that you can overcome your fear. Now go be a goalie."

Nathan started to cry. He let go of me though, turned, and slowly made his way toward the goal.

I got to my feet and said to Mom through my forced smile of encouragement, "I think I'm going to throw up."

"You'll have to get in line behind me," my mother replied, who was also speaking through her put-on smile for Nathan's benefit.

Nathan got into position and cast one last long, despairing glance at my mother and me. We were still beaming away like a pair of idiots.

"Tell you one thing, Mom. Once this game is over, I'm telling his coach that I'll rip his mustache off if he ever forces Nathan to be goalie again."

"There's the spirit," she muttered.

The game started up again. With the score tied, both teams were going at each other all out. Being the latest to have scored, the opponents were riding high with confidence, which translates in sports vernacular to their having the momentum. Our team simply could not get the ball out of our side of the field.

While I knew, rationally, that each rotation was only six minutes in length, this one was taking an eternity. So far, both teams kept managing to intercept each other's passes and keep the ball pretty much in the middle of the field. Neither team had gotten a hard shot on goal.

Finally, though, the other team's best player—a tall, string bean of a boy—got the ball away from our right wing and dribbled toward the goal. Nathan's eyes widened as the boy neared. The boy made a nice stutter-step that fooled our sweeper—the last defender other than Nathan as the goalie. Just as the boy tried to make a shot on goal, the sweeper blatantly pushed him.

The referee blew his whistle. "Goal kick," he cried.

"Oh my God," I cried.

"What's a goal kick?" Mom asked me.

"It means he's probably going to score on Nathan. It means he gets to take an unimpeded shot on the goal from close range."

"I can't watch," Mom muttered, turning her face. "Tell me what happens."

That meant that *I* had to watch, but it did seem like the least I could do for my son. It probably felt that way because it *was* the least I could do.

The other team whooped with excitement at the referee's ruling, one of the other team's members slapping their best player on the back and saying, "All right, Kyle! You never miss these!"

The teams got into position, only Nathan, his teammates

unable by rule to help him, between the ball and the goal. The other boy took a couple of steps back. He kicked the ball with so much force that I could have sworn I felt the vibrations in my feet from my stance on the sideline. Simultaneously, Nathan sprang to his left. He managed not only to block the shot, but to catch the ball.

With no hesitation, Nathan ran to the top of the semicircle in front of his goal and drop-kicked the ball. It went soaring to the center line of the field, where Peter, Gillian's son, gained control of it. Peter and ball kept going down the field. He juked past their sweeper and kicked the ball past their stunned goalie.

Peter raised his hands and cried, "Yes!"

The referee blew his whistle. "Game's over."

Nathan, Peter, and their teammates celebrated like the young children that they are, as did all of us not-so-young children on the sidelines. Gillian and I even hugged each other, which was truly silly, as we should have known better than to attach so much importance to our children's game. The team did their "Two-four-six-eight-who-do-we-appreciate?" cheer for the other team, and then finally stopped celebrating enough to join their parents.

My mother let out a big sigh of relief, as did my father. Dad said, "That was a little too nerve-racking for me."

"Me too."

It took a long time for Nathan to make his way over to me, for he first basked in Jim's and Grampa's praises. When he finally reached me, he said, "You were right, Mom. It's kind of fun to be goalie."

Several minutes later, Peter announced that he wanted Nathan to come to his house to play, which was a first. Gillian said that that was fine with her, and we arranged for me to pick him up in another three hours, which would correspond nicely with my running taxi service for my daughter.

The play arrangements made me a tad uncomfortable. I couldn't quite believe that Peter and Nathan were going to be able to bond on the strength of one soccer play, but there was no harm in giving the boys the latitude either to surprise us or to learn that lesson for themselves.

Jim and I went home, which was strangely quiet without dog and children. The message light on our answering machine was flashing. I pressed the play button and recognized Sam Dunlap's reedy voice as he identified himself, then said, "It seems I was wrong about the school board members having nothing dark in their pasts. I just now stumbled across something big that you'll find real interesting. If it pans out, it'll help you and your father considerably. I'm meeting with someone in Saratoga to discuss it this afternoon. If you get this message in time, meet me at the racetrack at two P.M. Otherwise, leave me a message at my office, and we'll make other arrangements."

"That's strange," I said to Jim. "I wonder why he'd choose a location like that."

"It's one nobody could miss, I guess. A public location, and all."

"But it's off season. I'd be surprised if the gates are even unlocked at this time of year. It strikes me as so ... fishy. Why wouldn't he just come over here or have me go to his office?"

"Are you certain it was his voice?"

"Positive."

"You'd better play it safe. Give Tommy a call and have him meet us there."

"Us?"

Jim raised an eyebrow and peered at me. "You don't honestly think I'd let you go meet a private investigator alone, do you?"

"Of course not," I said, embarrassed at the realization that I'd neglected to tell Jim of my previous meeting with Sam. "That would be foolish."

Chapter 15

I'm All Ears

Jim was not especially companionable as we drove into Saratoga. For the third time in fifteen minutes, he said, "We shouldn't meet with a private detective under these circumstances. We should wait for Sergeant Newton."

As I'd responded twice before, I said, "I know. I agree in theory, but it's way more likely the 'detective' is going to skip town before he gives me important information that could clear my father than he is to lure us out here to shoot us. I mean, come on, Jim. Do you think he's been plotting to do me in and figured he'd do it at the racetrack, just to add some . . . local ambiance or something?"

Jim furrowed his brow even further—his eyes were narrowed to furious-looking slits—and said nothing. I'd left a message on Tommy's machine, but I knew that he checked his machine so frequently that he might even beat us there by putting on his siren and speeding.

Despite the tense circumstances, I found myself appreciating the old-money classiness of the area and looking forward to seeing the track. Though the town is a mere twenty-minute drive from Carlton and my sister and I were wild about horses, we'd rarely been there when we were children. The races in August caused the population to swell exponentially, and my parents tended to consider the possibility of parking problems an unsolvable obstacle.

"This is a wonderful little city, isn't it, Jim? Everywhere you look there are these pretty redbrick buildings, wrought-iron gates, wood trim. I guess with those kinds of building materials, it's probably hard to build something ugly. Then again, there are plenty of unattractive prisons out there. . . ."

"Hmm," Jim muttered, not listening.

"Liberty Park," I said wistfully as I eyed the circular area directly in front of us. "If there's a prettier park in a city, I've never seen it. If we've got time after we're through with our rendezvous, we should take a stroll. There are all these marvelous gardens and natural spa fountains, stone carvings, benches—"

"Isn't there more than one racetrack here?" Jim interrupted, focused on the task at hand.

"Yeah, but I'm sure he meant the one right off Union Avenue." I wasn't paying much attention to where we were, and anyone who trusts me to give directions is in trouble, a fact Jim knows better than anyone. We soon saw the racetrack, looming in all its splendor alongside the road.

Knowing Jim's tendency to drive past places while erroneously anticipating well-marked entrances, I pointed. "Here's a public parking area, Jim. Let's park the car here and walk."

Jim put on the blinker, but grumbled, "You think he's going to meet you in the grandstands, right? That's clear on the opposite side of the track."

"I know, but I've never gotten the chance to be this close to the track when the place is deserted."

We parked and, while zipping my jacket to brace against the brisk autumn breeze, I dashed across the street and through an open gate to walk along the beautiful white picket fence. I kept an eye on the oval track, imagining the voice on the loudspeaker boom: "And they're off." I could almost hear the thundering hooves, feel the vibrations through the soles of my tennis shoes. Jim came along behind me and soon caught up. I'm not sure if he shared my sense of reverence—and judging from his mood, it was unlikely—but we didn't speak as we made our way along the track toward the wooden grandstands.

The stands themselves were part of an enormous structure. It hit me again how odd it was that Sam said to meet him here. If he was so paranoid about being seen with me that he wanted to meet me far outside of Carlton's city limits, a simple instruction to meet me at a restaurant would have made more sense. The racing season had ended a good six weeks ago, so I expected the chain-link gate around the grandstands to be locked, but it wasn't.

A chill that I couldn't explain ran up my spine as I entered the building. "Something seems wrong," I said to Jim. "Maybe we should wait for Tommy to get here after all."

"Wait where?" Jim asked. "Should we go back to the car?"

Part of me wanted to say yes, but I held my tongue, thinking again about how frustrating it would be if Sam Dunlap-cum-Jacobsen gave up on me while, merely out of paranoia, I was waiting across the street. I felt torn. I've learned to trust my instincts and yet am forever prone not to heed them. "Let's just . . . see if he's here."

"There's only the one car in the parking lot. Maybe that belongs to the . . . PI. What was his name again?"

"Sam?" I called, killing two birds with one stone. My voice echoed slightly. The place seemed completely deserted. "If that car is his, it seems strange that he doesn't answer." I was stating the obvious, but needed to hear myself talk. The eeriness of the place was getting to me.

I walked slowly and took in my surroundings. There were numerous betting booths and thick pillars, all built in white-painted wood. I felt dwarfed by the structure, which had a rare elegance about it. Maybe that was because there would never be a modern stadium like this. As was the case for the fence surrounding the track, the wood would be replaced by man-made materials.

My appreciation of my surroundings was broken when I glanced down. There were a couple of dark spots on the cement floor. I froze and stared. Jim stopped beside me. "Jim? What does that look like to you?"

His eyes widened, and he'd obviously drawn the same conclusion that I had. "It might not be what it looks like. That could be . . . paint, or grease."

"Sure. That's all it is. Watery red grease. I'll buy that." I was trying hard to convince myself not to panic. "Those . . .

grease spots seem to be making a trail in that direction," I said, pointing.

Jim put a hand on my shoulder. "You'd better wait here."

"I don't think so, Jim. I'm not staying here alone."

"Then let's go back to the car."

"Sam might need immediate help. Let's get this over with."

Grabbing onto Jim's arm, I kept walking, telling myself that it was my imagination that what we were following was a trail of blood, the drops of which increased in frequency as we proceeded.

The trail led to the last betting booth at the end of the row. Despite part of my mind, which was screaming at me not to look, I opened the door.

This time my scream echoed through the rafters.

It was Sam Dunlap, his lifeless eyes fixed in a horrific expression, his blood pooled around him from a stab wound in his midsection.

"Christ almighty!" Jim cried.

We stumbled out toward the parking lot. "We've got to find a phone. Call 911," Jim murmured, his face as pale as I'd ever seen it.

A police car was pulling into the parking lot of the grandstands just as we were heading outside. Jim flagged it down and ran up to the car, which I dimly realized was Tommy Newton's.

I sat down, feeling dizzy. A minute or two later, Jim returned and said, "Tom's contacting the local police on his radio. He says they're probably going to want to take us into the station house to get our statements."

I nodded. Jim sat down next to me. Tommy walked up to us. His normally placid expression looked stony. "Molly, we got to stop meetin' like this."

I gave him a glare, which he returned. "I'm serious. You find dead bodies faster than flies do."

"Charmed, I'm sure. And it's not as though I'm deliberately *looking*, Tommy."

Jim said forcefully, "Tom, there's no reason to take this out on my wife. She's already upset, and she certainly didn't ask for this to happen."

As if to himself, Tommy muttered, "I should've had someone from the Saratoga PD get over here and check the place out till I could arrive. Might've saved this guy's life." He glared at me again, then added, "Figured if I did, they'd arrest you on the spot."

"I'm sorry," I said. A lump formed in my throat. Was this man's death my fault? Had he died because his killer had found out he was about to give me damning evidence?

" 'Sorry' doesn't help my investigation any. And it sure doesn't help your friend back there."

Sirens in the distance grew near. I rose, shivering against the cold. Jim put his arm around me. He was shaking every bit as hard as I was.

There's some old adage about there being "no rest for the weary," or perhaps it's "the wicked," but in any case, there's definitely no rest for the parent. Nathan only knew that my arrival at Peter's house was late, and apparently the two boys had run out of sources of entertainment, so he was not pleased. Jim, meanwhile, picked up Karen and BC in the second car.

"Did Nathan have lunch?" I asked Gillian, in my numb state forgetting that my son was old enough to speak for himself.

"No," Gillian said, just as Nathan was answering "Yes."

She looked at him in surprise. "We made ourselves hot dogs while you were gone," Peter explained.

"I had to run out for a while," Gillian said with a shrug that didn't quite mask her obvious embarrassment. "Something came up. I was only gone for a few minutes."

"More like two hours," Peter grumbled, rolling his eyes.

"It was a few minutes. Kids can't tell time."

"We watched the entire *Star Wars* tape and had lunch, Mom!"

Gillian blushed a little as she met my eyes. "A friend of

mine was hospitalized, I just found out when I got home. I went to visit."

"No damage done. Thanks for—" I glanced back, distracted as Nathan stormed off and got into the backseat, "having Nathan over."

I got into the car, wondering about the coincidence. Could Gillian have gone to Saratoga to meet with Sam Dunlap? While we drove, Nathan complained that he'd have had more fun today if I'd gotten there on time so that he could have another friend over to play. "Now it's too late!" he went on.

His tongue-lashing was falling on deaf ears, as I realized how much danger I was in now. Two people had been murdered. If the killer had indeed murdered Sam rather than risk his passing along evidence, could I be next? I needed this person behind bars. That meant I needed a board member on my side to give me inside information. Dad wasn't cut out for the espionage business, but I knew someone who was.

Once the kids were fully engrossed in their own pursuits and Jim was preoccupied watching a football game, I grabbed the phone and dialed.

She answered and we exchanged a couple of words of obligatory small talk, then I said, "Stephanie, I need your help."

There was a long pause. "That has to go down as one of the most unexpected sentences I've ever heard."

"Nevertheless."

"I'm all ears."

I paused, mulling over whether or not I could use that phrase somehow in a greeting card. The front of the card would read: What did one cornstalk say to the other cornstalk? The inside would be: I'm all ears.

Stupid idea, I chastised myself—not only lame, but had been used in children's riddles for years. "I need you to help me get some information on the other board members."

"Information?"

"The latest gossip, really."

"Why, Molly. Suddenly you're speaking my language. I'll

get right on it." She was so excited about her new mission that she hung up without another word.

The next morning was Sunday, and to my surprise, Stephanie was waiting in the parking lot as we left the early Mass at the Catholic church a couple of miles from our house. Jim was the first to greet her and said, "I didn't realize you're a parishioner here. Are you early for the next mass?"

"No, I'm not Catholic. I'm here to speak to your wife." She grabbed my upper arm and started leading me away, calling, "I'll have her back with you in just a minute."

"You learned something already?" I said in a half whisper.

Dropping the more melodious tones she'd used while speaking to my handsome husband, she said under her breath, "That private detective that Sylvia hired was killed in Saratoga yesterday."

"Yes, I know. I found the body."

She stopped and released my arm. "And you didn't tell me? Molly, you're a rank amateur when it comes to gossip." She put her hands on her hips and studied me, giving her head a shake of disgust. "The rumor is that Kent and Michelle are longtime lovers and were pulling some sort of scam that was bilking the budget. I've alerted my accountant, who's looking into the financial end of it, but you should talk to the two of them. See what they have to say for themselves."

I nodded, Kent being someone I'd already realized I needed to learn more about. If nothing else, he had such a machismo attitude about him that he struck me as potentially violent. "I was thinking of going to football practice after school tomorrow and—"

"Kent runs practices on Sunday afternoons, too," Stephanie pronounced.

"Okay, I'll go scope things out today, then. Not that watching someone coach a football team would necessarily tell me whether or not he was a murderer. Which reminds me. Do you have any idea if it was a man or a woman who tried to strangle you?"

She shook her head. "All I know is it was someone with bad breath and strong hands."

Short of shaking everyone's hands while sniffing their breath, those weren't helpful clues. "Hear any other rumors about board members?"

"Only that the friction between Kent and Stuart is an object of some creative speculation. Word has it that their troubles go way back, before they were on the board. That Stuart has some past life that he ran away from, deserted his kids, that sort of thing, and that Kent called him on it."

I furrowed my brow, and Stephanie held up her hands. "That's all I know. I'll tell you more as the information comes in."

"Thanks, Stephanie. I'm impressed. How did you hear this so fast, anyway?"

"Oh, you give a few tidbits of information and you get a few back."

"What tidbits were you giving?"

"Nothing you don't already know yourself. I've got to run." She whirled around on one of her spike heels and strode to her car, leaving me to ponder just what it was that she or I knew that could be fodder for the grapevine. Maybe my alliance with Stephanie had been too rash a decision.

Later, with Jim now engrossed in a second professional football game on TV, I drove out to the high school fields and soon found the team. Kent Graham was making them run through various drills.

Only a dozen or so people were in the stands, watching the practice. I made my way across the first row, scanning to see if there was anyone I recognized and could pump for information. No familiar-looking faces, but I did spot a familiar back of a head. It was on the shoulders of a teenage boy Tiffany had once dated, and he was on Kent's team and sitting alone on the bench. He was such a fan of the Atlanta Falcons that he'd had his hair shaved in the shape of a falcon. In my opinion, it looked more like a bat than a falcon, but then, I doubt he had much chance to observe the back of his head. I made my way over to him, trying in vain to recall his name.

"Hi there. I recognized your . . ." What? His bird? His logo? ". . . head. I'm Molly Masters. Tiffany baby-sits for me."

"Oh yeah." He nodded then mumbled something that sounded vaguely like "Howzitgoin' " as I sat down next to him. I noticed then that his arm was in a sling.

"How's the team doing this year?"

"Not bad." He indicated his injured arm. "Course, I could be better myself."

"Sprained wrist?"

"Broken collar bone. Can't do shi—crap on the field, but Coach says I gotta come watch."

I made some sympathetic murmurings, then asked, "Can you tell me if Coach Graham's wife is here, by any chance?"

The boy looked back and scanned the stands, then shook his head. "Nah. Don't see her."

"What does she look like?"

"Kind of pretty, I guess. Kind of top-heavy." He gave me a sly grin, which I ignored. More important, Kent's wife did exist and the team members were not mistaking Michelle as the coach's wife. We watched in silence for a couple of minutes as the offense and defense scrimmaged.

"Do you like Coach Graham?"

"He's all right."

Kent blew his whistle and called out for his team to "hit the showers." My companion rose and trotted across the field to join his teammates.

Kent did a double take in my direction, then strode toward me. "Molly Masters. What brings you out to our practice?"

"I'm a football buff, actually."

"Really? That surprises me." He spat into the dirt, making like a baseball player. "I would assume you think sports are a waste."

I ignored his hostility, trying to "make nice" for the purpose of gleaning information. I stood up—a little too quickly for my still-sore muscles—and came over to stand beside him as we watched the last of his team jog toward the gym.

"You've got some great linebackers. They really seem to do a pretty good job on pass rush. The nose guard was being held on almost every play during your scrimmage, and he still managed to force the quarterback into throwing it away."

"So you weren't bluffing."

"Not about football. Horseback riding, maybe."

"You seem to be a little sore."

"I've felt better." In truth, a certain key area of my anatomy felt as though it might well be bruised beyond all repair, but this was not a matter I felt like discussing with Kent.

Kent raised an eyebrow. "You know, Molly, some people are just not meant to horseback ride after they reach a certain age."

"What the heck do you mean by that? I'm younger than you or Michelle."

"True, but unlike either of us, you've allowed yourself to get out of shape. See, skinny people have that problem. It's harder for you to realize when your muscles are getting flaccid."

I found being called "skinny" every bit as insulting as being called "fat" and snapped, "If you want to test how flaccid my muscles are, grab me a baseball bat and let me take a few whacks at your shin."

He chuckled. "I was just being honest. No offense, Molly."

"Oh, well, in that case, none taken," I said sarcastically. So much for my "making nice." In fact, I was at a loss for how to turn this around to pump Kent for information. Furthermore, someone was crossing the field toward us, so our conversation was about to be interrupted. I stared in surprise when I saw who it was. "Stuart?"

"Molly. I'm . . . surprised to see you here."

"You too, Stuart. Are you a football fan?"

"No, I'm here to discuss a personal matter with Kent."

Kent nodded and dismissed me with a flippant, "Thanks for stopping by, Molly."

"My pleasure." *Jerk face,* I silently added.

I left by way of the bleachers, which gave me some cover

as I walked behind them slowly, watching the two men converse. Not surprisingly, they were soon arguing. Unfortunately, the acoustics were nothing like those of Proctor's, and I couldn't catch a single word.

I decided to wait in the parking lot to see if Stuart would perhaps go for a sympathetic ear and tell me what the trouble was. To my surprise, though, it was Kent who returned to the parking lot, not Stuart.

"You're still here?" he asked.

"I was waiting to talk with Stuart."

Kent gestured behind him with a jerk of his head. "I doubt you'll see him for several minutes. He's pretending to be interested in jogging around the track. Of course, he's really only giving me time to leave so he won't have to face me. That worm."

"What did he do?"

"Nothing. He's always a worm. Half of the board members are. . . ." He let his voice fade.

"Do you have as high an opinion of my father? Or is that reserved for Stuart?"

He jabbed a finger at me. "We are all serving on the board out of sense of duty. To help the children of this community. For that, we deserve respect."

"I do respect you for that. But you've lost a lot more of my respect through your tactics. Nobody likes a bully, Mr. Graham."

Kent crossed his arms and gave me a haughty smirk. "Don't they? Try askin' 'em how well they like me at season's end, when we're in the finals. And what about the boosters? Ask them how well they liked me after my team went undefeated last year. Ask them if they'd call me a bully, or a winner."

"Life isn't the same as football. That is just a game, after all, Kent, regardless of how seriously some of us might take it. Whatever your coaching record might be, you've got to get along with your board members to get anything done. Or do you just try to plow over them, as well?"

The muscles in his jaw were working. "My strategies are successful. I'm going to get my way on this vote, too."

"How did you convince Michelle to switch her vote? Somehow, I can't believe she did so purely out of a change in heart. Did you force her to, in order to keep herself eligible for reelection?"

A vein on his forehead was bulging in anger. I had a feeling that, in his eyes, I'd just turned myself into an incompetent referee. "Watch yourself, Molly. You're already in dangerous waters. You're going to find yourself over your head in no time. I'd stop making enemies, if I were you."

He strode away at a furious pace. I headed to my car, thinking he was probably right about the make-no-enemies-unnecessarily part. It's just that the killer was moving closer now. A man had been murdered right before he could meet with me.

I was running out of time.

Chapter 16

An Affair to Forget

Later that afternoon, somebody rang the doorbell. BC rushed up from the basement, barking maniacally. I yelled, "I'll get it," to my otherwise inattentive and uninterested household. It was Lauren. She was wearing jeans and an oversize *Sports Illustrated* sweatshirt that I'm pretty sure was once mine, having claimed it from Jim as equity earned by virtue of his overuse of our bathroom while reading that particular periodical. Her round face bore a look of deep concern, so she didn't appear to be in the mood to want to trace her clothing's past.

The moment she stepped inside, she nervously combed both hands through her shoulder-length brown hair. "Molly, Tommy just told me what happened to you at the racetrack yesterday. I can't believe he didn't even tell me till just now. I'm so . . ." She stopped and took a calming breath, but with a voice still as agitated as before she asked, "Are you all right?"

"I'm fine. Though I'll be seeing that scene in my nightmares for a while yet."

She clicked her tongue and rolled her eyes. "This is so ironic."

"What is?"

Again, she combed her fingers through her hair and frowned, then met my eyes. "Well, you see, Tommy was home yesterday when he called his office for his messages and got yours. So he happened to tell me how he was heading out to Saratoga to meet you. That's what . . . ticked me off so much that he didn't tell me you . . . found the body. I asked

170

him last night how things were when he saw you and he just grumbled, 'Typical Molly Masters,' and I let it drop." She rolled her eyes a second time and shook her head sadly. "Anyway, the mention of Saratoga had given me what I thought was a great idea, so I went ahead and called, and now it's about the stupidest thing I could have done."

"What are you talking about, Lauren?"

"Your birthday a couple of weeks ago. I didn't get you a gift. And remember how I told you way back how much I enjoyed my trip to the spa in Saratoga?"

Uh oh. I didn't like where this was going. I wasn't a spa type of person. The very mention of the word gave me an image of a group of naked women being massaged by men with hairy arms, and I knew that I didn't want to be one of those women. Or one of the hairy-armed men either, for that matter. "I remember, but Lauren, you don't *need* to get me a gift. I thought we agreed we'd just take each other out to lunch on our birthdays from now on, and you already *did* that."

"I know that's what we agreed, but then I got to thinking about how you've been moving so gingerly for the last couple of days, ever since your horseback riding, and, well, I decided that this would be the perfect gift." She held out the envelope as if utterly discouraged. "Of course, that was before I knew what a horrible shock you got at the racetrack."

I opened the envelope. It was a gift certificate to the Jackson Mineral Baths. "Wow. Nobody has ever given me a gift bath before."

"I made out the certificate myself, just so I'd have something to physically give you. I actually charged the whole thing to my credit card over the phone. And I know that Saratoga is probably the last place in the world you want to return to, but they have a twenty-four-hour cancellation policy, and I already made the appointment for you for tomorrow, so I get charged whether or not you actually go."

"You made the appointment for me?"

"At one P.M. That was pushy of me, I know, and believe me, I regret doing it now. It's just that I knew you were going to be a little skeptical. I was, too, till I tried it. It really is great for sore muscles, and it's completely relaxing. Considering all the stress you've been under, this seemed like the perfect time for you to go. And I figured that, if I didn't make the appointment for you, you'd just stick it on top of your refrigerator and forget about it till the coupon expires."

"Just because I do that sometimes with fruit doesn't mean I will with a gift certificate."

"Sure it does. Molly, I've seen the top of your refrigerator."

She had a point. I use the top of my refrigerator as my last line of defense for important things that aren't to be chewed by the dog or thrown away by my son in one of his cleaning binges.

Lauren continued, "I'll understand if you don't want to use this. I'd have simply gone myself and not mentioned it to you, except I have to work tomorrow."

She looked so disappointed that I felt compelled to show my appreciation, which also meant feigning an enthusiasm that I didn't feel. "Don't be silly, Lauren. Of course I want to go. This was so thoughtful of you. Thank you. I'm sure I'll love it."

"Really?"

"Absolutely. It was a wonderful gift idea. Thank you so much."

She chuckled slightly and I found myself admiring the way the skin around her eyes crinkled when she smiled. On some people, that might be called crow's feet, but they were truly laugh lines on Lauren. She said, "I can tell you're lying through your teeth, but believe me, once you get there, you'll thank me for real."

"I already *am* thanking you 'for real.' I'm faking enthusiasm, not gratitude."

"Okay. You're welcome. All I ask is that you be sure to call me the minute you're home and tell me exactly how it was."

"Will do." Rats. My having to report the details to her was probably going to mean that I couldn't simply give the appointment to my mother and have her go in my place. Of course, Mom would have refused the offer. I don't get my non-spa-isms from nothing.

Cheered by believing she'd done something nice for me, Lauren left in considerably brighter spirits than when she'd arrived. Jim entered the living room just as I was shutting the door behind her.

"What did Lauren want?"

Even before I'd had the time to turn around and face him, the realization hit me that, while I wasn't a skilled enough actress to fool my best friend, I *was* good enough to fool my husband. "Guess what? She came by to give you an early birthday present. She got you 'the works' at the Jackson Mineral Baths."

He furrowed his brow. "What? Let me see that."

He snatched Lauren's certificate out of my hand before giving me the opportunity to lose it through a sleight of hand. The certificate bore my name.

"Nice try." He handed the certificate back to me and turned on his heel. "I hope you enjoy yourself tomorrow."

"Thanks, dear," I said dejectedly, feeling as though I was being killed by kindness all of a sudden.

Because the next morning was a Monday, it was an opportunity to talk to Agnes Rockman. If she had indeed sent me the fax about Sam Dunlap's not being who he said he was, Agnes could shed considerable light on things. After I'd failed so miserably to get any information whatsoever from Kent, I was in dire need of some light-shedding.

My theory was that, if the fax was from Agnes, Sylvia, too, had found out about Sam's ruse—*before* she'd told my father that a second board member had a checkered past. This went along with what Sam had said in his message to me before he was killed. If my theory was correct and Sylvia and Agnes had exchanged information about Sam's true identity, maybe they'd also shared information about the suspicious board member.

I decided to drop in at the Education Center. Maybe Agnes

would admit that she'd sent the faxes if I confronted her directly.

I peeked my head into her office, not sure if the superintendent's secretary had returned to work today, which would put Agnes back in the other office where she'd been when Stephanie confronted her.

To my surprise, Stuart Ackleman sat at Agnes's desk.

"Stuart?"

"Molly." He immediately blushed and shut the folder in front of him, then put his elbows over it in an obvious attempt to block me from reading it. "What brings you here?"

"I wanted to speak with Agnes about something. Are you . . . filling in for her?"

"Oh, no. She never comes in this early. She's on a staggered start-time schedule and won't be in for another thirty or forty minutes. No sense waiting for her."

"Late start for a school employee."

"Yes." We stared at each other for a moment, then he said, "It was good seeing you again. Tell your father I said hello."

I was not about to be dismissed that easily by someone who was acting as though I'd just caught him red-handed. "Actually, I'm perfectly happy to wait for Agnes to return. I'll just sit over here." I sat down in a hard-backed chair facing Agnes's desk.

"Ah. Well. Good. In that case, maybe you can tell her I was here and that I'll see her soon. In fact, she might be right next door in Superintendent Collins's office."

"Why would she be there if she doesn't start work until nine-thirty?"

"She . . . starts at eight whenever she has to fill in for his personal secretary, who had the flu last week. Maybe you should go check."

"I might do that. What are you doing at her desk, by the way?"

"Oh, we all share this office. Those of us on the board."

"I see you're reading a file."

From the hallway came the voices of two women approaching. One sounded like Agnes Rockman.

Stuart looked all the more disconcerted at the sound. "Yes, I'm checking into the records of the multicultural committee. I'll just put it back." He whipped the folder off the table and dropped it into a desk drawer just as Agnes entered.

She froze at the door. "Mr. Ackleman, what are you doing at my desk?"

"Nothing. I was just looking for the file on the multicultural committee in order to keep myself up to speed."

"That's in the file cabinet in the corner, as you well know."

"Oh. Right. Of course."

Agnes gave a little glance my way, but was not about to let Stuart off the hook even long enough to acknowledge my presence. Instead, she marched around her desk and stared down into a drawer of files in the bottom of her desk. "What were you doing looking at the board members' personal files, Mr. Ackleman?"

"It was my own file. I have the right to look at my own file."

"Why didn't you ask me for it? And how did you get a key to my desk?"

Stuart spread his hands. "I don't recall. You must have given it to me at some point. Or maybe your temp did when you were on vacation."

Agnes slammed the drawer shut with her foot, not removing her eyes from Stuart's. She held out her palm. "Give me back the key, Mr. Ackleman."

They stood toe to toe for a moment, then Stuart reached into his pocket and dropped a small key into her hand. He squared his shoulders. "Remember who works for whom, Ms. Rockman."

"I remember. We both work for the taxpayers of this city."

Stuart shut his mouth and left without another word. Agnes pursed her lips and dropped her pudgy, elderly body into the chair. "What a load of hooey," she said under her breath.

"What do you think he was really after?" I asked, hoping she would continue to take me into her confidence, though I'd given her no reason to do so.

"Probably information to use against one of his adversaries on the board. Unfortunately, Stuart's no worse than the rest of them." Then her eyes widened and she looked at me in earnest. "I'm sorry. I wasn't thinking about your father just now. I truly didn't mean to lump him in with the rest of them, especially now that . . . poor Ms. Greene's gone. Mr. Peterson is either more decent or too new at this to join in on the board's trickery and underhandedness."

"It's the former." After a pause, I prompted, "Stuart's behavior reminds me . . . I was at the football fields yesterday and saw Stuart and Kent get into quite an argument."

"It would only be news if they met and *didn't* argue."

"Just the same, though, I heard a rumor that . . ." I hesitated, deciding how to best phrase the information that Stephanie had fed me yesterday, "that Kent might be milking the school budget for his own private use. As the coach of the expensive football program, that might not be all that hard for him to do."

She paled a little but shook her head. "That's just not the case. The football program's funding is watched like a hawk, because it *would* be so easy for money to wind up in someone's pocket. Also, Kent's been offered positions at various universities, at several times his current salary, and he's turned them down. He says he loves his job too much to sell out."

"You're certain that he doesn't 'love his job' so much *because* he's making a fortune off the school budget?"

"I'm positive. Even if he were pilfering funds, which he isn't, he couldn't possibly steal enough to offset the difference in salary between a high school coach and a university coach." She studied my features, then asked, "What brings you here today?"

"I received a couple of faxes in the past couple of days. I'm wondering if you can tell me anything about them." I pulled my copies out of my purse and held them out for her to see.

Her cheeks grew pink, giving me my answer before she could deny it. She didn't take them from me, but was reading the first one as I held it out.

"Did you send them?"

"If I did, it would be because I didn't like the way things were going, but didn't feel that I was in the position or had enough evidence to go to the police."

"Evidence against whom?"

She shook her head. "I don't know specifically. Just that the afternoon before the board meeting, Ms. Greene told me she was scared and that she'd miscalculated. She was sitting right where you are now. She said, 'I've got to get this taken care of immediately, before the whole thing blows up in my face.' And that, otherwise, a lot of people were going to get hurt. I asked her to explain, but she said she wasn't at liberty to do so."

"Did you hear what happened to Sam Dunlap on Saturday?"

She nodded slowly, her wide lips in a frown. "I read about it in the papers. Such a strange thing. Someone must be desperate to keep some secrets buried."

"Is there something in those files in your desk that might indicate who?"

"No, Ms. Masters. I can tell you that much."

Playing along with her attempts at vagueness rather than admitting that she was the sender, I asked, "How might one have known about Sam Dunlap's family history?"

"Someone who was close to Sylvia Greene could have heard directly from her."

"And how did *she* find out? And when?"

"I don't know how, but she found out the day of the meeting, before she lost her life. I assume she had some contact with someone who told her about Mr. Dunlap."

"And there's nothing in this office that might tip you off as to who that might be?"

"Nothing except for the fact that Stuart broke into my desk. And that he lied just now about looking at his own file."

Though I hadn't permanently crossed Agnes off my list of suspects, she had moved farthest down on that list by virtue of my appreciation for the woman's character. I decided to trust her enough to ask, "Do you have any hunches as to which one of the files he was looking at?"

"Not a hunch. I saw its color-coded tab—it was Gillian Sweet's."

I thanked Agnes and headed out the door without even bothering to make a pretense that I was going anyplace other than to visit Gillian. Agnes could be pulling quite a number on me, lying about everything and setting me up, but I vowed to work harder to identify and trust my instincts. I trusted Agnes. I now no longer trusted Stuart and had never trusted Gillian Sweet.

By the time I arrived back in my own neighborhood and pulled into Gillian's driveway, I had formulated a legitimate topic to discuss with her. In her green dress and heels, she was positively dressed to the nines when she answered, which was a cliché that I've never understood. Wouldn't someone rather be dressed to the tens? Or to the eights? Though she swept the door fully open, she looked startled and ill at ease, as if she'd been expecting someone else.

"Hi, Gillian. Did I catch you on your way out?"

"Yes, as a matter of fact. What's up?"

"You said something about Stuart that night when Sylvia was killed. I'd all but forgotten about it. You said that he was a doctor. He denied it, but you seemed pretty sure of yourself."

She held her face immobile, but blinked a couple of times. My question had thrown her. "I must have been misinformed. I can't even remember who told me that he was a retired doctor. Someone on the board, perhaps."

"Sylvia?"

"I . . . don't know. Maybe."

"But you really don't remember now?"

"No. Why?"

"I was just curious. I'm still hoping something obvious has been overlooked that will vindicate my father."

"Molly, I'm sure you'd like that to be the case. But I've spoken to the police so many times about this that my throat is raw. I'm sure they investigated Stuart thoroughly. I wasn't in my right head at the hospital. I never should have . . . said what I did about Stuart's being a doctor. He wouldn't hurt a fly."

Confused, I studied her features. "Why would his being or not being a doctor have anything to do with his hurting someone?"

"It wouldn't. I'm just saying that he wouldn't kill anyone." She gestured with her chin at the still-open door behind me. "This isn't a good time for me to visit with you. I'm ... waiting for my ride to a meeting."

"I'll let you go then. Thanks." I returned to my car and backed down the driveway, too curious now to do anything other than plot my surveillance of her house to see just who showed up at her door. By the time I reached the bottom of her driveway, I realized how easy this would be as an often-recognized member of the neighborhood. Who just happened to be going for a stroll. Albeit on the opposite side of the development from her home and right behind Gillian's house.

I parked two cul-de-sacs down and walked back, trying to keep up a pace that made it look as though I were simply walking for exercise, yet trying to recognize the shape of her house. The more I thought about it, the stupider I realized this was. I couldn't see who drove up this way. Not even *I* had the nerve to stroll right through the woman's lawn to check for cars in her driveway, and if she was getting a ride someplace, the vehicle would be there for less than a minute.

I deserted the plan entirely, returned to my car, and was just about to head home in defeat, when Stuart Ackleman pulled in and parked directly across from me. I immediately ducked out of view, then watched him walk through the woods toward Gillian's house. There was only one reason I could come up with for him to be so averse to being seen by neighbors that he would park here. After a couple of minutes, Gillian and Stuart emerged arm in arm from the very same path through the woods that I had used.

They were deeply involved in a heated discussion, and Gillian shook her head and started to run away from him, but he grabbed her wrist and pulled her into a passionate kiss. She was crying, and Stuart seemed to be indicating that she should come with him to his car. This was when Stuart spotted me, sitting there, watching all of this. He froze, and Gillian followed his gaze. Her jaw dropped at the sight of me, then she darted back through the woods toward her house.

I started my engine, intending to leave the scene as quickly as possible, but Stuart stood there, torn between following Gillian or me, and opted for me. He knocked on my window, which I rolled down.

"It's not what you think," Stuart said, his face beet red. "I was just comforting her. She got a little upset about all of this trauma we've been in. The pressure is just so great and, well, you stumbled onto a one-time anomaly that would never happen again. Gillian is a happily married woman."

"That's nice," I replied, not knowing what else to say. Apparently it wasn't her husband who was accountable for the "happily" part of the sentence. I almost laughed when I looked at him—the glue job on his comb-over was not holding its own in a sudden stiff breeze. His hair was standing at attention like the flag on a mailbox. "I'll just leave now and we'll pretend like this never happened."

Gillian Sweet and Stuart Ackleman? Who would put those two together? And if Kent and Michelle were *also* having an affair, that meant that there were two couples on one board.

Stuart was still holding onto the frame of my window, however, foiling my attempt at a hasty exit. "I . . . get the impression that you don't believe what I just said."

I shrugged. "This is really between you and Gillian. And her husband. And their son."

"Don't remind me." He met my eyes. "You've got to keep this quiet, or her son will be hurt. The truth is, we've been managing to keep this a secret for the past couple of years. We didn't mean for it to happen, though."

I'm never one for excusing adultery, and figured that since Stuart was making me stay in his company, he deserved my lecturing him. "Please, Stuart. You're both responsible adults, in control of your actions." He frowned and reseated his glasses on his nose, but still had one hand on my window frame. "I can see saying that you 'didn't mean for something to happen' when you're talking about an accident versus a deliberate act. To me, claiming you accidentally became involved in a longstanding affair with someone is like claiming you accidentally shot someone, sixteen times or so. But this truly isn't my business. Unless, of course, your relationship led to murder. Then it's everyone's business."

Stuart reached through my window and laid a heavy hand on my shoulder. For the first time, I regretted our not having paid more to have the luxury of electric windows. "You can't tell people about this, Molly. A lot of innocent people would get hurt."

"I have no desire to tell anyone."

"What does that mean?"

"That as long as I'm not forced to talk about this, I won't. But if it turns out to affect the police investigation in any way, all bets are off."

He started to protest, then set his jaw. "Please don't tell your father."

I chuckled a little at the irony. "That's almost nostalgic. Back when I was a teenager, I'd always be the one asking someone else not to tell my parents."

"So you won't tell him?"

"I see no reason to say anything to him at this point."

"Thank you."

I didn't acknowledge his thanks, too uneasy at this latest discovery. I drove home and fixed myself an early lunch, still dreading my one o'clock appointment for "the works."

If I'd learned anything in the past few days, it was that this particular school board was not one with which I wished to be affiliated, nor with which to have my father affiliated.

The doorbell rang. There stood Stephanie Saunders, looking casual but especially nice in tan cotton twill slacks and a royal blue blouse.

"Stephanie, this is a surprise. Is Mike with you?" I asked in hope.

"He's at preschool." She wrinkled her nose in disapproval as she scanned my living room.

"I'm sorry I didn't have time to spruce up in honor of your

visit. My son does most of the cleaning and he's still at school."

She met my eyes. "Have you made any progress in determining who might have tried to strangle me? And killed Sylvia and that other guy?"

"No. I'm still working on it though." After weighing the pros and cons for a moment and realizing that I had no need to feel loyalty toward either party, I added, "I did find out that Gillian Sweet and Stuart Ackleman are having an affair, however."

She put her hands on her hips. "Huh. That's what I came over here to tell you. That, and the more I think about it, the more certain I am that Stuart's some sort of a con artist."

"What makes you say that?"

"For one thing, I'm excellent at discerning people's accents and am certain he's from Massachusetts, and yet he always claims he's from Connecticut and got his accent from his parents."

"That's possible, though, isn't it?"

"It would be, except he doesn't have the, well, social bearing of someone from Connecticut. And I did a little checking on the town. No one's heard of an Ackleman family there."

"You called the *town*?" That must have been quite a feat; I could only imagine trying to call, say, Boulder, Colorado, to ask if the Acklemans had ever lived there.

She didn't elaborate. "My sources tell me that Stuart and Gillian are trying to cool it, though. Gillian wants to prevent her husband from finding out."

Gillian was trying to end things. That fit in with the exchange I'd overheard at Proctor's the other evening. Which meant that Gillian was hiding some secret regarding Stuart's past, a secret which she was tired of keeping. "How did you find out, Stephanie?"

"Gillian's best friend is the homeroom mom of my hairdresser's daughter's class."

"Small world."

"Mmm-hmm." She glanced at her watch. "And speaking

of which, I'd best be going. I've got an appointment at my salon."

"That reminds me. Are you interested in taking my place at the Jackson Mineral Baths this afternoon? I've got an appointment already paid for, but I'd just as soon not go."

"Please, Molly. I have a personal massage therapist plus a skin consultant for my facials. I don't even share my bathtub with members of my own family. The last thing in the world I would ever do is take a mineral bath in the same tub where thousands of strangers' nude bodies have been."

The image turned my stomach slightly, but I replied, "I'm sure they wash the tub between customers."

"Just the same, I'll pass. Thank you for the offer, dear. I'm sure you'll enjoy yourself." Grinning, she gave me a visual once-over. "Immensely, even."

Chapter 17

Wringing Out the Sheets

One P.M. arrived far too quickly, but to my credit, I was at the spa on time. Technically, though, I was still in the parking lot debating the matter of actually going in at the top of the hour.

Before entering the building, I circled the outside and had one prolonged moment in which I realized that this place reminded me of some childhood image I had of an insane asylum. When I opened the door to the main entrance, I was instantly awash in that indoor-swimming-pool type of air—humid with the faint odor of chlorine. The lobby itself resembled a fancy swimming pool—a mosaic of tile on the floor and walls, furnished in bamboo patio furniture. (Not to say that most people put bamboo furniture in their pools.)

I dragged myself to the desk, where a smiling receptionist greeted me. "Hello. Welcome to Jackson." She spoke in a low, breathy voice that instantly set my teeth on edge. "Do you have an appointment?"

"Probably. My name is Molly Masters."

"Ah, yes. You're right on time for your one-fifteen."

"Actually, my appointment was at one P.M."

"No, your friend who made this appointment specifically said that you'd be late unless she told you to be here earlier than your actual appointment time. Have a seat, please, and Hilga will be right with you."

"Who's Hilga?"

"Your personal escort. She'll run your bath and guide you to each station for your full body-works experience. Please, relax. It is our job to pamper you for the next few hours."

"Goodie." I hate that word: *pamper*. Makes me think of diapers. I dropped into the nearest seat. Hilga. I was about to be diapered by some Swedish goddess type who'd make me feel like a member of an inferior species.

"Here's Hilga now," the receptionist said, as a stooped-over, prune-faced elderly woman shuffled into the room.

I got to my feet and found that I towered over the woman. Okay, I told myself, I'd made an off-base assumption about the woman's name. Maybe I'd find that I underestimated this entire experience. Lauren knew me well, after all, and if she thought I'd enjoy this, she was probably right. Much as I doubted it.

"This way," Hilga told me, her sharp voice a striking contrast to the receptionist's. I followed, straining to walk slowly as she led me down the hall. "You start with the mineral bath itself. Then the massage. Then the facial. By the time you're through, you'll look and feel ten years younger."

If this woman was anything less than a hundred and ten years old, I had serious doubts about this place's rejuvenating powers.

The hallway we inched along resembled an ancient and oversize airport bathroom—a badly maintained bathroom, at that. "The baths are in here. You got the middle one, here. You got your own private dressing room."

She pushed the metal stall door open for me, then stepped inside with me. The area was not much larger than a handicap toilet stall, but with a built-in bed/bench along one side. The thin mattress was reasonably clean, but looked like something from a prison warehouse sale. The Hilga person was still standing beside me. "Umm, if it's private, aren't you going to leave?"

"I got to run the bath for you and get you in. That's part of the service."

"But I've been running my own baths for years now. I really, truly know how to get into a bathtub. And out of one."

"It's also a safety issue, miss."

I looked around, desperate now to escape. At the back of this little dressing room was a second stall door, which had to lead to the tub itself. A small laminated sign on the front wall listed the suggested tip for one's bath escort. "Hilga, how much could I tip you to let me get into and out of my own bath?"

"Don't you want the hot sheet wrap? It feels great."

"Call me compulsively modest, but I have a thing about perfect strangers seeing me naked."

She flicked her pruny hand at me. "Miss, I been doing this job for twenty years now." She reached around the front stall door, then shut it behind us and handed me a frayed, once-white, rust-stained towel, roughly the size of a placemat. "Believe me, there ain't a body type I ain't seen, and I'm long past noticing or caring."

"I'm sure that's true. But the same isn't the case for me, and I'd feel stupid closing my own eyes."

"You'll be fine." She shuffled past me, entered the second stall, and turned on the bath water. I took a peek at the tub, which had to be the least-appealing bathtub I'd ever seen. It was an old-fashioned white tub with claw feet, but the insides were a dark, red-brown hue.

"Yow. Talk about rust stains."

"That's caused by all the minerals in the water. You know, some of our most famous presidents enjoyed these very same hot springs."

"I'm sure that's true. It's just that I'd hoped somebody would have cleaned the tub since then."

" 'Scuse me?"

Resigned to my fate and wondering just what Lauren had been thinking when she got me this "gift," I undressed and flattened my placemat-cum-towel against my significant body parts in the front, having to give up on any notion of hiding the fact that there was a full moon showing in the back. I'm sure that when these baths were first built, they were really elegant. At the moment, though, I would have been more inclined to take a dip in the toilet at a well-maintained truck stop. Hilga, my personal trucker lady, grabbed my arm and "helped" me maintain my balance as I stepped into the tub.

"You can just let your washcloth float on the water surface, since you're shy."

I took that to mean my placemat was actually a washcloth. She left without another word, or a guffaw, and I settled into the slightly rotten-egg-scented warm water, and watched the tiny bubbles form on my skin. I instantly resembled a gigantic Alka-Seltzer tablet. I concentrated on the concept of my body fizzling away entirely, while plotting how I could possibly reciprocate appropriately when Lauren's birthday rolled around next spring. And yet, despite the less-than-elegant surroundings, the water did feel wonderful on my aching muscles. I felt my body begin to relax, in spite of myself.

In the stall next to mine, a woman was having a conversation with her friend. They were speaking at a volume that indicated that the two women were not sharing a tub but rather had requested adjacent ones. I tuned them out, trying hard to relax and to assure myself that I hadn't done anything to tick off Lauren, but rather that from here on, my enjoyment would escalate. I pricked my ears up, however, when one of the women said, "They sure are having quite the problems in Carlton with that school board, aren't they? I mean, things were ugly enough before. Now they're murdering one another."

"I'll say," her friend responded. "Makes me glad my own kids are grown, so that I'm no longer affected personally by what goes on."

I gritted my teeth at that, knowing exactly what she meant, and yet also knowing what a false sense of security it was ever to dismiss education as not having an impact on one's own life. It only stood to reason, too, that these "splashy" murders would be the subject of conversation in a bath house. I had instantly lost any hope of relaxation.

"I can't believe they're not kicking that murderer off the board," said one woman.

"They don't even know who did it yet," said the other.

"Of course they do. It's obvious that the killer's that man who was written up in the papers. Charles Peterson."

In an example of how far I had to go till I could take remarks such as that one lying down, even while soaking in a tub, I sat up, hoisted myself partially out of the tub enough to pound on the metal partition that separated us, and cried, "Hey! That's my father you're talking about in there. And he's innocent!"

There was a momentary silence. Then the woman said, "I'm sorry. I didn't mean to offend anyone. I didn't realize . . . you were in there."

"What made you leap to the conclusion that my father is guilty?"

"Nothing. I don't know. I, uh, sorry." She called out loudly, "Hey, lady with the towels? Isn't it about time we got out of here? I'm getting all pruny."

"Me too," her friend called.

"Be right there," someone answered, probably Hilga, but I couldn't say for certain.

There were various rustling and bumping noises as the women got out of their tubs. After a couple of minutes, the room was completely silent, and I took this to mean that I was the last bather in the place.

Suddenly my door opened, and I tried to hide beneath my rusty little washcloth, then laughed. The person had a sheet draped over her entire body, with just the holes cut out for the eyes.

"If you're the bath attendant, this really is not what I intended toward protecting my modesty. *I'm* supposed to be the one under the sheet."

The sheeted person walked up to the edge of my tub and knelt without a word. Her hands were covered by rubber gloves, and she grabbed me by the shoulders and pushed. In a tribute to how strong my sense of disbelief was, even after she'd shoved my head completely under the surface of the water, I was thinking: *If she thinks I'm giving her a tip after this, she's got another thing coming. She's shoving me* under *instead of helping me* out!

An instant later, it dawned on me that this wasn't a joke. Someone truly was trying to drown me.

I had automatically gasped and had a lung full of air when the sheeted person shoved me under. That precious breath of air was not going to last me for long.

I flailed madly, trying to get myself free. My assailant had a grip on my hair, close to the scalp. I grabbed the attacker's hand to protect my scalp and tried to pull myself around sideways, using my elbows while kicking up with my legs.

It was no use. I couldn't get any leverage.

My toe caught on the chain. I kicked the plug out and hoped that the water would drain before I lost consciousness.

My lungs were already burning, and I had a strong urge to take in another breath, even though I knew that I'd only be filling my lungs with water. My eyes began to sting.

Suddenly the person rose, and I managed to get up, sputtering and coughing for air.

"Hey! What are you doing to her?" someone cried.

Hilga! She had caught my assailant in the act and saved my life.

My assailant, still under the sheet, barreled into the elderly woman. Hilga let out a grunt of protest as she fell, smacking backward into the partition.

I was struggling too hard to regain my breath to do anything else. Instead of chasing after the person, Hilga looked at me. "Are you all right?"

My head felt as though it would explode, my pulse was racing so, but I managed to nod. "You okay?"

"I'm too old for this nonsense," she muttered, rubbing the back of her head where she'd smacked into the wall. "Who was that?"

"I don't know. The person was covered by the sheet."

Hilga was not going to be able to give chase, and I got to my knees, gripping the edge of the tub.

"Can't you trip an alarm?" I asked.

She made her way out of the stall, and I stepped out of the tub, shivering, wrapping my arms around myself as best I could. She came back a moment later. "He's long gone. Went out the emergency exit. Nobody saw him. I'm sorry."

"Him?"

"Well, yeah. That's what I figured. Didn't you?"

I shook my head, my teeth chattering as I dripped all over the floor. "Hilga. Could you please call the police? And get me my heated sheet? Or better yet, a freaking towel?"

"No need to be surly," she grumbled as she went back to the hallway.

I gritted my teeth at the etiquette lesson, reminding myself that this woman had just saved my life, plus she'd taken a conk on the back of her head as a result. I made my way into my "private dressing room" and found to my immense relief that my clothes were still there.

Hilga returned and handed me both a towel and a hot bed-sheet, both of which I used merely to dry myself off somewhat. She watched me dress, then said, "Does this mean you ain't goin' for the massage and facial?"

Wanting to save time and walk with some sense of purpose, I found my own way to the lobby, currently empty except for the receptionist, and demanded that she let me use her phone. I hesitated before dialing 911, considering the grouchy officer who had questioned me after the racetrack, and instead dialed Tommy's number.

To his gruff "Sergeant Newton," I replied, "Tommy, I've had an incident at the Jackson Mineral Baths. Someone in a makeshift disguise just tried to drown me."

After a silence, he asked, "Is this a public pool or something?"

"No. A private bath. Semiprivate, anyway. They have a thing about watching you get in and out of the tub. This person—I think it was a woman, but my one witness, who works here, thinks otherwise. Anyway, it was impossible to tell because he or she was wearing a sheet with holes cut out for the eyes. The sheeted person shoved my head under the water and tried to drown me."

There was a pause. Meanwhile, the receptionist was staring at me with her mouth ajar.

"Tommy? Are you still there?"

"I'm gonna have to develop a separate Molly Masters task-force unit, aren't I? I'm gonna have to assign a whole team to nothing but following you around."

"Tommy, I'm serious! I need your help. I was going to call the Saratoga police, but I thought maybe you'd come help me again. I've gotten the impression from Saturday's police interrogations that they don't especially care for me out here."

"That's just 'cause they don't know you like I do. Course, if they did, they'd've banned you from the entire town."

He hung up before I could formulate an appropriate response.

The receptionist rose and said in her still-affected but now decidedly shaken tones, "Ma'am, can I get you anything? Herbal tea, perhaps?"

"No, thanks." I began to pace. This couldn't have been an isolated incident. I didn't believe that any more than I believed that Stephanie's partial strangling had been—

I interrupted my own thoughts. "Stephanie!" She knew I was going to be here at one P.M. If she happened to speak to one of the board members about me, and that person happened to be the killer, that explained how someone had found out where I was.

"Ma'am? Perhaps we can find you a private room to use until . . ."

While she was speaking, I grabbed the receiver again and dialed, this time hoping for the actual person and not the machine. I got her machine. "Stephanie? It's Molly," I said at the sound of the beep. "I have to know if you told anyone on the board about my appointment at the mineral baths today. Call me as soon as—"

There was a *click* as she picked up the phone. "Molly, my dear, what possible reason would you have to care about whether or not I happened to mention your trip to the mineral baths?"

"Someone tried to drown me, that's what!"

"Oh my. Unsuccessfully, I take it?"

She was playing dumb blond in an attempt to shift my

focus. "Stephanie, don't mess with me. If I were contacting you to seek revenge from my watery grave, I can guarantee you I *wouldn't* use the phone. Just answer my question. Did you tell anyone on the school board where I'd be this afternoon?"

In the meantime, a middle-age couple had entered the lobby, and the receptionist rounded the desk to speak to them. I covered my free ear to better hear Stephanie's response.

"Just Gillian Sweet. I happened to bump into her after leaving your place. She was going on a walk and, well, I didn't think anything of it. She lives right in your neighborhood, after all."

Great! Stephanie tells Gillian about my vulnerable location, right after I discover her affair! "*Why* did you tell her about a thing like that?"

"It was just on my mind, that's all. I happened to be chuckling to myself at the thought of you getting a full-body beauty treatment. No offense, Molly, but you're just the last person I could imagine doing that. And there Gillian was, coming down the block, and you said yourself how I need to try to be more friendly toward my fellow board members."

"Did I? What I seem to remember is the fact that you realized that one of those board members is a murderer, so you weren't going to be speaking to them." I glanced over my shoulder and noticed that the receptionist and the two customers were gawking at me. I gave them an apologetic smile, the best response I could muster.

"I . . . do hope I wasn't indirectly responsible for what happened to you. But look at the bright side, Molly. We've flushed out the killer. It has to be Gillian Sweet, because she's the only one who knew you were there."

"How very clever of you to use me as bait," I retorted, lowering my voice.

"Much as I'd like to take the credit for finding the killer, it was purely by accident. I didn't intentionally set you up. And I'm merely pointing out to you that you should be happy that we found the killer."

"I'm overjoyed, Stephanie." I slammed the phone down into its cradle.

The receptionist immediately grabbed my elbow and began ushering me back into what I now could only think of as the bowels of the building. "Let's just find you a nice, comfortable waiting room, shall we? You've obviously had a very rough day."

She was using such a patronizing voice that I began to suspect she thought of me as a raving lunatic. "There really was a person in a sheet who tried to drown me. Just ask Hilga."

"Oh, I will. But let's just get you all comfy till the police arrive."

I stopped in my tracks when she seemed to be leading me back into the baths. "I'm not going back there again."

"Of course not. But there's a nice office you can have all to yourself, right around the corner."

I didn't trust her, but to my relief, she did indeed deposit me at a rudimentary office. I sat down on the edge of the couch, determined not to let my guard down. The receptionist said, "I'll bring the police to you the moment they arrive," and closed the door behind me.

I mentally replayed my conversation with Stephanie. She was, of course, only partially correct. Whether or not my close call proved that Gillian was the killer depended on whether or not Gillian had shared this information. Far-fetched as this scenario was, if Stephanie innocently managed to pass along the less-than-compelling news of a visit to a bath house, Gillian might have done the very same thing.

What would be tricky was determining whether or not Gillian actually told anyone where I'd be this afternoon. For, if she was in fact the killer, she'd probably have found a way to announce it to everyone and cover her own tracks.

Twenty minutes later, I was still pondering the matter when Tommy arrived. He was in uniform but holding his cap, which had left the customary band-shaped mark around his red hair. To my utter and unpleasant surprise, I added the final capper to my Sojourn into Humiliation by bursting into tears at the sight of him.

Having known me for most of my childhood, and even
better during the last five years or so, Tommy had to have
been at least as surprised by my outburst as I was. Word-
lessly, he whipped out a white handkerchief from his pocket
and handed it to me, then sat beside me, slowly rotating his
cap in his hands while I struggled to collect myself.

My self-control returned after a minute or two, and after a
brief silence, Tommy said quietly, "Molly, I was thinkin' as I
drove here. My first dozen years on the force, I only investigated one, count 'em, one murder case. Then you moved
back to Carlton. Nowadays they might as well call me Detective Death . . . when I'm not watching you nearly get yourself
killed, that is. I've been saving up for my sons' college, not to
mention Rachel's. But I'm thinkin', why not let 'em fend for
themselves? So, even though you're indirectly responsible
for me 'n' Lauren getting together, plus you're her best
friend, and I'm kind of fond of you myself, I'll give you my
entire life savings if you'll leave town. Permanently."

Tommy had a twinkle in his eye that let me know this was
just his way of cheering me up. I dried the last of my tears.
"How much money are we talking about?"

"Twelve thousand, give or take a couple bucks."

"Right about now, I'd settle for a bus token and a large
order of fries."

"Deal. I'll even throw in the handkerchief." He stood up
and prompted, "Come on. I'll take your statement at the
nearest McDonald's." He put his arm around my shoulder
and escorted me to the door.

"By the way, have you checked into the cost of a college
education lately, Tommy?"

Chapter 18

Can't You Just Draw a Cat?

Back home, hours later, after having recuperated from my near drowning in my Alka-Seltzer bath and awaiting my husband's return from work, Lauren came over, very despondent on my behalf. She explained that "the boys," Tommy's teenage sons, were home with Rachel, but that she had to apologize in person for the way things turned out.

"I can't believe this happened," she said for the umpteenth time. "How could Stephanie have been so stupid as to tell a suspect that you'd be completely vulnerable, a sitting duck?"

"In bubbling water, no less."

"For all of her faults, she's normally brighter than that."

"She claims she inadvertently blabbed, though she also pointed out that her doing so helped to track down the killer."

"How did you happen to tell Stephanie about your mineral bath in the first place?"

I was saved from having to answer that question when the doorbell rang. I promptly went to answer it. Tommy was still in uniform, though his workday had probably ended. Or else he was on dinner-break.

"Lauren here?" he asked.

"Yeah. Come on in."

He smoothed his hat-head red hair as we made our way back to the kitchen. "Just got through chatting with Gillian. To save you the effort of retracing my steps, I'll just tell you: She says she never mentioned your agenda for this afternoon to anyone."

"That's interesting," I replied. "Do you think that that makes her look more guilty or less guilty?"

He frowned and took a seat at the counter, next to his wife. "I just collect the evidence 'n' try to determine who could've done it. I leave all the postulating about intangibles up to you."

I crossed my arms and leaned back against the stove, which of course wasn't on, or I'd have found a cooler resting place. "'Postulating about intangibles?' Sounds like you've been scanning a thesaurus. But all right, then. What about the 'evidence'? Did anyone else on the school board know where I'd be this afternoon?"

"'Fraid so. Seems someone who identified himself as your father called the receptionist to ask when you'd be through so he could pick you up on time."

"My father? But he wasn't supposed to pick me up, and he never even knew I'd be there in the first place."

"Uh-huh. And your dad said he placed no such call. I asked the receptionist if it could possibly have been a woman deliberately speaking in a low voice. She said no. So all we got to go on now is, it sure appears to be one of the men."

"You've crossed Superintendent Collins off any list of possible suspects, right? He never had any opportunity to poison Sylvia, did he?"

"Right. Collins wasn't with Sylvia till the open meeting. Never touched the water or any of the glasses."

I was relieved to hear that. The last thing I wanted to consider was that we had a killer running the district.

"That means it was Kent or Stuart. And Stuart's the only viable body type." Plus the likelier to have been conversing with Gillian this afternoon. "But even if that's accurate, how could either of them have known where I'd be? The only persons other than myself and Jim who knew were Gillian, Lauren, and Stephanie."

"Thank you for your startlin' insights, Dr. Watson," Tommy all but snarled at me. "I wasn't serious about my leaving the postulating up to you. It's not your job to solve this case. I'm just tellin' you what I know, to see if it helps you remember something that might turn out to be a clue. Such as another person you told or could have overheard you tellin' Stephanie."

"Tommy, I've already staked my life on that one. There wasn't anyone else."

"I didn't tell anyone," Lauren said, "and I made the reservation on our private phone, where nobody could have overheard. Not even Rachel."

"And if it was Gillian, disguising her voice despite what the receptionist says, she'd be pointing a finger at herself, all but announcing that she did it."

Tommy rose, then looked at Lauren. "You comin' home soon? I'm gonna head back."

"I'll come, too." Lauren reached out and gave my wrist a squeeze. "Again, Molly, I'm so sorry that my gift backfired."

"Don't give it another thought. Until next year at my fortieth, that is. A trip to Bermuda would compensate nicely."

That night, after the children were in bed and I was working on some cartoons, my right wrist hurt a little bit. Maybe it was possible to get carpal tunnel syndrome from drawing too long on a badly positioned notebook. That notion led to my sketching out a truly silly cartoon concept. Four people in a car are emerging from a tunnel and are all crying, "Oww! Oww! My wrist! My wrist!" The caption reads: *Carpool Tunnel Syndrome*.

Afterward, I spent some time just staring at my sketch, wondering if my parents had been disappointed whenever they'd first realized that the particular bent of my mind would lead to my cooking up idiosyncratic cartoons instead of, say, formulas for world peace or cancer cures. No, my daughter doesn't save lives. She creates cartoons about carpool tunnel syndrome!

That thought pattern led me to drawing yet another cartoon, wherein a toddler with wild hair is scribbling mathematical equations on the wall. With his crayon poised from having written $E = MC^2$, he is looking up at a woman in old-fashioned clothes beside him who laments, "Oh, Albert!

Can't you just draw kitty cats and doggies like normal children?"

This cartoon made me feel a little better—emotionally, that is. My wrist was now really killing me, and I decided that, yes, I'd developed enough of an equivalent to carpal tunnel that I was going to knock off on the drawing and call it a night. Jim was already in bed. We hadn't spoken much that night. He'd been less than pleased at learning about my latest mishap in Saratoga.

He wasn't asleep, though, for as soon as I'd settled into my half of the bed, he asked, "How are you feeling?"

"Okay. I'm just . . . appalled at what is going on with the members of the school board. The more I get to know them, the less I think any one of them is competent to make decisions that control the fate of our children. Not counting my father, of course."

"I meant how you felt physically. If you've discovered new bruises."

"Oh, that. No, I'm fine. Though my hair still smells like rotten eggs. And I'll probably be seeing tiny bubbles in my sleep." I thought more about my father, picturing him in the midst of the other board members, all of them fairly despicable, in differing degrees. Thinking out loud now, I murmured, "Maybe that's why they set up him up. Because he was the only sane one, so he didn't fit in."

"Your father, you mean? You think the murder was a conspiracy?"

"I don't know." I paused and considered the question more fully. "No, I don't. I just think all of the board members had something to hide. And that Sylvia was truly so single-minded in her intentions that she was willing to threaten and coerce anyone and everyone till she got her way."

"You can't risk pushing everyone's buttons the way that you do. Molly, you don't know which of these people killed Sylvia. You can't keep risking your life like this."

"I know. And I'm also worried about my father's safety. Maybe it really would be best if he'd just . . . resign."

"Ironic, isn't it?" Jim murmured. "That's how all this

started, Sylvia's trying to force him to resign. Now you want that, too."

"Don't tell my parents I said that."

"You've avoided the issue about how you're exacerbating the situation."

For a moment I was distracted at the word "exacerbating." Jim must have been thumbing through Tommy's thesaurus. "I'll try to take up a new hobby and get out of the habit of caring about justice."

"Somehow, I doubt you mean that. Good night."

The next morning, even after a reasonably full night's sleep, I couldn't get past my feeling that the person under that ghostlike sheet had been a woman, not a man. It just hadn't struck me that the person was all that large or strong. And yet it had been a man who'd called the spa. That could only mean that my energy had to be focused away from Kent Graham, toward the man with a much slighter build: Stuart Ackleman.

I concurred with Stephanie's opinion when she said that Stuart had a Massachusetts accent, and if she'd checked into this so-called hometown of his in Connecticut and found he'd never lived there, he probably was covering up for something. Gillian had said that Stuart had been a doctor. Of course, she later turned out to be Stuart's lover, so maybe this whole doctor thing was a line Stuart had fed her. Still, I needed to start by determining as best I could if Stuart truly was a retired philosophy professor.

After giving the matter considerable thought, I hit upon a possible litmus test for Stuart and called my mother to get the necessary details. Fortunately, she answered instead of making me listen through her machine's message. I immediately asked, "Mom, remember that really annoying thing you were always saying to us while we were in junior high and you were taking that philosophy course at SUNY?"

After a pause, Mom replied stiffly, "I'm never annoying, Molly. You must have me confused with someone else's mother."

"It was something like, 'So blow your nose, slave.'"

"Oh, that. Somebody whines that he has a runny nose, and the philosopher retorts, 'Then wipe it, slave,' meaning that you become a slave to your illness when you let yourself obsess over—"

"Yeah, that's the one. But, believe me, Mom, it was darned annoying to have to listen to when you're suffering from a bad cold. But who said it?"

"Epictetus."

"Epic who?"

"Epictetus. He was Roman, one of the many Stoic philosophers, as in stoic with a capital S. They all presented a basic, 'quit whining and buck up' style of philosophy. They probably came from some region named Stoicia, or something similar."

"Well, that certainly wouldn't be a place I'd care to have my car break down near. Imagine trying to find a good mechanic there, let alone a little sympathy. But would any philosophy professor know that quote?"

"No, there were so many Stoics who—"

Cutting her off before she could turn this into a full lecture, I asked, "But any philosophy professor would know who Epictetus was, right? And that he was a real Stoic, with a capital S?"

"Oh, absolutely. Why?"

I didn't want to get another lecture about how I shouldn't be investigating this myself, so I quickly said, "Because Karen's coming down with the sniffles. Thanks, Mom. I'll talk to you later."

I hung up, planning on apologizing for my abruptness to my mother once this was all over, then called Stuart. I identified myself, then said, "I've been thinking about the whole thing of my stumbling onto you and Gillian like I did, and I just wanted you to know that I've decided to drop the 'So, blow your nose, slave' attitude."

"Pardon?"

"Sorry. I meant, 'wipe it, slave,' I think. Are you familiar with that Epictetus quote?"

"Who?"

"Epictetus." There was a long pause, but Stuart never responded or indicated that the name meant anything at all to him. "He was one of the Stoics."

"Good for him," he said, clearly annoyed. Apparently this particular quote had that kind of effect on us non–philosophy majors. He went on, "But what are you trying to tell me? Are you going to tell the world about Gillian's and my relationship, or aren't you?"

"No."

"Good. Because we're calling it quits anyway. That's why I'm a little . . . edgy. I'm just not myself today."

That was exactly what I was beginning to suspect.

Stephanie suspected that he was really from the state of Massachusetts. But how could I check that—call information and ask for every Ackleman listed in the state and hope to stumble upon a relative? It was bad enough having to always come off as a fool to my mom and others who know me; intolerable to also have to ask inane questions of total strangers.

After ending my conversation with Stuart, I decided to take a real long shot and try the white pages of my Internet provider. Though I was thinking that the name "Ackleman" was probably so common as to bring up a few hundred listings in the state of Massachusetts alone, to my complete surprise, there was only one listing: Linda Ackleman, which gave her address and phone number in a city called Westfield. Figuring that this would be pretty low on my scale of embarrassment factors, I dialed the number. A woman answered and I said, "Hello. May I speak to Stuart please?"

There was a pause. "Stuart hasn't lived here in years. May I ask who's calling?"

I hadn't taken the time to consider the possible consequences of answering truthfully. I decided not to risk doing so. "Oh, I'm sorry. I must have an old number here. Is the more recent number the one I have for upstate New York?"

"Yes, that's right."

Making a fast, reasonable assumption, I asked, "So I must be speaking to his ex-wife?"

"Yes, who is this? What's this in regard to?"

"I'm sorry. I meant to identify myself earlier. My name is Marilyn Smith and I'm with . . . Information Retrieval Services. I've been trying to locate—"

"You people again? Don't you ever take no for an answer?"

"Ma'am, I'm new at my job, and I—"

"Then you need to talk to your employer. I told that man to leave me alone. The case was resolved years ago and Stuart is no longer practicing medicine. Everyone has suffered enough."

She hung up.

I began to pace the floor. Okay. I needed to get to the bottom of this. The woman was obviously very upset about whatever Sam had uncovered.

How could I possibly find out what that was? Drive out to Westfield and go through their old newspapers until I discovered Stuart's name? If Stuart had been a doctor, he'd surely have to have been certified, or licensed, or whatever. Maybe there were some public records of all court cases involving doctors. I didn't know how to go about finding that kind of information.

What I needed now was some contact in the community of Westfield—some doctor or lawyer who'd be willing to pass information on to me.

Though part of me inwardly chastised myself for being so devious, I grabbed the yellow pages and located a national doctor referral service, who, upon my request, gave me the number for a local service in the city of Westfield, Massachusetts.

I procrastinated for a few minutes, wondering if I was really taking this too far. I'd already lied about my identity to Linda Ackleman, an innocent person I'd never met. At length, though, I decided to ponder my sense of ethics at a time when my father's freedom and reputation weren't at stake and two people hadn't lost their lives.

A woman with an elderly—but decidedly nasal—voice answered the doctor-referral service number in Westfield, and I said, "My name is Marilyn Smith. I'm moving to Westfield,

Massachusetts, and I'd like some information on physicians in that area."

"All right, ma'am. Are you looking for a general practitioner, family physician, or a specialist?"

"Actually, I'm interested in finding out about one particular physician by the name of Stuart Ackleman. He had a practice in Westfield several years ago."

I waited through a pause as I heard the clicking of computer keys in the background. "There's no Dr. Ackleman listed. I'm sorry."

"I heard he retired. There may have even been a lawsuit involved."

"Oh, yes!" she cried. "Dr. Stuart Ackleman. I remember that myself. I was still working as a nurse at the time."

"What happened?"

"My memory is too fuzzy to rely on, but I can tell you this: I sure can't recommend him, even if he's still practicing medicine, which I doubt."

"Why?"

"He was a GP. He nearly killed a patient, accidentally, when he overlooked an allergy and prescribed the wrong medication. He wound up losing his medical license and moving out of town. The whole thing caused quite a hubbub around here, let me tell you. Broke up his marriage and everything."

Chapter 19

I Suppose You Think This Is All My Fault

Twenty minutes after hanging up the phone, I was sitting in Tommy's office, rehashing what I'd uncovered about Stuart Ackleman. We were playing our typical game—Tommy pretending that none of this was of any interest to him, me pretending that I didn't notice his lack of attention to my every word.

Sounding as though he were half asleep, Tommy droned, "Let me get this straight, Molly. You think that Stuart could have killed Sylvia Greene and Sam Dunlap—"

"Jacobsen," I interrupted. "That was his real name, remember."

"Jacobsen," he patiently corrected, "rather than have his reputation in his new hometown get tainted by his past?"

"Yes. He denied being a retired doctor when Sylvia collapsed. Obviously, then, he truly didn't want everyone to know about it."

"And yet he hadn't even taken as minor a preventative measure as to change his name. But your theory is: Why go through the effort of changing your name when you can simply murder anyone who discovers the truth about your past, right?"

His smugness made me clench my fists, which were below his line of vision because of his desk. Still maintaining a measure of calmness in my voice, I asked, "Are you saying that killers are always rational and intelligent about their decisions? Maybe Stuart *isn't* rational about the whole thing. I mean, he knew CPR better than anyone, yet he let my father administer CPR, rather than risk revealing any medical expertise. How rational is that?"

"That's not at all irrational, if you hate the person in need, just immoral and despicable. But I can't go arresting the guy just 'cuz he's a less than stellar human being."

"Right. And at the very best, we have a 'less than stellar human being' running our school board." An even less appealing thought occurred to me an instant later. "Tommy, if Stuart is the killer, Gillian Sweet is in mortal danger."

"How do you figure?"

"Remember how, after Stephanie's choking incident at Proctor's Theater, I told you about the couple I overheard arguing? I'm now sure that it had to have been Gillian and Stuart, and Gillian said that she was 'sick of keeping his secret.' Or something to that effect."

"I'll talk to her and to Stuart. But I got to warn you, Molly. It's not going to make any difference. I interviewed Gillian personally that evening after speaking with you, and she denied being anywhere backstage and having had any discussion of that nature."

"Did anyone else confess to, as you put it, 'having had a discussion of that nature'?"

"No."

"Well, then . . . ?"

He pushed back from his desk. "Like I said. I'll talk to both of 'em. You could be right. Gillian might've still been trying to protect Stuart then. Now that they've had a falling out, maybe she'll change her tune."

"Thanks. Because, while I can't identify the person under that sheet at the bathhouse, I can rule out Kent Graham. He's just too muscular and broad-shouldered to have disguised himself that way. And we're certain it was a man who pretended to be my father who called the place. It sure wasn't my dad, and the private investigator wound up as the second victim, so the only male suspect that leaves is Stuart Ackleman."

Tommy remained silent. His features were so cross that I couldn't help but point out, on my behalf, "At least you've got to admit that I've given you some potentially helpful information about one of the suspects."

"Since you brought it up, Molly, truth is, Stuart told me this himself, way back when I first interviewed him at the hospital. He was feeling guilty for not performing the CPR himself. Pleaded with me not to spread it around to his peers on the school board. The guy was in tears over the whole thing. Furthermore, Kent told me the same thing about Stuart. Called Stuart a worm for not trying to save Sylvia's life, and that if that got out to the press, it'd destroy Stuart's reputation."

"How did Kent find out?"

He gave a small shrug. "Unintentionally overheard a private conversation."

"Oh." My cheeks were instantly blazing hot. "You couldn't have just told me that when I first started telling you about Stuart?"

He stared at me, a blank expression on his face. "See, Moll, there's some folks out there who, believe it or not, actually respect this here uniform." He tugged on the fabric of his sleeve.

"That must make you feel really proud. I'm happy for you."

"Tell you what. You get yourself accepted into the academy, get yourself in shape physically so you can pass the tests on the obstacle courses and so on, endure a few years of traffic patrol, work your way up the ranks, and you should be qualified to take over my job right around the time I'm ready to retire. How's that sound?"

"What? And give up the glamour and excitement of the faxable greeting card business? Don't be silly. I'll see you later, Tommy."

I got into my car and sat there for several minutes, trying to figure out what to do next to prove once and for all whether or not Stuart was the killer. I couldn't just drop by Gillian's house again, and I'd pushed Stuart about as far as I could. That meant I had to either leave the evidence-gathering with regard to Stuart up to Tommy, or discuss Stuart with the two board members I had yet to talk about him with: Carol Barr and Michelle Lacy.

I had no ready excuse I could use to set up a meeting with Carol. Michelle, though, had her decorating business. I could always feign interest in hiring her, while I picked her brain regarding what she knew about Stuart.

By consulting an interior designer, once again, I would be the proverbial fish out of water. The only fun part of home ownership for me is in picking out furniture that fits my family and the house itself. I could not conceive of paying someone else to do this for me. It was tantamount to announcing, "I don't know what I like and have lousy taste anyway, so dress my house for me."

I went home and called Michelle, who, try as I might to change her mind, insisted upon making a house call. I hadn't wanted her to see how very non-decoratorish my house was, and so I'd told her that a house call was "pointless," because I wanted her services for a future sunroom. She countered that she needed to get a feel for my taste and needs before we could proceed, and that she was going to be in my neighborhood anyway, as she had some paperwork to drop off at Gillian's.

Hence, at two P.M., I found myself furiously tidying the house, all for a bogus appointment with an interior designer to discuss her ideas, which under no circumstance would I implement, for a nonexistent room that I had no intention of actually constructing. Though the exercise did lead me to question my judgment, if not my sanity, at least my neatnik son would be happy when he got home in an hour or so.

Plus, it gave me at least a vague idea for a card: the image of a pilot of a small airplane that has crashed. The pilot glares at his terrified wife and says to her, "Damn. I *knew* I should've postponed takeoff till half-time! This is *your* fault for buying me a portable TV!"

The doorbell rang, and I tossed my dirty dust rag and spray bottle into the coat closet and opened the door. Michelle, holding a couple of thick three-ring binders, was wearing such an attractive pale yellow skirt suit, and such a flattering hairstyle, her dark hair swept up, that I instantly felt under-dressed and inadequate, and had to remind myself that this was, after all, my home, and there was no dress code here.

I smiled. "Hello, Michelle. Thanks for meeting with me on such short notice."

"Not a problem, Molly. As I said earlier, I was in the neighborhood anyway." She stepped inside, and I found myself wanting to delay having to show her around, so I kept my place directly in front of her as she shut the door.

"Everything went all right for you with Gillian?"

Michelle raised an eyebrow, but said only, "Yes, of course. I was merely dropping something off." She waited a moment, and when I still didn't step aside, asked, "Were you interested in having me assess just the one room, or the entire house?"

"Just the one room. Which hasn't actually been built yet. But if you'd like, I can show you the part of the yard that it would probably eventually occupy."

"I don't think that would be particularly helpful. I brought along some eight-by-tens of sunrooms that I especially like, since you said that you felt you wanted to get a feel for room possibilities before you did anything else. I thought we could flip through those for a minute, and you could show me a couple of rooms on your main floor. That's really about as much as we can do, at this stage."

"Okay. Well, I'll take you on the two-cent tour, then."

I showed her the living room, dining room, and kitchen. She nodded politely and, in the family room, said, "I like this room. You've done a nice job here." The remark was probably pure salesmanship on her part, but it made me feel good nonetheless.

We took seats at the kitchen table, and she slid her albums over to me and asked me to flip through them. "While you're looking at the photos, let me get some rudimentary notes. What do you think you might want your room to say?"

"My rooms don't talk much, but if they did, I think I'd like them to tell me where I put my car keys." Michelle stared at me, and I reminded myself that she didn't appreciate my sense of humor. I returned my attention to her photo album and mumbled, "I'm always losing my car keys, you see."

"Let me rephrase. What kind of look are you going to be aiming for in this room? Since this is a sunroom, perhaps you're thinking southwestern. Or tropical, perhaps."

"I like people to feel like they can be comfortable in my house, primarily. But I also want the room to look nice. And I want the kids to be comfortable as well. So I guess my main priority is that everything be cleaned easily and hide the dirt."

"Hide the dirt." She sighed and jotted something in her notebook.

"They do make products for people like me, right? Scotchgard?"

"Oh, sure. Though it's an unusual top priority when you're talking to an interior decorator. As opposed to a house cleaner."

There was a moment of silence, during which I bristled at her "house cleaner" jab and looked through more room photographs, not really seeing them. My thoughts were now beginning to focus on how I could turn this conversation around to Stuart. I should have given the matter more thought earlier, but I'd been too busy cleaning.

"Let's talk a little about your budget, Molly."

"Budget? That's got to be just about your least-favorite subject, considering all the controversy regarding the school's budget." I had to fight back a smile of pride for my smooth segue.

"Yes. And just to warn you, I've made my mind up, though I know you and your father won't approve."

"Meaning you're making the mistake of cutting art and music programs?"

Not surprisingly, she gave me the evil eye for that remark. She pursed her lips and said nothing.

Thinking of Stuart and Gillian, I said, "I heard the rumor that there were some . . . strange liaisons on the school board."

She furrowed her brow. "I keep mistakenly thinking that people will come to realize that it's okay for a man and a woman to just be friends. And, to be honest, Kent and I really aren't even that. He's too self-absorbed to have friends. I simply find him a pleasant riding companion. Most of the women who board their horses there seem compelled to talk incessantly while we're trying to ride. I'm quite certain our horses are closer friends than Kent and I are."

"To tell you the truth, Michelle, when I heard rumors that there was a romance on the board, I assumed—"

"The same thing everybody does. That it was Kent and me. Sylvia never did believe that he and I were just friends, so she watched us like a hawk. When rumors of a romance surfaced, everyone assumed that it had to be two of us young board members. That's exactly wrong."

That was a strange comment. Gillian was younger than Kent or Michelle. Nevertheless, I feigned surprise and asked, "You mean Stuart and Gillian are having an affair?"

"No," she said, seeming utterly confused. "Stuart and Carol Barr. Why would you think I meant him and Gillian?"

"Because . . . I stumbled across them the other day and caught them . . . embracing."

"You're kidding! I've kept quiet about this, but I've caught Stuart and Carol 'embracing,' as you say, on more than one occasion."

This was really hard to fathom, if Michelle was telling me the truth—and she certainly appeared to be. "So . . . Stuart has, at one point at least, had a thing going with both women? It's lucky for him he wasn't the one to get killed."

Michelle, too, seemed disconcerted by the revelation that Gillian and Stuart were also a couple. "Well. There's no accounting for taste, as they say. Stuart has that gentle, fatherly thing going for him, and Gillian and her husband have been on the skids for a long time now. I guess she was lonely. Still, though . . ." She shuddered and said slowly, "I never have been able to understand Stuart and Carol's relationship. Carol's husband is much better looking than Stuart. And she's a nice enough woman, of course, but I'm surprised that both of them are attracted to her."

"I think she's not only 'nice enough' as you say, but reasonably nice looking."

Michelle grimaced a little. "Only when she's fully dressed. I ran into her at a swimming pool clear down in Albany one day last summer. Her body is terribly disfigured. That's why she always wears slacks and long-sleeve blouses. She told me she was in a fire when she was a kid. Her house burned down."

"Really? That's so awful."

"Yes. But let's get back to you and your sunroom, shall we?"

"Yes, let's," I said cheerfully, though that was the last thing I really wanted to discuss.

"Let me just get my calculator and I can run some very preliminary figures for you." She rummaged through her purse, then stopped, and her eyes suddenly widened as she pulled a palm-size object out of her purse. "That's odd. I wonder what this is?"

I rose and looked at what she was holding. "Oh. My son has something similar. If it's the same thing, it's a toy tape recorder. You can store a minute or two's worth of your voice, and play it back."

"I wonder who could have put it there?"

"It's not yours?" I asked stupidly.

"No. Someone must have . . . put it into my purse by mistake, somehow."

My thoughts instantly turned to how someone had planted the vial of poison that was in my father's jacket. "That could be evidence in the murder." I considered warning her about fingerprints, as well, but decided that any prints would have been smeared with Michelle's by now. "You were just at Gillian's house. Were you with any of the other board members lately?"

She shook her head. "Not since clear back at Proctor's Theater."

"And you've been through your purse since then, right?"

"I . . . must have been. Sure. I think I'd have discovered this sooner if it had been here all that time."

"Can I see it?" I asked. She handed the toy to me.

Unlike Nathan's toy, this one had an up and down arrow, and I didn't know its purpose. I pressed a small button marked "Play." Though the device seemed to be operating, there was no sound whatsoever on the tape.

"Huh. There's nothing recorded on this at all. That's unusual. Even if you buy one of these brand new, there's almost always some kid's voice on the tape who was fiddling with it in the store." I pressed the record button and held it up to my lips, while pressing the down arrow. I said into its built-in microphone, "I wonder what these arrows do."

I pressed the play button a second time, and it played back my short recording. My recorded voice had been drastically lowered. I sounded just like a man.

Chapter 20

Is It My Imagination?

Michelle stared at me. "What's the matter, Molly? What's the significance of that little . . . recorder thing?"

"It means that I've probably been wrong about some things. Michelle, it's absolutely critical for you to recall when the earliest and the latest time was that this device could have been placed in your purse."

"You're thinking that the killer could have planted it there?"

"Yes."

She rose, apparently disconcerted at having been set up, and began to pace beside my kitchen table. "Like I said, I had my purse with me at Proctor's Theater. I'm certain that this device couldn't have been there sooner than that, because I remember searching through all of the compartments to see if I could find any loose change for the parking meters. Then I found out meter money wasn't needed that late at night, anyway. I suppose it's possible that this . . . toy has been in the bottom of my purse ever since."

I looked again at the recorder. It had a pause button. "I need to test a theory," I murmured to Michelle. I recorded myself saying, "Hello, I'm Mr. Jones. Could you tell me what time Mrs. Jones will be free?" I waited a moment, then said, "Thank you." I played the first part back while holding the down arrow, then pressed the pause button, waited for a good thirty seconds or so, then released the pause and pressed the down arrow again. My test worked perfectly. A woman could easily have used this device to make herself sound like a man when she called the spa yesterday, pretending to be my father.

I returned the little recorder to her. "You need to call Sergeant Newton at the police station right away and give this to him." I got up. "Thanks for your help, Michelle."

"What about the decorating job on your sunroom?"

"Oh, right. I'll give that some more thought and get back to you soon."

Michelle gave me a half smile as she gathered up her notebooks and purse. "Sure you will. It's been a pleasure almost working with you, Molly."

"Thanks. You too." My thoughts had me too distracted to formulate a better reply.

I let Michelle out the front door and watched through the window while she drove off. This could all be a setup, I thought. Michelle could have faked discovering the device, having used it herself, and was now trying to make herself look less suspicious by producing what could be a crucial piece of evidence. She was a tall woman, though, and I didn't think it could have been her under that sheet. Then again, having been prone in a bathtub at the time, my vantage point certainly could have distorted a person's height.

On the other hand, the voice-changer might also have been a last-ditch effort by Stuart to deflect attention from himself, once he realized that yesterday's phone call to the mineral baths had let all the women on the board off the hook.

If only the person who tried to drown me hadn't been wearing those rubber gloves. That alone would have given me a much better idea if it was a man or a woman. For that matter, if only someone had seen the person before he or she donned the disguise. But why try to kill me? Did the killer think I knew something, held some key piece of evidence that even I didn't realize I possessed?

If so, maybe that was the link. Carol Barr had rummaged through my desk. Was she looking to see if I had damning evidence against her? Was hers the voice arguing with a man I'd assumed was Stuart? It was so hard to tell. If Tommy were to instruct all of the suspects to whisper those same words, maybe I could pick out the voice.

Or could that argument have been staged? Could someone have intentionally positioned herself so that I, or the next person who happened down that hallway, would overhear an "argument" that was really only between one person and a prerecorded, altered voice? How well would the voice-changer work with the up arrow? Would a man sound like a woman?

Carol searches my desk at home. Or not. Stuart looks through Gillian's personnel folder. Or not, if Agnes Rockman was the killer and pointing fingers at others. Stephanie gets choked at the theater. Sam Dunlap-cum-Jacobsen calls me to set up a rendezvous and then gets killed. Was I so sure that was really his voice?

There were too many pieces to this puzzle to put together by myself. I needed a sounding board. Lauren was usually my first choice for such a role, but Stephanie might be the better choice this time. After all, she'd had an encounter with the killer herself. Plus her loose lips had nearly turned me into the third victim. The woman owed me.

I called her and waited through her machine's message, then said, "Stephanie. We need to talk. Are you there?"

Just when I was about to conclude that she wasn't, she picked up. "Molly, I was just getting Mikey down for his afternoon nap. What do we need to talk about?"

"The murders. I need to run some thoughts by you. Since your son is napping now, can I come over there?"

She sighed. "I suppose so."

Several minutes later, I pulled into Stephanie's circular driveway. I reminded myself as I climbed the steps onto her elegant front porch that, despite her attitude on the phone, she wanted to solve this thing, too, now that an attempt had been made on her own precious neck. She was the perfect person to talk to right now: definitely innocent, knowledge-able about all of the suspects, and possessing a devious mind that could easily put her into a criminal's thoughts.

She opened the door before I could ring the bell, looking

several shades less than thrilled at my having disturbed her. Before she could annoy me into rethinking my visit, I said, "Stephanie, I need your help. Brainstorm this thing with me, would you please? I really think I must know something important that I'm unaware of."

She gave me—in jeans and T-shirt—a disapproving visual once-over, but stepped aside so that I could enter. "Such as how to dress like a mature woman instead of a twenty-year-old?"

"Truce, all right?" I fairly shrieked at her as I shut the door behind me. "Just walk me through this. Here is this person who manages to slip poison into Sylvia's water glass in the private meeting of board members. So it's got to be someone Sylvia trusts enough to handle her glass or who manages to create a subtle diversion so that nobody sees that the water's being contaminated. That person also puts a vial of poison into my dad's jacket pocket before the police temporarily confiscate the board members' possessions. Follow?"

"Go on."

"Then this person puts a thumbtack into the stirrup of Michelle's saddle, succeeding in getting the horse to throw her, though she's basically uninjured. Then the killer stabs the private investigator, just before he can give me damaging evidence."

"Don't forget how I was nearly choked to death."

"Right, but you managed to scream, even so."

"It was just a quick thing. I felt his hands on my neck, then they released me, and I screamed."

"You said 'his' hands. Are you thinking now that it was a man?"

"Not necessarily. Except that I'm fairly certain it had to be someone roughly my height."

The shortest person on my list of suspects was Agnes. "So that lets out Agnes Rockman."

"Oh, please," Stephanie scoffed. "Agnes Rockman? She worshiped Sylvia Greene. She'd never kill her. Although . . ."

"What?"

"My accountant did have an interesting theory about some

funds that had disappeared a couple of years ago and then reappeared. He thought Agnes Rockman might have swindled the district, but since the money had been returned, he didn't feel he had the justification to pursue the matter further."

"Huh." Even if that were true, I couldn't see how that could be grounds for her to resort to murder. Furthermore, why had someone choked Stephanie? Mistaken identity? Was she supposed to have been me? She was taller, though, especially with those high heels she always wore. The only per-son she could easily be mistaken for in the dark was Michelle Lacy.

The thought of Michelle jogged my memory. "You told me on Sunday that there were rumors that Michelle and Kent had been pilfering monies from the school budget. Did your accountant look into that?"

"Yes, as a matter of fact. He's told me that he's absolutely certain that they were innocent, and the only irregularities could all be traced back to some funds that Agnes had access to and, again, that the money did eventually turn up. He's going to call me when he has some solid facts about the budget's overall status. He was talking about how the school's insurance premiums are just so astronomical that that alone is a huge budget hit."

"So I've heard. They had that fire a few years ago," I murmured to myself, thinking.

"I remember that. The arson case at the high school. They never did solve that. I wouldn't be half surprised if it was one of those dreadful boys that Tiffany's former boyfriend used to hang out with."

Carol Barr had scars from a fire, which Michelle had seen when they had run into each other clear down in Albany. Could that have been related? Could Carol be a closet arsonist—if there was such a thing—and had Sylvia somehow found out that her scars weren't from a childhood accident, but rather from that fire at the school? That could be a motive for the attempt on Michelle, and perhaps on

Stephanie, too. Still, not much of a motive. What could seeing someone's scars possibly prove?

"How long ago was that fire, anyway?"

Stephanie shrugged and looked at her nails, losing interest in the conversation, now that it had drifted so far away
from herself. "Four years ago, I think. Cherokee, Tiffany's
ex-boyfriend, would have been a freshman."

And Carol Barr would not have been a member of the
school board. In any case, if Carol was an arsonist, who'd
gotten caught in her own fire, how had her hands not been injured? Michelle had been the one to tell me about Carol's
scars. If she was the killer, she could have staged that fall
from her horse, maybe even lied to me about Carol's scars to
point me in the wrong direction. It wouldn't be that hard to
find out. Surely all I would have to do was ask Agnes. She
probably had enough personal knowledge of the board members that she'd know if Carol had been hideously scarred in a
childhood fire.

Stephanie's phone rang, startling me a little. She must
have added a few more phones since I'd last been there, for I
could hear at least four separate ringings from various rooms,
one of which was very close at hand. Stephanie excused herself to sweep up a portable phone that was resting, out of its
cradle, on an occasional table in the foyer.

Stephanie looked at me wide-eyed and said into the phone,
"Why, Stuart, we were just speaking about you. My, uh,
friend Molly invited herself over and was asking if you and
my accountant have made any progress in going over the
budget." She paused and smiled. "Of course I would. I can
come right away." She winked at me, then said, "Thank you
so much, Stuart. I'll be right there."

She hung up the phone and said, "Ta dah," while pirouet-
ting and hugging herself.

"Good news?" I asked in a monotone.

"Absolutely. The best. I need you to baby-sit."

"My, that *is* good news," I said sarcastically.

"On second thought," she said, returning her attention to
her phone and pressing buttons, "I'll get my neighbor to

come over here to watch Mikey. Come with me to the Education Center, Molly. We're about to bask in the glow of my having saved the day once again."

"I can hardly wait."

"Superintendent Collins has called a meeting for the school board so that he can make his announcement today."

"So we're going back to the scene of the crime again," I said, feeling a tad anxious at that thought, especially since another murder had occurred.

"Yes, and they're televising the meeting. This means I'll have my first opportunity to be on camera as one of the board members."

Her neighbor must have picked up, for Stephanie said into the phone, "Hello, this is Stephanie. Be with you in just a moment." Then she held her hand over the mouthpiece, while giving a fashion-model's gesture with her free hand to indicate the lovely blue dress she was wearing, "This is why I'm always so well dressed, Molly. I think, if you dress as though wonderful things will happen to you, they do indeed happen."

I muttered, "In that case, you must have chosen the wrong shade of shoes the night someone tried to choke you," but she'd already returned her attention to the phone, instantly insistent, because Stephanie had "an absolute dire emergency."

Within minutes, the poor, trusting soul rushed over, and Stephanie promptly gave her instructions on what to do, should Mikey awaken soon. In the meantime, I'd realized that my own children had been home alone for too long now. I called Lauren and explained the situation, who said that she'd either go get them and bring them to her house or bring Rachel over.

Stephanie's neighbor, a pleasant-looking woman in her early thirties or so, had apparently been listening to my conversation with Lauren. She glared at Stephanie and said, "I thought you said that this was a 'dire emergency'!"

"There are all kinds of emergencies, my dear," Stephanie explained as she strode out of the room toward her garage. "This just happens to be a happy one."

The neighbor let out a little puff of protest, then put her hands on her hips and shifted her gaze to me.

"Recently moved into the neighborhood, by any chance?"
I asked, my cheeks warming from my embarrassment of guilt
by association.

"Yes. And allowing Stephanie Saunders to manipulate me
is a mistake I won't make twice."

Wishing that were as easy as it sounded, I made my way
out the door.

In her own typical style, which, thank goodness, was in-
imitable, Stephanie raced off in her BMW, leaving me to in-
hale her engine exhaust as I got into my Toyota. I was soon at
the Ed Center.

My father was already in the small auditorium by the time
I arrived. He was standing near the front of the room, looking
a bit disconcerted. Perhaps that was because my mother
wasn't with him, and she'd been such a fixture on his arm of
late. He was wearing his jacket and fishing hat. I went up to
him, battling feelings of déjà vu. "Where's Mom?"

"Making dinner. You know how she is about sticking to
her daily schedule and everything."

I scanned the room. The other board members were just arriving, dropping off their coats and so forth at their seats on
the dais. "Do you know what this is about?"

"Some big breakthrough in the budget situation," Dad answered quietly.

Stephanie was chatting with a nicely dressed man in the
front row. This would likely be her accountant, who, like
Stephanie, was dressed for "good things to happen." If he'd
managed, somehow, to save the day for the schools, we'd
never hear the end of it from Stephanie, but that was a price I
would be more than willing to pay.

Stuart banged his inherited gavel and requested over the
microphone that everyone please take their seats. Stephanie
marched across the dais with the confidence of someone who
expected to be coronated. I took a seat near the center aisle, a
couple of rows back. Agnes, however, was still setting things
up, placing some printed report or memo in front of each
board member. I couldn't help but notice that everyone de-
clined Agnes's offer of water. I noticed, too, that Carol Barr

still hadn't arrived. I glanced around behind me, but she was nowhere to be seen.

Agnes seemed unduly tense. She came up to me and said, "Let's meet in my office fifteen minutes after the meeting is over. All right?"

My initial reaction was to ask her why, but she was already heading to her seat, so I just said, "Okay. Fine."

"The meeting is now in session," Stuart announced, the moment Agnes had reclaimed her seat.

"Wait a moment, Stuart," Stephanie said. "Where's the cameraman? Shouldn't we wait for him?"

"He couldn't come and, apparently, neither could Carol Barr, though I left a message on her machine. We'll just have to proceed without them."

Stephanie's expression fell, but she nodded.

Stuart Ackleman pounded the gavel. "Superintendent Collins has an important announcement to make."

Within a couple of seconds, the room was dead silent and the superintendent spoke into the mike. "With the help of a skilled accountant, whose services were generously provided by our newest board member, Stephanie Saunders, we discovered that extra monies do exist within the budget. This allows us to continue the current budget for next year, without cutting programs."

Mr. Johnson from the local paper, my least-loved journalist, leapt to his feet. "How did you—"

Stuart pounded the gavel a couple of more times. "If we allow Mr. Collins to continue, he'll tell you."

Superintendent Collins proceeded to explain at great length about retirement-fund estimations and various escrows that could be moved and manipulated, but I lost my train of thought, feeling as though I was sitting through a geography lesson—which probably explains why more than just my "train of thought" gets lost so often. Next Stephanie spoke about how what she did "was nothing," which didn't stop her from making a speech about how noble and glorious she was.

Meanwhile, I watched the other board members for their

reactions. They all seemed to be obliged to indulge Stephanie in her self-congratulations.

When Stuart adjourned the meeting, ebullience seemed to pass across those on the dais. My father sported a wide smile and shook each of his peers' hands, as well as Superintendent Collins's and Agnes's. Michelle and Gillian hugged each other. Even Kent and Stuart shook hands. Stephanie then managed to make herself the center of attention, although she looked immensely disappointed when she realized that all of the reporters were following her accountant out of the room, rather than seeking quotes from her.

The small audience filed out, and I went up to the dais and gave my father a hug and congratulated him. He was clearly delighted and soon returned his attention to his fellow board members. "I'm taking all of you out to dinner tonight," he announced. He looked thoughtful, then added, "Pity that Carol still isn't here."

It was also a pity that Mom was currently home, dutifully making their supper, but I had no doubt that he'd remember this in time to insist that she join them.

"I'm going home to be with my children, Charlie," Stephanie said. "But thank you for the offer." While the others left in one group—for the first time since they'd been elected—she gathered her purse and coat.

I touched her shoulder. "On behalf of both myself and my children, thank you, Stephanie. You've just saved this community untold grief."

Instead of the annoying comeback I was bracing myself to hear, she met my eyes, smiled genuinely, and said, "You're very welcome, Molly."

I watched her leave, her head held high, her long blond hair perfectly in place, and thought what a wonder she was. Surely she was one of the most singularly annoying humans on the planet, and yet she did have her moments and her methods to attain success.

I realized then that I was the last person in the room and glanced at my watch. I had no idea what time the meeting had ended and how much time had passed.

The building felt almost eerily quiet as I headed down the hall toward Agnes's office. The security guard's little office was someplace around here, so even if Agnes had given up on me and left, I surely wasn't the last person in the building.

Agnes came out of her doorway, shutting the door behind her just as I was about to enter.

"Oh, Ms. Masters. I just have to go to the little girl's room. I'll be right back. Go on inside. It's not locked."

There was a slight smoky scent when I opened the door, which I dismissed as someone having lit up a cigarette. Someone nearby in "the little girl's room," perhaps. The odor gave me an idea for a possible cartoon. A couple of women are staring in horror as a third woman, whose hair is in flames, asks with a smile, "Is it my imagination, or is my hair really on fire?" Unfortunately, while I could picture the drawing, I couldn't picture how to possibly market the idea.

I took a seat in front of Agnes's desk and waited, feeling vaguely antsy, but not knowing why. After a couple of minutes, she entered the room. She took in a couple of audible sniffs. "That's odd. Do you smell that?"

"Yes, but I assumed it was coming from one of the bathrooms. Someone smoking a cigarette."

"That's possible, I suppose." She sniffed again. "It seems to be coming from the superintendent secretary's office, though, and no one should be in there at this hour." She started to cross the room toward that second door and said over her shoulder, "So what did you want to meet with me about, Ms. Masters?"

"I have no idea. You're the one who said you wanted to meet with me."

She froze and said, "I did no such thing. There was a note on my desk, saying that *you* wanted . . ."

She let her voice fade, as we both caught sight of a puff of smoke snaking toward us through the crack under the door.

I put my palm on the door's surface. The wood was warm. My heart started pounding. "Oh, God. There must be a fire on the other side."

"I should have seen this coming," Agnes cried. We both

turned, intending to leave immediately through the door to
the hallway. Carol Barr stepped inside before we could cross
the room. She immediately snapped some kind of metallic-
domed contraption over the doorknob.

She wiped beads of sweat off her forehead, her white
hair unusually grimy. She gestured at the doorknob. "Do you
like this? It's my own invention. Got the idea from those
child-proof locks they put on doorknobs. You can break it
in two eventually, of course, and get out. But it takes hours.
And there's already one of these on the exit to the adjacent
room. Which, as you've probably guessed, is burning rather
rapidly."

"Carol!" Agnes shrieked. "What have you done?"

She stared dully at Agnes. "Oh. I guess you're still a step or
two behind. I started a fire in the next room, which will
spread to this room momentarily."

Agnes brushed past Carol and tried to turn the knob. "This
is senseless," Agnes said. "The fire-alarm system will kick
off any moment, and we'll get drenched."

"No. I disconnected the system. Quite some time ago, in
fact. Just after the last visit from the fire marshal." She turned
her attention to me and said, "I have an engineering degree.
Back from before that was the vogue thing for women to do."
As she spoke, she swiped again at her damp forehead, then
pulled her shirtsleeves up. I found myself staring at her
hideous scars.

"Carol, we were just . . . talking about you," Agnes said
nervously. Her words had all the calm of a mouse squeaking
at the cat who has hold of his tail. "And the other board members. And how delighted we were that the board has managed
to . . . to . . ."

"Pull a workable budget out of the fire, so to speak?" Carol
said with a sad smile.

"Yes."

More smoke was coming under the back door, and Carol
started to head toward it. I knew that she intended to open it,
fueling the fire. I stepped in front of her, blocking her path.

"What are you doing, Carol? This is silly. The security guard will smell that smoke and be here to help us before you—"

"He's incapacitated, I'm afraid."

"You killed him?" I asked.

"I tried hard to seek help. I really did. I even thought I was cured. Oh, but the allure of fire. You can't begin to know how compelling it is."

"Sylvia found out?"

"Yes." She narrowed her eyes at Agnes. "Along with Agnes. Sylvia and I had had an argument the day before her final meeting. She'd ... caught me in the act. Just a little wastebasket fire, but ... I had no choice, after that. I slipped the poison into her water glass in the back room, and afterwards in the confusion, I dropped a vial into your father's jacket. That would have been the end to all of this, if it hadn't been for your interference, Agnes. I warned you that I'd reveal your petty thefts, but you just couldn't keep quiet, could you?"

Agnes was whimpering and shaking her head. Anger surged through me. Though we were two against one, Agnes wasn't going to be of any help in her current emotional state.

"Michelle Lacy," Carol spat out, curling her lip. "I've always hated her. Her smug superiority. Looking at my scars as if they were ugly. Then that Stephanie. They were cut from the same cloth, those two. But I just wanted to scare some sense into them. That damned private investigator, who you found out was Sylvia's ex's brother-in-law, once you saw him face-to-face with Sylvia and recognized him from the funeral."

Agnes sputtered, "How did you—"

"I bugged your phone, Agnes. And I found out that you gave him all of the mental-health reports from my childhood. That was supposed to be *our* secret."

"You told me you were cured," Agnes whined. "It wasn't till Sylvia told me about the wastebasket fire that I knew you weren't. So I told her how you'd started the fire at the school."

"Yes, and it was just a matter of time till you told Molly.

I've been checking the log on the fax machine and knew that you sent her a fax." She glared at me. "You just wouldn't let it go, would you, Molly? Nobody ever suspects the kindly old lady, you know. Stuart underestimated me, too, like so many others. I've had Stuart wrapped around my finger, even used him to spy on the other board members for me, so that I could keep my secret. Came in handy when Gillian told him to go join you at the spa and soak his head. And guess who Stuart told? It took some effort to track down which spa and what time, but you see, Molly, you're not the only one with investigative skills."

Agnes quietly made her way to her desk and picked up the phone. She was sobbing. Her face was a picture of terror. She let the handset drop. "The phone's dead." She grabbed her head with both hands and stared wild-eyed at Carol. "Are you crazy?" Agnes exclaimed, a redundant question if ever there was one. "You've blocked your own escape as well!"

"I want to die. I deserve it. But so do the two of you. If you'd just let this go, no one else would have had to die. It's your fault every bit as much as it is mine."

"Let us go, Carol," Agnes said, still sobbing. "I didn't tell anyone except Sylvia. And when you killed her . . . I kept quiet, just like you told me to."

"Just like I *forced* you to, you mean, you little thief!"

"I told you, I was just in a jam! I gave the money back!" She looked at me and at the door. "Molly's got two young children."

"Too late now." Again she gestured at the door to the hallway. "My invention there doesn't come with a key." She tried to step around me, but I blocked her path again. "Let me open the door. Let the fire in. This will all be over sooner that way."

"No!" I grabbed Carol. In the corner of my eye, I caught sight of Agnes's coat on a rack in the corner. "Agnes, push your coat against the door. We've got to block off the smoke."

Agnes grabbed her coat and came toward us, just as Carol pried her wrist free and then tried to lunge past me. I grabbed at her again and wound up falling, knocking us both to the floor. Agnes quickly got her coat into place. Then she helped me overpower Carol, fighting Carol so savagely that I yelled, "Agnes, just hold her down."

This was a windowless, interior room. The door to the adjoining room where Carol had started the fire was so hot to the touch that we would probably have to make our way through a wall of flames to reach its windows.

I scrambled to my feet and scanned the wall to the hallway, now our only means of escape. It appeared to be made out of Sheetrock. I kicked through the inside piece with little effort, intentionally not putting much force behind my thrust until I knew where the studs were.

"No, Molly! What are you doing?" Carol shrieked from behind me. In spite of myself, I looked back to see her getting to her feet.

"Agnes! Don't let her go!"

It was too late. Seeing that I'd made the beginnings of an exit for us, she ran toward it and me.

Carol, instead of trying to stop us, kicked Agnes's coat away from the door to the burning room, grabbed the now red-hot doorknob, and threw the door open.

I automatically shielded my face and didn't look, my own screams blending with Carol's and an unbearable heat blasting through the air.

Kicking and clawing desperately, Agnes had enlarged the hole I'd started. She managed to jam herself through the gap between the studs in the wall. Immediately after her, I jammed through, as well. Coughing, barely able to see with my stinging eyes, I made it into the hallway, which was deserted, unaffected by the mortal combat taking place in one of its rooms.

Agnes, whimpering and sobbing in fright, ran toward the building's main exit.

"Agnes! We have to find the security guard!"

She kept going, bolting out the door as if she hadn't heard.

A somewhat muffled male voice called from a nearby room, "Help! I can't get out of here!"

The man began banging on the door, which I threw open. It

was the security guard. He grabbed me by both shoulders.
"How'd you . . ." He examined the doorknob, which was un-
encumbered on the side facing the hallway. "Damndest thing
I ever saw. That elderly lady on the school board marched in
here a while ago, yanked my phone clear out of the wall, stole
my radio, and slapped this damn thing on the doorknob. I
couldn't get out!"

"We need to find a phone for 911 and get out of here!" I
cried, my insides reeling.

The guard said, "Come on," and pulled me along. "I got a
second radio in my car. I'll call for help from outside."

Within moments, I was standing in the parking lot of
the Ed Center, watching smoke ascend from the back of the
building, all the while taking deep breaths of sweet, cold air.

Hours later, Betty Cocker sat on my lap in the loveseat
with Jim beside me and Karen and Nathan on the adjacent
couch. Despite my change of clothes after a lengthy shower,
the smoke seemed permanently emblazoned into my sense of
smell.

Our local regular programming was soon interrupted to
broadcast a report about the fire and its cause at the Ed
Center. The story confirmed for the first time what I feared—
Carol Barr had died. I sat with tears streaming down my face,
but felt too numb, somehow, to sob. I'd always liked Carol.
She'd seemed so caring and capable. How could she appear
to be so sane and competent, and yet secretly be so mur-
derous and crazily obsessed by the horror of a raging fire?

I dried my eyes and sighed. When I looked up, Karen was
watching me. She smiled and said, "Good job, Mom," and
gave me a hug.

"Thank you, sweetie," I answered, my throat still considerably sore from the fumes.

"I never get to be on television!" Nathan grumbled.

"Let's hope none of us do, ever again," I murmured.

An hour or so ago, my mom had been over to see if I
was all right and to tell me that Dad would be over later.
The doorbell rang. I promptly announced to Jim and the

kids, "Let me get this," pushed BC off my lap, and got up to answer.

Indeed, my father was standing on the porch, a stunning bouquet of long-stemmed white roses in his arms. Caught off guard at the sight of the flowers, I stammered, "Hi, Dad. Come on in," and pushed the screen door aside for him.

His eyes were a bit bloodshot and red-rimmed, and if I didn't know better, I would have thought that he'd been crying. He stepped beside me, his expression both weary and sad. "I'm sorry about what happened to you."

I nodded. "I'm just glad it's over."

He averted his gaze to the flowers in his arms. "Back when I was in school, Latin was a requirement. I thought I'd forgotten all of it, but one line came back to me when I was in the floral shop, getting these for you." He sighed, searched my eyes, and said, " *'Saepe creat molles aspera spina rosas.'* I believe it means that the sharpest of thorns can often produce the gentlest of roses." Dad handed me the bouquet, then put his palm on my cheek and said quietly, "You're *my* rose, and I am so proud of you, Molly."

For once, I was struck speechless. I set the bouquet on a nearby table and hugged my father in silence.

In Conversation...

LESLIE O'KANE AND MOLLY MASTERS

LESLIE: Today I'm interviewing Molly Masters, a thirty-something, happily married mother of two who creates faxable greeting cards for a living, and who has a propensity for turning up dead bodies. Thank you for consenting to this interview, Molly.

MOLLY: Does that mean I had a choice?

LESLIE: Actually, no. I was just being polite. So tell me, Molly, what is it with you and murder? How do you keep managing to stumble across all of these dead bodies?

MOLLY: Leslie, I really fail to understand that myself. It all seemed to start the moment I moved back to my hometown in upstate New York, and my least-favorite high school teacher was murdered shortly thereafter. Since then, two of my neighbors have been murdered, as was this guy that I couldn't stand. Plus the former owner of my house. Shot dead on my front lawn, I might add. That's part of the reason I went away on a nice vacation to Colorado . . . a working vacation, really. I'd decided to run a greeting-card writing workshop up in the mountains north of Boulder, which is where I went to college and lived for a number of years. Sounds like such a great idea, doesn't it? A whole group of women who don't know one another, off in a nice cabin retreat in a lovely, remote mountain setting? Except that the woman in Boulder I'd hired to help me organize things wound up having to get acquaintances of hers to fill in at the last minute, but I soldiered on and held a brain-storming session in which participants anony-mously toss their ideas for cards into a hat. Want to know what one of the very first card ideas was? "Violets are blue. Roses are red. One of you bitches will soon be dead!" And then guess what happened?

LESLIE: **Someone was murdered?**

MOLLY: Exactly. I'm really getting a complex about this. I'm turning into the Lizzie Borden of the greeting card world.

LESLIE: **Let's change subjects, then. How's your busi-ness going?**

MOLLY: Terribly. I mean, I ask you, Leslie: Why would you pay somebody to design a personalized faxable greeting card for you, when everyone in the world is on-line, and you can send a personalized e-card for free? Do you have any other questions for me? Because, I've got to tell you that you're getting me so depressed I might need to go on Prozac by the time this interview is over.

LESLIE: **Tell me about your children, Molly. You have a daughter who is twelve and a ten-year-old son, right?**

MOLLY: Karen and Nathan. They're the greatest, both bright and articulate, though Nathan is both a compulsive cleaner and a full-time pessimist. Karen is happy and well balanced, does well at everything, and is a delight to be around; though she's showing signs of teendom creeping up on her. In fact, have you ever noticed how similar they are to your own children?

LESLIE: **Yes, and that is an interesting coincidence. But what about the other people in your life, Molly? Your best friend, that police sergeant you're always butting heads with, your parents? They aren't anything like anyone I know, are they?**

MOLLY: Not really, though they do seem to share some characteristics of people you know. Which is something I've heard said about the two of us, by the way.

LESLIE: **Well, yes, but then, if I were to discover a dead body, I'd call the police and keep myself safe and away from anyone who might have done it, at least until the killer was caught. You, on the other hand, seem to keep poking at things, even when that means putting your own life in jeopardy. Why is that?**

MOLLY: I honestly don't know, Leslie. And you're quite right. At some point, I always do seem to be all but engaged in hand-to-hand combat with the killer, fighting for my very life. That's generally because there's some compelling personal reason for me to investigate, which winds up taking precedence over my own safety. And nowadays I've gotten a reputation for being able to solve these things, so it's getting even harder for me to stay away from police investigations.

LESLIE: **Final question: What's next for you, Molly? Are you happy living in Carlton, New York? Are you going to rejuvenate your business in some way, or perhaps try your hand at something else? Do you think you'll be able to avoid those darned murders from now on?**

MOLLY: All of that remains to be seen. Time will tell, as they say. Though some people I know seem to get really crabby when I use clichés. And that was four questions, by the way. Frankly, I see myself as just your everyday, average middle-class soccer mom, doing the best I can, who's had some extraordinarily bad luck when it comes to staying safe and sound, and at having the other people in her life do the same.

LESLIE: **Ah, yes. That latter piece is probably the rub for you.**

MOLLY: Which reminds me. Did you take my favorite drawing pencil? It seems to be missing. Leslie? Hello?